MUSCLE
memory

Vicky,

Love never forgets

xx, Stylo

STYLO FANTÔME

Published by BattleAxe Productions
Copyright © 2017
Stylo Fantôme

ISBN-13: 978-1975672607
ISBN-10: 1975672607

Critique Partner: Ratula Roy

Editing Aides: Barbara Shane Hoover

Cover Design: Najla Qamber Designs
najlaqamberdesigns.com

Interior Design: Champagne Book Design

Copyright © 2017

DEDICATION

To strange thoughts while driving on lonely stretches of highway,
and to sometimes even remembering them.

CHAPTER
one

He couldn't remember.

He was left handed and he could speak pretty tolerable Spanish. He knew how to shave properly and he could prattle off most of the New York Yankees' batting averages. He knew his favorite food in the whole world was authentic Mexican and he was positive he'd been to Prague at some point.

I don't remember.

He could remember his first day in the hospital. It had been very sunny out, and the blinds had been up. He'd blinked his eyes rapidly in the glaring light, then looked around the empty room. It was a shared room, but the curtains were pulled back, exposing a vacant bed next to him. A TV was on up in the corner, and next to him lay a remote attached to the bed. He found the button for the nurses station and pressed it. A moment later, a young woman in well worn scrubs came into the room.

"Hi," he said in a shaky voice. Her face was full of shock, but he took a deep breath and carried on. "I'm sorry, but I was hoping you could tell me what I'm doing here, and …"

"I'll get the doctor, right away," she said, backing out of the room. She was already running down the hall when he finally finished his sentence.

"… who I am?"

The first week was rough. And not like first day of school, or bad day at work, rough. More like "I want to scream until my soul starts bleeding" rough.

He couldn't remember his name. He couldn't remember how he'd wound up in the hospital, or even where he'd been before—he couldn't remember where he'd grown up, his parents, his home, his friends, *nothing*. It was an impenetrable fog.

So of course it was a mystery to him how he'd fractured his skull and broken his humerus.

"I what!?" he exclaimed. A large nurse was sitting in the chair next to his bed, cutting coupons out of a newspaper. She was on her break, but she'd taken a shine to him for some reason, and she often came in to keep him company.

Because she knows how scared I am when I'm alone.

"Mmm hmmm," she replied, twisting the scissors around in her hand. "You could've died. You were waiting for the L at Bedford Avenue when you fell off the platform, went down almost four feet straight onto your head. Cracked your skull open on the tracks and broke your arm. You're lucky a train wasn't coming, either. Caused quite a problem, shut down the lines for a couple hours."

"I just … fell?" he asked, feeling around at the back of his skull. Stretching from just above his neck and arching up towards his right ear was a wicked feeling scar. She shrugged.

"You were probably high. You're almost lucky in a way, I bet you didn't feel a thing."

Another thing he'd forgotten—he was a drug addict. Or at least, that's what they told him. He couldn't remember. He did have a mark on the inside of one arm. It had started out small, he'd been told, and under normal circumstances would've healed right up and he'd never have known it was even there. While he'd been unconscious, an infection had caused it to open and become sore, ugly, and red. It was now a permanent scar, and apparently it was from a needle.

"I don't get it. How can I not remember doing drugs? Shouldn't I be jonesing or something?" he asked, scratching at the scar.

"You were unconscious for over two weeks, honey. You detoxed while you were out, which trust me, makes you one of the lucky ones."

"Do you know what drugs I did?"

"That's something you should talk to your doctors about."

But he didn't like talking to his doctors. It was already weird enough not knowing his own name, but being treated like a case file, a number, just made it worse. Most of them just strolled into his room and looked at a chart and prattled things off to him he didn't really understand.

"Don't worry," the kindly nurse said as she climbed to her feet. "It'll all come back to you, Jon."

Jon. It wasn't his name. Well, he supposed it could be, Jon was a pretty popular name in the United States. He preferred it without the *H*, though, so he spelled it that way when he needed to sign off on anything. In all honesty, *Jon* wouldn't have been his first choice, if he'd had any say in it. But he hadn't—he'd had no identification on him when they'd brought him to the hospital, not even a wallet. So during the two weeks he'd been unconscious, everyone had referred to him as *John* because it was the name on all his medical charts.

John Doe, case number 438643.

He smiled goodbye as the nurse walked out of the room. Then he fidgeted around in bed. Turned on the television. Scratched the area around the scar on his head, then hissed when he bumped a staple. He had to use his right hand to itch—his left arm was in a collar and cuff, stabilizing the break. The doctors told him he only had to wear it for a couple more weeks, but it was driving him nuts.

A couple more weeks, where will I be then? Where do you send someone like me?

He asked that question to one of his doctors later in the day when, he was wheeled up several floors for a check up.

"I mean, I don't know if I even have an apartment. And even if I do, I don't know where it would be," he said while the neurologist looked at x-rays. "The cops took my fingerprints, but nothing turned up. No DNA sample matches, either. I guess that means I wasn't a criminal, which is good. But I almost wish I was, because not knowing anything sucks. Where am I supposed to go when you guys kick me out?"

"We don't 'kick people out', Mr. Doe," the doctor replied, turning around to face him. She was a very small woman, and surprisingly young. "Your case worker, the one from social services, will help with your transition. You can call them at any time and ask these kinds of questions."

His social worker couldn't answer all his questions, though. He thought back to the nurse he'd spoken with earlier in the day.

"Hey, I've been meaning to ask. What kind of drugs was I on?" he blurted on. Dr. Anand's eyebrows went up.

"Well, you were on morphine for the pain, but they stopped that, I'm pretty sure. You're on co-codamol now, a range of antibiotics, also some—"

"Not what I'm on *now*, I know those ones. I was told I was a drug addict before I came here, but I can't remember. My lab work should say what I was taking, right?" he asked. She glanced around her, then spotted his file and picked it up. After flipping through a few pages, she glanced at him.

"When you were admitted to the emergency room, you were

well over the legal limit for alcohol. You also had THC in your system, oxycodone, cocaine, ecstasy, and speed," she prattled off in a fast voice. Jon's jaw dropped.

"All of those? How am I alive?"

"The human body can surprisingly handle a lot. It's not a good mixture, though—alcohol is a depressant, and that quantity of it mixing with so many stimulants, well … it 's almost a good thing you fell, it probably saved your life."

"That's … good?"

No, it wasn't. It was fucking depressing. He was a drug addict who'd fallen onto the train tracks. He was also clearly a loser, because no one seemed to be looking for him. No one had shown up at the hospital asking about him. A local news crew had even interviewed him, but nada.

Maybe I threw myself onto those tracks, hoping for a train to come along.

Dr. Anand seemed to read his mind and she closed his file with a snap, then smiled at him.

"Maybe you had been to a wild party," she offered, moving around so she was behind his wheelchair. He could walk perfectly fine, but because of his head injury, the hospital staff was insisting on using the chair. Normally, an orderly or a nurse wheeled him to and from places, so he was surprised when the doctor grabbed the handles and started pushing him.

"I don't think so. One of the cops showed me a picture of myself, from when I was first brought in."

Based on the photo, Jon had been a wild party all by himself. The man in the picture was foreign to him. He'd had thick, coarse brown hair, which had all been twisted into long, neat dreadlocks. Very bohemian, he supposed. He'd been unshaven and he'd looked dirty. His clothes had certainly been filthy. They were still hanging up in the closet in his hospital room, he avoided touching them. Based on the way he looked in the picture and the state of those clothes, he almost thought maybe he'd been homeless.

The person he saw in the mirror—Jon—looked completely different. They'd shaved his head, as well as his face, before he'd gone into surgery to deal with the nasty skull fracture, and in the three weeks that had passed since then, he'd grown a thick stubble all across his scalp. He'd also been thoroughly cleaned while unconscious, and with the aid of a chair and a plastic bag for his arm, he showered regularly, and he continued shaving his face. He had gray-green eyes which stood out starkly against his olive toned skin and dark hair. All of it combined gave him a very striking look, he supposed.

Jesus, I don't even know what nationality I am. Puerto Rican? Maybe some African American? Italian? Greek?

"Then think of this as a fresh start, Jon," Dr. Anand urged as they rode down a couple levels on an elevator. "The man they brought into me three weeks ago had looked like a train wreck. But the man sitting in front of me right now, he seems pretty smart. Do something with this, make sure not to go down the same path."

He thought about her words long after she'd deposited him in his room. Of course she was right. He *was* lucky in a way, he knew. He'd gotten to detox without being conscious for any of the withdrawal symptoms, and if he had been homeless, he now got to sleep in a warm bed every night.

He also knew that after his little spot on the news, someone had set up a crowd-funding page for him. Complete strangers were donating money to the John Doe Fund and he already had almost ten thousand dollars to his made-up-name. The news spot was a double bonus, actually. The TV station offered to pay most of his medical bills. He'd refused to do any TV spots at first, the idea of being on camera had made him nervous. But when one network finally said they would pay his bills in exchange for an exclusive, he didn't see how he could possibly turn them down. Sixty minutes of sweating through an interview was worth it to have the pressure of bills taken off his back.

Life was still scary, though. Not knowing who you are or where you came from or what you were going to do with yourself, it was awful. It woke him up in the middle of the night in a cold sweat. He would find himself reaching out for someone—but who? Someone who'd apparently lain on his left side, but he couldn't remember them. A woman? A man? Jon Doe found quite a few of the female nurses rather attractive, but who knew about Dude X, the hobo he used to be in a past life.

But Dr. Anand was right. He would take the donated money and he would do something good with it. Get himself an apartment. Get a real job. Get a life.

It will be scary, but it's got to be better than whatever I was doing before.

BEFORE

"**H**ey!"

Whoever was yelling, they repeated themselves a couple times before he realized they were yelling at him. He turned around and finished lighting his cigarette, then squinted through the smoke.

"You talking to me?" he asked.

He watched as a bubbly looking brunette hurried towards him.

"Yeah, yeah, hi," she panted when she finally came to a stop.

"Do I know you?" he continued, blowing a stream of smoke over her head. She was a lot shorter than him. He was fairly tall, but she only reached to maybe the middle of his chest.

"No. I'm Delaney," she said, raking her fingers through her thick hair. She had massive amounts of it, and it was all wavy and coarse, like it wanted to curl, but couldn't make up its mind.

"Good for you."

She was hot, he'd give her that, but he didn't know her, and she had "good girl" rolling off her in waves. He wasn't into good girls, and he wasn't into people wasting his time. Whatever she wanted, he wasn't interested.

"Okay," she shrugged her shoulders and continued on. "Um, you were at Crash's party tonight."

That surprised him a little. What had a girl like her been doing at Crash's?

"Yeah, I was."

"Yeah, I saw you leaving."

"Look," he sighed, flicking his ashes at their feet. "Is this going somewhere? I have a train to catch."

"It's just ..." she seemed nervous. She fiddled with a strand of her hair, and her big blue eyes were looking everywhere but at him. "Okay, I'll level with you. I've only lived here for a few months, so I don't know how this works."

"Jesus christ," he muttered, rubbing at his eyelids with his free hand. "How *what* works?"

"I heard you were holding," she said, leaning towards him and speaking under her breath. His eyebrows shot up.

Is this chick for real?

"Holding?"

"Yeah."

"What? My dick?"

Her cheeks turned a faint shade of pink, but to her credit, she didn't back down.

"I was hoping for something more exciting," she snapped back.

I'm almost impressed.

"What is it you want. I'm not a cop, so just say it," he sighed.

"Coke. I heard you had some coke, but before I could ask you for some, you left the party," she blurted out. He barked out a laugh.

"You want some coke? Have you ever even seen drugs in real life?" he asked, deliberately looking her over. The blush on her face grew stronger, but she still stood her ground.

"Have you ever seen a hair brush in real life?" she asked back, staring up at his unruly mop of hair. It was a lot like hers, thick and course and a little wavy. He couldn't be assed to go to a barber shop, so it had grown down to his shoulders.

"Alright, tough guy," he said, and he stepped closer to her before chucking his cigarette into the gutter. "Let's say I do have some blow. What are you gonna give me for it?"

"I don't know, how much money do you want?" she asked.

She was actually *very* hot. She had an angelic face with dark lips—he could already tell they looked most natural in a big smile. Her blue eyes popped against her porcelain skin and dark hair. She was wearing a pair of skinny blue jeans, Chucks, and a thin tank top. It was only early March, but New York was having a very unusual heat wave. Jackets weren't necessary on that night. He let his eyes wander over her body. Her rounded hips and high, firm breasts.

"Maybe I don't want money," he replied. She snorted.

"Well, I could kick you in the balls a couple times, then check your pockets. Sound good?" she offered.

"Kinky."

"Look, are you going to sell me the stuff or what, douchebag?" she asked in an impatient voice.

"Hey, I don't gotta do shit—I'm not the one looking to score," he snapped back. "So if you want to get high, you better learn how things work around here."

"Enlighten me. How do things 'work' around here?"

"It means if I say you need to suck my dick for blow, that's what you're going to do."

She slapped him across the face, hard. He felt the sting long after she'd started walking back towards the party.

"Suck on that, ass wipe!" she yelled back, holding up her middle finger in the air.

He rubbed his hand against his cheek and realized he was smiling to himself.

Goddamn. I like her.

His smile turned into a full on grin and he started walking after her.

"Hey!" he called out. She didn't acknowledge him, so he jogged to catch up.

"Go away," she snapped when he reached her side.

"Let's start over. What was your name again?" he asked, having already forgotten her introduction.

"Bitch Who Will Mace You," she replied, and he was a little surprised when she started reaching for her back pocket. They'd stopped at the front gate to the party, so he grabbed her arm and gently pulled her aside.

"Seriously. Sorry I was an asshole. Really. Take pity on me, I'm not well."

"That's obvious," she snorted, yanking her arm away from him.

"Look, I'll *give* you the coke," he said. "Just tell me your name again, I wasn't paying attention the first time."

She glared at him through narrowed eyelids for a moment, then she let out a deep sigh.

"Delaney," she said.

"Delaney. Unusual."

"Give me the coke."

"Don't you wanna know my name?"

"Not really. Drugs, please."

*I like her **a lot.***

"Jayson," he offered, taking her hand in his and forcing her to shake it. "Jayson Fairbanks."

"Lovely to meet you. Coke. Now. In my hand," she replied, holding her free hand out, palm up.

"You know, Delaney," he sighed her name as he grabbed her other hand. She glared and pulled at his grip, but he didn't let go. "I think you and I are going to be good, good friends."

CHAPTER
two

Things I Know About Myself:

I am most likely somewhere between the ages of 24 and 28.

At some point in time, most likely when I was young, I broke my leg. I still have a scar.

I have four fillings, all in molars. Most likely done when I was young.

I have four tattoos—one on the inside of my left forearm, by my elbow. One on the top of my right hand thumb. One on my back at the bottom of my neck. One on my left rib cafe, right under the pectoral muscle. No one recognizes them or what tattoo shop they may have come from. None appear to be new.

I fell (or jumped or was pushed) off a subway platform in Brooklyn on October 31ˢᵗ. I was waiting for the L train at the Bedford Avenue Station (though I don't know if I was coming from somewhere, or going to somewhere, or what I was doing in Brooklyn).

I was taken to NYU Langone-Cobble Hill Emergency Room in Brooklyn directly after the accident. They were unable to provide the medical care my injuries required. Due to the holiday, all affiliate and surrounding hospitals were overcrowded and/or couldn't provide the medical care I needed.

On November 1ˢᵗ, I was transferred to Lenox Hill Hospital in New York, because they were the closest hospital that had an open bed and a neurology team ready to take my case on immediately.

On November 16ᵗʰ, I woke up. I have virtually no memory of anything before that day, except for basic things like eating, walking, writing, reading, speaking, etc.

On November 29ᵗʰ, I was told I would be discharged within a few days. I have no identity. No social security card, and no possibility of getting a new one, which means no job. I have no name, no birth certificate, no credit score, no references. I HAVE NO IDENTITY.

On November 30ᵗʰ, I fully realized I was totally and completely fucked.

"You are not fucked," Mrs. Sloan sighed.

Jon had discovered hospitals assigned social workers to certain patients, to help with their cases. Jon was one such patient. She was tasked with keeping his medical file organized and helping him understand it. She also helped him schedule meetings with different doctors and specialists, as well as getting him in touch with a pro-bono attorney to help him understand his rights and what he could do about his situation.

That meeting hadn't gone very well.

"Explain to me how I'm not fucked, Sloany," he snapped, throwing a file full of papers onto his bed. "The U.S. Government won't issue me a new social security number because technically I already have one. It's not their problem I can't fucking remember it. With out that number, I can't get a job. I can't even get a fucking I.D.! So what the fuck am I supposed to do? They're making me leave here in a couple days! How am I going to survive?"

"Your case is unique, Jon," she said in her calm tone of voice. He figured that's how Sloany had gotten her job. She had a very soothing voice which matched her very soothing appearance. She was thick and curvy, always wearing tailored pant suits or professional skirts with heels. Her blonde hair was most often swept up into some type of twist or bun, but that particular day she'd left it down. Her warm hazel eyes were usually smiling at him, never hinting at the razor sharp wit and sassiness that hid behind them.

"Yeah. Amnesia is pretty fucking unique," he grumbled.

"No it's not—a lot of people suffer from retrograde amnesia after brain trauma, but they usually, eventually, remember. The amnesia is almost always temporary. What makes *you* unique is your memories haven't made any sign of returning. Despite what movies and books would have us believe, it's not a common occurrence. You could get your memories back tomorrow, or never. We just don't know, and so … yeah, the U.S. Government can't really help you."

"See? Fucked."

"*No,*" she insisted. "You're lucky they sent you here. Lenox Hill is a great hospital, and a lot of people here want to see you do well, and none more than me. I have some plans for you, and I want to go over them today."

"Oh, *good,*" he groaned, falling into his chair. He ran his hand over his head, scratching at the ever thickening coat of hair, but avoiding his scar.

"Okay. You're healing up great, as you know. Spectacularly, even. You should be able to use your arm on its own in the next week or so. Your head is fine. So really, there's no reason you can't work," she said, opening a thick binder she had sitting on her lap.

"Except for the whole *I don't have a fucking identity* part," he snarled. She clicked her tongue at him.

"Attitude gets you nowhere, Jon. You must have been an annoying little shit in your last life."

He gave her a hard time, but he really did like Sloany.

"I wouldn't doubt it," he chuckled.

"Now, this is kind of wild, and not by the books at all. I had to call in a few favors, and we may have to fudge some stuff on your file, but I think I can get you into Benson House," she told him while she put on a pair of reading glasses.

"What's Benson House?"

"It's a halfway house."

"A what?"

"Technically, it's a *residential reentry center*, but let's be real, no one calls them that—everyone says halfway house. It's where they put prison inmates and recovering drug addicts prior to full release. Sort of reintroducing them to society," she explained.

"You want to put me in a house with a bunch of criminals," he clarified. She shrugged.

"Better than sleeping on the streets. You're right, there's nothing I can do about a job, and that's usually a requirement for the house. But you can also volunteer, so that's what we'll have you do. You must do at least fifteen hours a week in order to keep your room. Breakfast and dinner are provided for in the home, and you'll have assigned chores that will need to be done. There's a curfew, and no women allowed. If you break any rule, even once, they can kick you out, and there's nothing I can do for you then," she said.

God, it sounded awful. He was picturing some broken down piece of shit building, complete with a leaky roof and flickering lights. A parole officer bursting into rooms at random hours, shaking people down and looking for drugs in mattresses. A curfew? *Chores!?*

Would you rather sleep on the streets?

"How long do I have to stay there?" he sighed, rubbing his fingertips against his eyelids.

"Honestly, I have no idea, but I'll be right there with you the whole time, and you know you can call me day or night. I'm going to fight for you, Jon, even if it means calling the Social Security office every damn day. And I have some other ideas—we could get the media involved again, there's always interest in a crazy story like yours. The power of the press and all that," she said, sounding excited.

Jon frowned and turned to stare out his window. He didn't like her idea one bit. The one news spot he'd done, he'd felt like a circus freak. He got fan letters full of all kinds of strange things. Women who wanted to fuck him. Men who wanted to fuck him. It gave him the creeps. But it had also gotten him ten grand and his medical debt taken care of, so if he had to go through it all again, he guessed he could deal with it.

"Sounds peachy, Sloany. You're awesome, you know that?" he asked, looking back at her.

"Duh. So I've got homework for you, kiddo. I want you to really think about what you like doing. Do you think you're good with your hands? Do you remember anything about working with cars? Building stuff? What about food, can you cook? Can you clean? Are you any good at math? Can you do accounting? Computers, data entry, anything at all. It can help us place you somewhere for the volunteer work, and then later, help us fight to get you a job."

"Can do. I'll start making a list."

"Is there anything you want me to do?"

"Yeah," he said, and he started absentmindedly chewing at the side of his thumbnail. "I was wondering—the website fund thingy? The money all those people donated? They want to release it to me, but I need a bank account for it, but …"

"But you can't get a bank account," she finished for him. "I've thought about this, and I have a suggestion. You should get a conservator, or possibly give someone power of attorney for you, but in a limited capacity. They can open bank accounts and manage money for you, but it should be someone you trust."

"Someone I trust, that's funny. The only people I know are the ones in this hospital, you, and that lawyer prick," he snorted. He could tell she was fighting not to smile.

"I'd be happy to do it for you, but I want you to really think about it. Maybe there's a nurse or a doctor you've grown close to, I don't want to seem like I'm trying to run your entire life," she said.

"But you are running my life, and thank god because you know I'd just drive it straight into the ground. Please, it makes sense. I'll be seeing you all the time, at least until I get my memory back. *If* I ever get it back. If you don't mind, that is. I guess you probably have lots of sad cases begging for your help," he told her.

"Awwww, is this a pity party I hear? You're almost cute when you're being pathetic," she teased as she stood up. "Of course I'll do it for you. I'll look into what all needs to be done and I'll give you all the options, okay? And again, try not to worry. Stressing about all this on top of your injuries *on top* of your condition, it just makes things worse. You're not gonna be homeless, I won't allow it. Things *will* get better," she assured him while she packed up all her paperwork.

"You keep saying that. I'm not sure I'll ever believe it," he said, moving to chew on his index nail.

"Believe it, achieve it, dream it, whatever. Insert sunny motto here," she said. When she had all her stuff together, she took off her glasses and looked around the room, then sighed.

"What?" he asked.

"Next time I see you, it'll be to take you to your new home," she replied, walking towards him.

"God, my new home is a halfway house."

"Stop complaining, you ingrate. And stop *that*," she snapped, and he was shocked when she slapped his hand away from his mouth. "Chewing your nails is a nasty habit."

Jon stared at Sloany as she walked out of the room. Then he grabbed the paper he'd been writing on earlier, before she'd interrupted him.

I have at least one habit—I bite my nails.

BEFORE

Jayson Fairbanks hurried up the stairs, his hands shoved deep into his pockets. The unseasonably warm weather from early March had disappeared. Mid-April was rainy and shitty. He emerged from the underground station and squinted as he looked around.

"Jay."

He whirled around at the sound of his name, then broke into a smile.

Delaney Carter was hurrying towards him. She was bundled up like she was going to the north pole, wearing a parka with a fur lined hood. She had what looked like a padded tackle box hanging at her side, with a messenger bag strap holding it to her cross body style. She gingerly tiptoed around a puddle, then came to a stop next to him.

"Hey," he said, finally pulling his hands out of his pockets and jerking the collar of his jacket upright, trying to keep out the dampness.

"I didn't think you'd actually show up," she laughed. "I would've left my shit at school."

Delaney was going to beauty school. She was originally from Connecticut, but Brooklyn had always sounded "cool" to her, and she liked makeup. So a couple months after her twenty-first birthday, she'd moved to the big city and she'd yet to look back.

She was actually pretty good at it, as far as Jay could tell by looking at the makeup she did on herself. Like that day she looked like a '50's pin up girl, with cherry red lips and huge wings on the sides of her eyes. Other days, she could almost look like a Kardashian. Sometimes she even had wild colors going across her lids and neon shades on her lips.

She always looked beautiful, but if he was honest, he really did like her best without any makeup at all.

"Why didn't you think I'd show up?" he asked, cupping his hands together and blowing into them. She started walking and he fell into step beside her.

"You've bailed on me the last three times," she reminded him.

Right. The last time had been legit—he'd been delayed at his job. They'd been mad at him for being late and being high at work. He'd gotten mad because they were making him miss a date with Delaney. They'd asked what was more important, his job, or a piece of ass?

He'd quit the job, but by the time he'd gotten to the bar he was supposed to meet her at, she'd been long gone.

He had no real excuse for the other two times, though. He'd gotten high as fuck and simply forgotten.

Not that day, though. Something about this chick, she was special. He didn't want to let her slip away, so he was trying to be a good guy for a change. Maybe not a great guy, but at least better than he was before—so he'd shown up for their afternoon date totally clean and sober.

Well, for now, anyway.

Though they'd spoken on the phone a lot and messaged each other quite a bit, they'd only gone on a handful of dates since they'd first met. She'd played hard to get—he'd had to extort her number from one of her friends. Then, between their two schedules, it had been difficult to find times to meet. They both lived in Brooklyn, but not close together. In the month and a half since their first run in, they'd only gone out alone maybe three times total.

Three times was enough, though. He was going to marry this girl someday. She was sexy, she was funny, she didn't take any shit, and she liked to party. Jay *loved* to party. He'd been afraid at first because upon first introductions, she came off so clean and wholesome. Now he knew it was just the way she looked. She could drink like a fish and cuss like a sailor. It was *awesome*.

"So where do you wanna eat?" she asked, moving away from him so she didn't have to walk through a pile of slush.

"Hey, you asked me out, so it's your choice," he pointed out. She laughed at him, but he didn't care. He loved the sound of her laugh. It was almost like she was singing.

"Yeah, but I didn't think you'd come! I don't know, do you like Thai?" she asked.

"Not really."

"Okay, sushi? Or there's this great Korean place by my apartment."

Her apartment, hmmm. He'd hadn't gone there yet, didn't even know her address. Just knew she lived close to her school. Maybe if they went to Korean food, they could go up to her place afterwards, and he could finally relieve some of the sexual tension brewing between them.

"Korean sounds good," he said in an innocent voice. She snorted.

"You're not getting laid, jack ass."

He barked out a laugh. Another awesome thing about Delaney, she was fairly psychic. It was either that, or they shared a brain. She often seemed to know exactly what he was thinking.

"Okay, okay, fine. How does Mexican sound?" he asked, eyeballing a festive looking sign for a restaurant a couple shops ahead. She nodded.

"Mexican sounds great. You wanna grab a table while I run home and put this stuff away?" she asked, holding up her makeup "tool kit".

"Yeah, sounds good. Want me to order drinks?" he asked as they came to a stop in front of the restaurant. He rubbed his hands together, trying to create friction.

"Yeah, just get me a beer."

So unpretentious. He loved it. He didn't even care that he could in no way afford to treat her to dinner. He'd figure it out later, after he made her fall in love with him.

"One beer, coming up," he said through chattering teeth.

She laughed her awesome laugh again, then she stepped up close to him. She fussed with his collar, forcing it upright again, then she buttoned his jacket all the way to the top.

"You never dress for the weather," she said, unwinding a black knit scarf from around her neck and looping it around his. "I worry about you, you're gonna freeze to death one of these days."

He stared at her while she tied the material in a knot around his throat. She wasn't looking at him, she was concentrating on what she was doing, the corner of her mouth crooked up into a sideways smile.

He didn't pause to question his next move. He leaned down and covered the distance between them, catching her off guard with a kiss. She didn't pull away though, just gasped softly, then leaned closer. They didn't touch anywhere else, just their lips.

Just our souls.

"So a beer, huh?" he asked in a scratchy voice when he pulled away. But only a little, his nose was still brushing against hers. She didn't move, either. Just stared up at him with wide eyes.

"Yeah. I'll be back as fast as I can."

"You better."

CHAPTER
three

Jon twisted his fingers together. What he really wanted to do was chew on his nails, but he was trying to break the habit. He thought it was grossly unfair—his brain couldn't remember his own name, but it could remember he liked to chew his fingernails? What was that bullshit?

And also, Sloany would slap him if he did it.

"So you really think I'll like this place?" he asked, trying to keep his nerves out of his voice. She glanced over at him, then went back to concentrating on driving.

"Yeah. I took a tour a couple days ago. It's not the Ritz, but it's nice, Jon. The people were nice, too."

He was officially no longer a ward of the hospital. Dr. Anand had claimed they didn't just "kick people out", but it had only been a half-truth. If a person was seriously sick or injured, no, they would not kick them out.

But if a person was healthy and could fend for themselves, like

Mr. Jon Doe, then the hospital sent them packing without so much as a backward glance or saying "good luck".

Since he didn't know anyone and couldn't remember his family, there'd been no one to call to pick him up. Sloany had gotten his clothes cleaned, so he'd put them on and then a nurse rolled him downstairs. Sloany had been waiting for him in the parking lot with her silver Corolla.

"Can I start calling you Mom?" he asked. She made a choking sound.

"God, no! Jesus, Jon, I'm probably only ten years older than you, at most!" she snapped. He shrugged.

"I don't have a mom, really. And you take care of me," he pointed out.

"Because it's *my job*," she reminded him. He grinned at her.

"C'mon, admit it. I'm your fave."

"I admit nothing."

She was smiling when she said it, though.

She parked a couple blocks away, then led him to a nondescript building. It was in a fairly nice area of Harlem. Not upscale, but not run down, either. Solid middle class. Both the Lincoln Correctional Facility and Edgecombe Correctional Facility occasionally sent former prisoners to the Benson House, as it was situated somewhat between the two of them.

It also wasn't terribly far from Lenox Hill, so he could go for check ups easily. He still had physical therapy for his arm, and doctors and therapists still wanted to see him regularly to check in on his amnesia.

The house was large and clean, if a bit shabby. A woman greeted them at the door, shocking Jon a little. Where was the scary parole officer? This woman looked like she could be Everyman's mother. She was on the heavier side, with a floral pattern dress and an apron, and he had an overwhelming urge to hug her.

She led them into the building, where they met Mr. Gary Tupper.

He ran the house alongside the woman, Ms. Gaines. She showed up at six every morning and was gone by seven o'clock, and did all the cooking.

Mr. Tupper was surprisingly nice. He was older, probably in his sixties, but he was a retired Marine. He had a loud laugh and a great smile, but Jon could tell the man could kick his ass six ways to Sunday and not even break a sweat.

"I know you're not from any of the rehab centers or prisons," Mr. Tupper was saying as he took them upstairs. "But I expect you to follow all the same rules as our other inhabitants. You certainly won't be treated any different."

"No, sir, I wouldn't want to be," Jon said quickly. Mr. Tupper glanced approvingly at him, then nodded and unlocked the fourth door down the hall.

"This is your room—it will never be locked again while you stay here. If you attempt to change the lock, or to block the door in anyway from the inside, your door will be removed for a week long period. If you attempt either again, you will be expelled. Understood?"

"Understood."

They walked into the room. It was small, with a full sized bed, a scratched dresser, a filmy mirror, and a tiny closet. There was a window, though, and it looked out over the back garden. Ms. Gaines kept an herb and vegetable garden out there, so it was actually a pretty nice view.

"Take a look at this room as it is right now—whenever you aren't here, it should look like this, okay? Failure to keep your room in an orderly manner will result in losing your door. Repeated failures will result in expulsion. Understood?"

"Yes."

"No weapons, drugs, or alcohol are allowed in this house. We do weekly random inspections of all the rooms. If we find anything like any of those in your room, it will result in immediate expulsion. If you are found to be using drugs or alcohol, inside or outside of the house, you will be expelled. If you are engaging in criminal activity, inside or outside of the house, you will be expelled. Understood?"

Jon felt like he was going through boot camp, but he still answered, "yes, sir."

"Curfew is ten o'clock at night, sharp. That does not mean ten-oh-one, or ten-oh-two. That door locks at ten o'clock on the dot, and if you're not inside it, you have to find somewhere else to sleep. You break curfew once, you lose your door and your curfew changes to seven o'clock. You break it twice, you're expelled.

"On the bottom floor, outside the kitchen, you will find our chore board. You are assigned weekly chores. You will do them, and you will do them well. All the men here are required to have jobs, and they report to me with proof of hours worked. You will do the same with volunteer hours worked. I understand you've already found a volunteer job, you will need to get a supervisor to sign off on your hours each days. If you fail to bring me your hours or keep up on your hours, it will result in—"

"Expulsion," Jon finished for him. "I'll make sure to keep on track with them."

"I'm real sorry about your situation, son, but it has to work this way. The other guys see someone getting special treatment, and it turns into Attica in here. Besides, room and board aren't free anywhere. You want to eat, you gotta give back to society somehow. But as long as you play by the rules and do everything you're supposed to, I think we'll get along just fine," Mr. Tupper told him. Jon nodded.

"Of course, sir."

"Oh! And one more thing," the old vet said as he started to leave the room. "Absolutely positively no women, you hear me? I know it's hard for good looking guys like yourself, but it's the rules. Ms. Gaines is the only woman allowed on the premise, with the exception of parole officers and social workers visiting. If you're caught with a woman in here, well ... let's just say I can think of more embarrassing things to do to you than removing your door."

With a wink and a cackle, the man disappeared around the door frame and they listened to him stomp down the stairs.

"Charming, don't you think?" Mrs. Sloan asked, smiling big at Jon. He stared back at her with wide eyes.

"I'm going to die here."

"God, you're such a baby!" she groaned. "I mean, look! Nice big bed, and hey! I think they're growing tomatoes out there!"

"Oh my god, *tomatoes!?*" Jon explained, pressing his hands against his cheeks. "Fuck what I said before, this is like heaven adjacent."

"I suppose I could find you a nice bridge to sleep under. Ever been gang banged by homeless dudes? I bet it's super fun," she offered. He grimaced and sat down on the edge of the bed.

"No," he sighed. "No, I'm sorry. Really, it's great. I have nothing to compare it to except where I've been, and it's a lot better than that, and certainly a lot better than being homeless. They're nice people, I'll get used to it. Thank you, honestly."

Mrs. Sloan smiled at him, then sat down on the bed, too.

"It's not forever, Jon," she assured him, bumping him with her shoulder. "And in three days, you start volunteering. It'll be fun, you'll see. You'll get to socialize, and I know a lot of the volunteers are right around your age. Won't that be nice?"

"Sure. Just like summer camp. *Can't wait.*"

While he'd been in the hospital, he'd done what Sloany had asked. He'd thought long and hard about things he thought he might like. Cars didn't spark much interest in him, but food did. Despite being pretty trim, he had a voracious appetite, and he'd watch the Food Network a lot. So he'd written down chef/cook as a job option.

After Sloany had gotten conservatorship over him, he'd had her use some of his donated funds to buy him a cell phone, as well as a decent laptop. He'd remembered how it worked, how to open it, turn it on, and surf the web, but that was about it. He was pretty sure being good at watching cat videos didn't qualify him for anything, so he hadn't written down computers.

He was, it turned out, pretty good at math, though. Algebra seemed very familiar to him, and anything with weights and measures. Had he worked in a lab? He'd written it down as a possibility, as well as accountant.

Then he'd written down his Spanish speaking abilities, and the fact he seemed to have an obsession with cartoons—could he have worked in a daycare? Been a babysitter? He was pretty sure no, because the idea of being around kids made his skin crawl, but he'd written it down anyway.

As it turned out, there wasn't a big volunteer pool for semi-bilingual lab working accountants who babysat. There were, however, a lot of soup kitchens and food banks. Sloany had gotten him work in a huge community center that worked with the homeless. He would be assigned to the kitchen, but there would be lots of other jobs for him to do and look into, if he wanted.

"Shut up, you really will love it. They have a gym you can use," she told him, pulling a brochure out of her ever present binder. "A rec hall—look, ping pong!"

"*Yay.*"

"I'll come by tomorrow and we'll go shopping, get you some more clothes," she said, looking him over. She'd grabbed him some pajamas and t-shirts to get him through the night and next day, but those were all the clothes he had. "Then before your work starts, I'll come get you and we can go get you coffee and prep you for the day."

"Sounds scintillating," he sighed, putting his elbows on his knees and his head in his hands.

"Seriously, Jon. Get your shit together," she grumbled, dropping the brochure on the bed and standing up. "You can either make the best of what's been handed to you, which is a bunch of awesome stuff, or you can just give up right now and lay down and die. All because you don't have a name."

Jon didn't say anything as she left the room, slamming the door shut behind her. He stayed hunched over for a moment, then he laid back on the bed. Stared up at the ceiling.

… all because you don't have a name …

It wasn't that simple, of course, but she was also right. He could have it a lot worse. He could be out on the streets with no one to care about him, which pretty much sounded like what his life had been like before he'd had his accident.

Now, he had great doctors and an awesome social worker looking out for him. He had total strangers offering to pay for stuff for him. Life wasn't perfect by any means, and it probably wouldn't be for a long time, but it wasn't awful. He wasn't in control now, but someday, he would be.

And right now, there was something he *could* control.

At least I can fucking name myself.

BEFORE

Jayson prowled from room to room, peering through the dark lighting. Almost every light bulb in the upstairs part of the house had been replaced with a red one, making it a bitch to see anything. Everyone's faces looked the same. But he was pretty sure Del wasn't among the crowds, so he headed back downstairs.

She liked to play hide-and-seek. Whenever they went to a party, it was only a matter of time before she disappeared. He always threatened to just leave, but he never did. He always looked for her, and he always found her. One time hiding in a shower, the water even running. Another time in a seedy den, hiding behind a couch—the smoke trail from her joint had given her away.

The worst time had been when he'd come upon her in a garage. Some other guy had found her first and had been trying to talk her into doing heroin. Jay had beaten the shit out of the guy, which had resulted in the cops being called, which meant everyone had scattered. Delaney had called him from her apartment an hour later; she'd run through a bunch of back yards, then doubled back to look for him and almost gotten arrested.

It was the end of April and they were back at their friend Crash's place. The dude had inherited a big old house and regularly held some crazy ass parties. The houses on either side of his were condemned, so there were no neighbors to really complain.

That weekend, it was really rocking. Most of the rooms upstairs were filled with people either dancing or getting high. Downstairs wasn't much different. The living room walls had been covered with black trash bags, then splashed with the liquid from glow sticks. Bodies danced and writhed under black lights.

Del wasn't there, though, so he went into the kitchen. Someone was attempting to make a grilled cheese, and he prayed the house wouldn't catch on fire. A gaggle of girls were snickering by the pantry doorway, but immediately stopped when he came around the corner.

Gotcha.

"Alright," he sighed, lifting his hand to rake his fingers through his hair, then stopping himself. He couldn't do that anymore—Delaney had given him dreadlocks the week before. "Game's over. C'mon out, Del."

"We don't know what you're talking about," one of the girls, a blonde, said around a lungful of smoke. She passed a joint to her friend.

"We don't know any Del," the other girl said.

"Delaney. Come out here. Now," he said.

"I told you, we don't—" the girl started saying again, but she was interrupted.

"*No!*" a voice shouted from inside the pantry. "Don't come back here!"

"What? Why not?" he asked, walking forward. The girls formed a solid wall in front of him.

"Just ... don't come in here!"

He was actually a little nervous. Was she high? Was she with someone? Was she with a guy? Was she hurt?

"This game is super cute, but we're done here," he said, and before the girlfriend brigade could reply, he simply picked up the blonde chick and deposited her behind him.

He stepped into the pantry, then fell short. Delaney was sitting on the floor and she was surrounded by snacks. An open bag of Oreos was in her lap, and a bag of Goldfish Crackers was next to her. A whole smorgasbord of ungodly goodness spread away from her feet.

"Nooooo," she moaned, hugging the Oreos to her chest. "I don't want to share!"

Jay barked out a laugh, then bent down and grabbed her by the arms. She squirmed for a moment, then let him pull her to her feet.

"So greedy!" he teased, fighting with her to get at the treats.

"Can you believe Crash has all this stuff!? He's been holding out on us!" she said, finally offering him a cookie.

"Where did you find it all?"

"It was just out in the open, behind the door over there, the one with the lock on it."

Broken lock, she must have meant. He laughed again when he took in the hanging hinge and padlock. She'd probably kicked in the door, hoping to find a good hiding spot, but had instead found Crash's secret stash of goodies.

"You're awful, you know that? How stoned are you right now?" he asked, looking into her eyes. They were clear and bright.

"Not even a little," she replied. "I found all these snackies and was good."

"Yeah, I'm sober, too. But we can fix that," he assured her, then he started to reach for his pocket.

"No, wait! First, let's go dance," she insisted, dropping the Oreos and grabbing him by the hand.

"What? No, I told you, Del. I don't dance," he reminded her.

"Tonight, you do. C'mon! It's dark in there, no one can see you!" she said, dragging him into the living room.

Some techno remix of a current hit was blasting through the house, the heavy bass making the windows shake. He could barely hear himself think, let alone listen to what she was saying. But she was smiling and she was happy, so he smiled, and he was happy.

She held onto his hand and started moving to the rhythm. Singing along to the lyrics. She would dance close to him, pressing her body tantalizingly against his for a second, then she would dance away. Rub shoulders with another happy party-goer. Laugh at some wasted dude wearing a tutu. Then she'd be close again and he could smell her perfume surrounding him.

The next time she danced against him, he put an arm around her waist and held her close.

"You're a good dancer," he said in her ear. She nodded, circling her hips against him.

"I know," she replied, and he shivered when he felt her hand sliding up his back, underneath his t-shirt. They'd only been seriously dating for a couple weeks, and they didn't often spend time alone together. Usually it was party after party, or she was at school, or at work, or he was wasted on someone's couch and didn't answer his phone.

But tonight, he was very sober and very present and thinking very clearly.

"I don't want to be here anymore," he said loudly.

"Where else would you rather be?"

"Anywhere alone with you."

It was as simple as that, apparently. So much for playing it cool all those weeks. She simply nodded and walked away, still holding his hand. He followed in her wake, moving up the stairs behind her. She must have planned it all out, he realized later, because she took him to the only empty room in the house. Crash's bedroom.

Jay stood in the open doorway while she wandered into the room. He wasn't sure what was going on—was she getting her jacket? A purse?

"How long were you gonna take to make a move?" she asked him, her voice just barely audible over the music. He chuckled and leaned against the door frame.

"A while," he was honest. She walked over to the bed, which was just a single mattress on the floor with some blankets and pillows scattered on top of it.

"Why?"

"I don't know. You just … you're a good girl, Del. I didn't want to rush it or fuck it up or freak you out."

"Hmmm, maybe I like it fast," she said, turning around to face him.

"Thank god."

"Jay," she said, unbuttoning her pants.

"Yeah?"

"Shut the goddamn door."

He kicked the door shut behind him and quickly locked it before storming across the room. She'd barely gotten her last button open before he was crashing into her. He held her face in his hands and kissed her without any hesitation.

She moaned and he felt her nails raking down his back. Then she was pushing and shoving at his jacket and he had to let her go so the material could fall to the floor.

"God, I was beginning to think this would never happen," she groaned as she pressed her whole body to his.

"Hey, this is a modern world, you know. You could've made the moves on me," he pointed out while he toed off his shoes.

"*I did*, jack ass. If I hadn't, we'd still be downstairs dancing," she laughed, pulling at his t-shirt.

They stumbled around the room in their hurry to get undressed. Pushing and pulling at each others clothing. She sat up on the dresser while he struggled to pull off her ridiculously tight pants. She giggled and leaned back against a mirror till he'd finally yanked the material free from her feet.

"God, Del, your body," he groaned, moving to stand between her parted legs. She was in her underwear, just a simple black bra and matching cotton panties. She was a small girl, but shapely and proportional. Rounded and soft.

"*Your* body," she whispered, trailing her fingers down his chest and stomach. His lifestyle and his genetics kept him lean, and his living habits kept him tone. When he wasn't stoned out of his mind, he was always walking, always running, always moving.

"You sure you want to do this here? Good girls don't usually get fucked in a random bedroom at a drug fueled party," he teased, planting his hands on the dresser and kissing his way along her shoulder.

"Good girls are boring. I love getting fucked in random bedrooms," she informed him as she tugged at his pants.

"Wait, how many times have you been fucked in—"

He was cut off by her hand on his dick. No, she most definitely was not a good girl, he decided. She was fucking *bad*, and he loved it. He moaned as she started stroking him, making him even harder.

"I think we have more important things to worry about right now," she breathed in his ear.

You're goddamn right.

It was all tongues and teeth and lips from then on. He couldn't stop kissing her. He wanted to crawl inside her. There was lots of panting and whispering. Promising each other different things, most of them of the sexual variety. Some of them of the forever variety.

He didn't want to come in his pants, though, so he finally pulled her hand free and pinned her wrists to the mirror above her head.

"Delaney Carter," he whispered into her mouth as he held her wrists with only one of his hands. "You are a bad, bad, girl."

"I am," she agreed, then she shuddered when his free hand landed on her breast.

"What should we do about that?" he asked, moving his hand inside the cup of her bra and finding her nipple, rolling it between his fingers. Her eyelids fluttered shut.

"Um …" she mumbled. "Anything you want?"

"Good answer."

His hand continued its journey down into her underwear, where she was very hot and very wet. She must have been thinking about this moment long before she'd brought him upstairs. She scooted her butt to the edge of the dresser and wrapped her legs around his waist, giving him as much access as he could possibly want.

"Oh my god," she moaned. "Jayson. *Jay.*"

She was the only person who ever called him Jay. The only person he'd ever been close enough with to warrant a nickname. He loved hearing her say it.

"Again," he whispered, sliding one finger inside her.

"What?" she asked, her breath catching and stalling in her throat.

"Say my name *again,*" he urged, now thrusting two fingers in and out of her.

"Please, Jay," she groaned, struggling with his grip on her wrists. "God, I love this, but please …"

"Please what?" he asked, pressing his thumb down hard at her core. She yelped and squirmed, undulating her hips against him.

"God, I want you so bad, Jay. *Please*, I can't take it. I *need* you."

"You got me, babe. Anyway you want me," he told her, leaning his head down to trail his tongue across her breast.

"I'm dying here, Jay. I want you to fuck me," she begged.

"Goddamn, Del. Your mouth," he growled, hurrying to comply with her request. He pulled his hand free from her panties and let her wrists go. While he struggled to get the black cotton underwear off her, she pushed and pulled at his pants.

"I don't care," she was breathing heavy as she kissed and licked at his chest. "I've wanted this for so long. Since I first met you."

Fuck it, he didn't care, either. He left her underwear dangling from one of her ankles and he held her legs wide apart, stepping back into the space between them.

"Liar, you hated me. You slapped me," he chuckled, rubbing his erection between her thighs.

"You deserved it, but fuck, you were so hot. And you were look-ing at me like I was garbage," she told him, sucking on the side of his neck.

"I thought you were just some good girl who didn't know what she was getting into," he said.

"Well then, do you still think that?"

"No."

"What do you think about me now?"

"I think you're a very naughty girl who's about to get fucked."

Before he could do it himself, Delaney grabbed him by the base of his cock and it was her hand that guided him home. They both moaned when he started sliding inside her. Fuck, she was so warm and tight and all the things that were good and right in the world.

"Oh my god, I can't breathe," she gasped when she finally took him to the hilt. She'd leaned back again and she had her hands on her chest, playing with her breasts through her bra.

"You better learn to hold your breath, then," he said, his voice strained with the effort it took him not to pound her through the wall.

"Oh, I fucking will."

She just keeps surprising me.

He pulled away, then slowly slid back. He kept it up for a few strokes, in and out. Back and forth. Getting to know her all over again, from the inside out. It was fucking fantastic, but it wasn't enough for him, and it clearly wasn't enough for her.

"Harder," she moaned, scratching her nails up his chest before leaning close.

"Like this?" he asked, pumping his hips faster.

"Harder," she said it again. The lace of her bra was tickling him, so with one hand, he wrenched and pulled awkwardly at her straps, forcing the material off her chest and down to her waist.

"Fuck, this feels good," he groaned, thrusting harder still and reveling in the feel of her nipples brushing against his bare chest.

"God, yes," she cried out. "Don't stop. Don't hold back. *Fuck me harder.*"

He'd always said she was psychic, that she knew what he was thinking or wanting or needing. He wanted to pound her through the wall, so he figured she must know already; *that's* what she was really asking for. What kind of gentleman would he be if he denied her?

So he began fucking her as hard as he could. His fingers dug into her thighs as he held her legs as wide apart as they could go. She screamed and cried out, her hands gripping him by the neck so strongly, he could feel a friction burn from them.

"Fuck, babe, you feel so fucking good," he hissed, staring down between their bodies so he could watch them together.

"So good. This is better than good. This is the best," she panted, tracing her tongue along his bottom lip. He groaned as nerve endings fired and shot off sparks.

"Shit, we should've done this weeks ago," he groaned. "Our first date. Fuck it, the first time we met."

"Yes, yes, yes," she chanted to the rhythm of his thrusts.

One of her hands fell away from his neck. He was biting down on her earlobe when he felt it again. Her fingertips, sliding around his cock as it pumped in and out of her. They would disappear for a second, then touch him again, then disappear again. Over and over. He realized she was playing with herself *and* him, at the same time.

"Fuck, you're gonna make me come," he warned her. She let out a throaty laugh and her hand moved.

"I want you to," she urged, pumping her hips back against him.

"Fucking dirty girl, wanting me to come," he chuckled, leaning back enough to grab one of her legs. She gasped and shuddered as he pushed it up, almost far enough that it was touching her chest. Then he rested the back of her calf against his shoulder.

"Holy shit, Jay, you're so fucking … deep …" she groaned, cracking the mirror when her head fell back against it.

"So fucking deep," he repeated, kissing along the edge of her leg.

He could feel it starting. Her pussy tightening around him, almost convulsing. Her whole body started to shake, and even in the dim lighting, he could see a faint blush start to spread across her tits. He cupped them in his hands, squeezing gently.

"Oh, please," she whispered, her fingernails clawing him. "Please, fuck me, I'm going to come. Jesus, Jay, I'm going to come so fucking hard."

"Do it, do it, do it," he demanded, pumping as hard as he could. The whole dresser was moving and shaking, pounding into the wall behind them. She couldn't catch her breath and she squeezed her hands over his, catching her breasts in a death grip.

"Oh my god, Jay … Jayson … *Jayson, I'm coming.*"

Beautiful words to hear from any woman, but coming from Delaney, shit. He actually felt *proud* of himself. Like he'd done his duty to god and his country, now he could die happily. While she screamed and her pussy turned into a vice around his dick, he fell forward onto her. He dropped their hands from her chest and took one of her nipples between his teeth, biting down. She cried out again and convulsed, her limbs cramping up and locking around.

"Fuck, Del. I can't … I can't … I'm gonna come in you," he growled, his whole body flush with hers as his hips pumped away.

She didn't respond and she didn't let him go, so when he came a second later, it was deep inside of her. He shuddered and groaned and bit into her shoulder. All of his muscles clenched and locked together while his orgasm went through him like an electrical current.

"Jay, Jay, Jay," she sighed his name over and over again, and he realized her hands were on his head, holding him close.

"Holy shit, Delaney," he gasped for air, turning his head to the side and laying his cheek on her abused shoulder.

"That was … better than anything I'd fantasized it would be," she told him, still trying to catch her breath.

"You've fantasized about us fucking?" he asked, a little surprised.

Of course he'd fantasized about it. More than was healthy. But for some reason, he'd never thought about her doing it.

"God, all the time," she chuckled. "I'm gonna wear out the detachable shower head at my apartment."

"That is *So. Fucking. Hot*," he informed her. She purred and rubbed her body against his.

"Want to know what I fantasized about? What I imagined you doing to me?" she whispered in his ear, and then she started telling him.

He'd just fucked her so hard, he was pretty sure he was going to collapse once he let her go. But the feel of her body against him and the sound of her voice in his ear and what she was doing to him with her words …

Seriously. Fucking marry this woman.

CHAPTER
four

Jon was trying to be a good sport. He'd trailed behind Mrs. Sloan through a Ross "Dress for Less!" store, but when she'd told him to grab whatever he normally wore, they'd both fallen into an embarrassed silence. Jon didn't know what he normally wore. So he just tried on a bunch of different clothing she helped him pick out, trying to figure out his sizes. They walked out with a lot of polo shirts and jeans, and even a couple pairs of shoes.

Then he let her talk him into going to a salon, where he was asked what style he normally wore his hair in—short? Long on top? Styled? He couldn't answer, so Sloany just asked them to give his short hair some kind of shape, just neat and trim. After a trip to a department store for some decent cologne, which she picked out all on her own, she finally took him to Starbucks, but she left him alone at the counter.

"What can I get for you?"

Who would've thought it could be such a crippling question? He stared helplessly at the huge menu. Did he like lattes? Americanas? Espresso, or no? Flavor, or no? Iced, or no? The barista stared at him, so Jon gave up and just ordered a regular coffee, black, and a bagel for himself.

Jesus, do I even like coffee?

Not a great start to his first day at "work", he decided when he sat down. He was already in a bad mood, and worse, it turned out he didn't like coffee. He was sipping at his bitter, unpleasant drink when Sloany finally came back from the bathroom.

"Ready to tackle the day?" she asked in her smooth voice, smiling big at him while she slid into her seat.

"Thrilled. Where am I working again?" he asked, stuffing pieces of bagel into his mouth.

"The, uh … oh, here—the Peter Blakeman Community Center. A Miss Katherine Beaumont will be your supervisor, she'll get you set up and tell you what to do and sign off on your hours," Sloany explained.

"And what exactly am I gonna be doing?"

"Meal prep, kitchen help, things like that," she told him, looking over a sheet of paper. "You'll be there from noon to three, I'm just taking you early so you look good to everyone."

"Appreciated."

"I'll make a success of you yet, Jon Doe," she assured him. He cleared his throat.

"I made a decision about that."

"What?"

"My name. I thought about what you said last night, and it still sucks, not remembering. Not knowing. But I figure maybe having a real name will help. Mentally, or whatever. And *John Doe* just sounds so stupid, like I'm making it up," he said. She nodded.

"I like this. What have you decided?" she asked. He was glad she didn't just laugh at him.

"I'm used to Jon now, but no *H* in the spelling. And since Doe is what everybody already knows me by, I didn't want to get too far away from it. How does Jon Doherty sound?" he asked. She smiled broadly.

"Sounds like an incredibly successful, smart, sexy as all get out man," she assured him. He laughed.

"You only want to help me for my body," he joked.

"I'm glad you finally caught on," she rolled with it, then she glanced at her watch. "Well, c'mon *Mr. Doherty*, let's go make you a productive member of society!"

Jon grumbled, but he followed her out to her car. He was still nervous. If he could barely handle a Starbucks, how he was going to live through doing an actual job? What if he got in the kitchen, and he didn't know how anything worked? In his mind, he could picture a stove, and picture how it worked, but putting it into practice might be totally different.

The community center was a large brick building and the grounds were well manicured. A tennis court sat to the side, though the net had been removed and two battered basketball hoops had been put up at either end.

Inside there was a gym, just as Sloany had said, and a proper basketball court. Everything was very clean and well maintained, but dated looking. Down a hallway there were rooms with all sorts of things—computers filled one, a large work tables another, and one was almost wall to wall sewing machines.

At the very back of the building was a large cafeteria, filled with round tables and a bunch of chairs stacked against the back wall. Long, buffet style tables were against a different wall. Off to one side they found a large kitchen which was full of shiny, intimidating look-ing industrial appliances.

"Can I help you?" an older woman asked as she peeled off a pair of plastic gloves. Her mouth curved down at the corners and she looked at Jon reprovingly.

Great, looks like Miss Beaumont is gonna be a laugh riot.

"Hi, I spoke with your director about my client, Jon," Mrs. Sloan said, gesturing to him in introduction. "He's going to be volunteering with you. They said for him to be here at noon today, but he wanted to come early to learn about the place."

"Right, I remember hearing about you. Follow me," the grumpy woman sighed and started walking towards the back of the kitchen.

Jon was cursing every deity he could think of, wondering what he'd done to deserve this. How awful a person had he been that his memory had been wiped and he'd been placed in a job with a goblin for a boss? He kept his mouth shut as they walked down a hallway and stopped at a door.

"Katherine!" the goblin barked, knocking sharply. "The charity case is here!"

Huh?

He was confused at first, but quickly realized it must mean the ol' grump *wasn't* his boss.

"Please don't talk like that, Geraldine!" a light voice said from inside the room, then the door was ripped open. "It's just mean, and what if they heard …"

Jon stared at the woman in the doorway, a little shocked. She looked young, possibly younger than him. She had long blonde hair falling around her shoulders in perfectly curated waves and warm brown eyes that smiled at him, even though her jaw was hanging open. She was *stunning*. Like a model. He instantly felt the need to impress her. Wanted to say something professional and assuring.

"Too late," he blurted out, then was instantly embarrassed.

*Sloany was right, I must have been an **awful** shit in my past life.*

But the blonde girl laughed and pressed a hand over her face, then stepped out into the hallway. The other woman, Geraldine, walked off with a grunt.

"I'm sorry about her," the girl sighed. "She's just started a week ago, and she's having trouble adjusting. Her personal life is a little rough right now."

"Honey, whose isn't?" Sloany joked, and they all laughed again. "I'm assuming you're Katherine Beaumont?"

"Lord, where are my manners? Yes, that's me, I think we spoke on the phone," Katherine said, quickly shaking Mrs. Sloan's hand.

"Nice to meet you, I'm Bev Sloan, and this is the man we spoke about," Sloany said, turning towards him.

"Yes, John Doe, I heard saw you on the news once. I'm so sorry you're going through this," Katherine said, offering her hand. He took it gently in his own, like he was afraid he'd get her dirty or hurt her.

"Oh, no, this isn't John Doe," Mrs. Sloan said quickly. "This is now *Jon Doherty.*"

Jon was a little embarrassed, but Katherine seemed to roll right with it.

"Oh, well, it's a pleasure to meet you, Mr. Doherty," she said, pumping his hand up and down. He finally smiled at her.

"You, too, Katherine," he replied. She shook her head.

"Not Katherine, please. I always feel like I'm in trouble when people call me Katherine. Call me Kitty—everyone does," she urged. His smile got bigger.

"Okay. It's really good to meet you, Kitty."

She smiled back at him and he realized they were still holding hands.

"You, too, Jon."

BEFORE

"I want to know everything about you."

Jay looked down at his chest. Delaney was sprawled across it, drawing lazy circles on his skin with her fingertip. They were both completely naked, laying on top of her bed. If it hadn't been for her talking, he would've been knocked out. Having sex all day can do that to a person. They hadn't left the bed for anything, except using the bathroom. Not even to smoke the joints he'd brought over—he was shockingly sober and clearheaded for a Saturday afternoon.

Maybe this chick will be good for me. Get me on the right track.

"Like what, specifically?" he chuckled, running his fingers through her hair.

"Where you come from, what your family is like. Who your first love was, where you went to school," she said. He took a deep breath and glanced out the open window. It was mid-May and New York was starting to heat up for real.

"I'm from Iowa," he started, and she burst out laughing.

"You? You're from *Iowa?*" she asked. He looked down at her.

"Why is that so hard to believe?"

"You're just so … exotic. I don't picture people like you living in Iowa."

"Very narrow minded of you, Del," he teased. She bit him on the chest.

"Shut up and explain what a hottie like you was doing in farm country."

"My mother was a Mexican migrant worker at a farm there, wheat or some shit. My father was from Denmark, he has degrees in agriculture and botany or whatever. The farm she worked at, it's huge, like part of a corporation. He was hired to help with whatever botanists do on farms. He met her and it was end of story. He never went back to Denmark, she never left Iowa. She stopped working, they got married, they had me, and then two girls," he explained in a rush.

"Wow, Jay, that's pretty amazing! Danish and Mexican, huh?" she commented, brushing her fingertips across his forehead.

"Yup."

"So what happened? You keep saying 'was' and 'had'—did they die?" she asked. He shook his head, but didn't respond right away. He didn't want to tell her the truth.

"No. We're not close, we haven't spoken in a while. They're still in Iowa, still doing their thing," he answered evasively.

"What happened?"

"Just some bullshit."

Bullshit like he stole money and jewelry to pay for his habit. It was all in the past—he didn't do speed anymore—but they'd kicked him out and they'd never invited him back. Never even tried to check up on him. He hadn't seen his little sisters in over four years. But he didn't want Del to know that about him. She knew he was a hardcore partier, but he didn't think of himself as a drug addict, and he didn't want her to think of him that way, either.

"You can tell me, I won't judge you," she assured him, then she planted a kiss on his breastbone. He trailed his fingers up and down her spine while he stared at the ceiling.

"But I haven't answered your other questions," he distracted her. "Family was good growing up, my sisters are a riot. We all look alike, people thought we were triplets. I was pretty good in high school, got good grades, and got into Kirkwood Community College on a scholarship."

"I never knew you went to college," she commented, resting her cheek against him.

"Yup, Jayson Fairbanks ain't as stupid as he looks."

"Shut up."

"I only went for like two years, though," he said, going back to brushing his fingers through her thick hair. "I wasn't really into it, so I dropped out. A year or so later, I decided to move to New York with a bunch of friends. We wound up in Brooklyn, and I've been floating around Williamsburg ever since."

"Mmm," she mumbled. "And what about the love of your life? You didn't answer that question—I want to hear all about her."

He spread his fingers across the back of her head, holding her tightly to his chest.

"She's a crazy girl from Connecticut who seems like the girl next door, but fucks like the bad girl from the other side of the tracks. Just looking at her turns me inside out and I swear, I'm gonna fucking marry her someday," he said simply.

There was a long silence, but Jay wasn't nervous. He was rarely ever nervous, especially when it came to his feelings. They couldn't be helped and he couldn't control them, and he certainly couldn't control hers, so what was the point of being nervous?

Still, when she lifted herself and crawled up his body and planted a gentle kiss on his lips, his heart swelled.

"And when you finally ask her, she will definitely fucking say yes," she whispered.

CHAPTER
five

The weeks went by and Jon was surprised to find he was actually enjoying life.

He and the tough old guy who ran the halfway house, Gary Tupper, got along shockingly well. Mr. Tupper sort of took him under his wing. They would go running in the mornings, and at night they went down to a weight room he'd had set up in the basement. Jon had lost a lot of weight while in the hospital, but he quickly started putting it all back on in muscle.

Part of the weight gain was also thanks to Ms. Gaines, chef extraordinaire at Benson House. She managed to make some amazing meals out of the meager supplies they had—lots of carbs and protein, everything a growing boy needed. Jon helped out in the kitchen often, and took a real liking to her garden. He spent lots of time out there, weeding and raking and learning the basics of gardening.

The other guys in the house weren't so bad, either. A couple had massive chips on their shoulders, and there was an incident in the hallway which ended with Jon having a split lip and the other guy having a broken nose. A week without a door was punishment enough and after his one fight, he made sure to let nothing provoke him.

The rest of the guys, though, were honestly trying to better themselves and do right. They had a game night every Thursday. On Saturday nights, when the urge to go out and get into trouble was at its strongest, they would set up a poker game in the kitchen. They played for pretzels and peanuts, but it was nice. A strange sort of comradeship was built out of moments like those ones.

The best, though, was his volunteer work. He looked forward to it every day, and was genuinely bummed when it was over. He often worked longer than the three hours he was scheduled for, often as many as six, before he would remember he had chores he had to do at the house. Sometimes, though, breaking the rules almost seemed worth it, if it meant getting to spend more time with her.

Kitty was amazing. She was smart and she was kind and she had a good soul. It shone out of her face, anyone who spoke to her could see it. He showed up early and he stayed late, just to be in her beautiful presence. Just to stare at her for a little longer, just to flirt with her a tiny bit more. Sometimes she could be a bit bossy. A tad controlling. Maybe even a little, dare he say, snobby. But she *was* the boss, so she had to be that way at the community center. He wondered what she was like outside of her volunteer work.

She was one of those women who was always put together, and he realized he really liked that about her. She always had her hair and makeup done, no matter what time of day it was or how she was feeling. She was always dressed in nice clothing that complimented her great figure. And she always, *always*, wore a tiny gold cross around her neck.

"What's with the crucifix? You're here even on Sundays, so I know you're not going to church," Jon asked one day. She smiled sweetly but didn't look up from what they were doing. They were serving spaghetti and meatballs for dinner, which meant they were rolling hamburger into a million little balls.

"You don't have to go to church to serve," she replied simply.

"Good little southern girl like you, not going to church?" he clucked his tongue at her. "What would your mother say."

"You could ask her—she's right over there," she laughed, gesturing to a tall woman on the other side of the room who was directing other workers.

Kitty and her mom could almost pass as sisters. Same blonde hair, same figure, same warm eyes, and the same southern accent. Kitty's was a lot less noticeable, she'd been living in New York since she was eleven, and the years had softened it. But Mrs. Beaumont sounded like she was straight out of Baton Rouge.

"No, no, I'd hate to get you in trouble," he laughed. He loved teasing her and flirting with her. It seemed to get her flustered, like she wasn't sure what to do with herself. Her cheeks would turn pink and she wouldn't meet his eyes. But then she'd always surprise him by turning around and dishing it out right back to him.

"And what about you, Mr. Doherty? Why isn't an upstanding boy like yourself in church on Sundays?" she questioned, finally looking at him and raising an eyebrow.

"I don't know if I'm religious," he answered honestly. "For all I know, I was a satanist in my last life. Or worse—Scientologist."

"I wouldn't judge you if you were."

"Thank you."

"I mean, at least not to your face."

It almost felt weird, talking so normally about something so bizarre. She was standing next to a man with a made up name. Made up, because he couldn't remember his own name. But since day one, she'd acted like it was no big deal, as if it was just another fact about him. Like "you have green eyes, you're six-foot-three, and you have amnesia. Pass the lemonade, please." It was awesome. Even Sloany wasn't so good at acting like he was normal.

"You know what I think," he started, turning to grab a towel and wiping off his hands.

"Oh, I can feel it, I'm about to be enlightened," she snickered, wiping off her hands, as well.

"You look like a good girl, and you act like a good girl, but really, you're not even close," he called her out. She playfully narrowed her eyes and plunked her hands on her hips.

"You caught me, Jon. I'm not a good girl at all," she took the tease even further, stepping well into sexual tension territory when she moved closer to him.

"Not even a little. Nope, I think you're most definitely a *bad girl.*"

A shudder ripped across his shoulders after he said those words, startling him. His eyes flared open wide and he felt a strange, sinking sensation in the center of his chest. It was ... *familiarity*. But why? Something about those words, that term. *Bad girl.* What did it mean? Had he said those words before, to somebody else?

What the fuck does this all mean!? Jesus, was I really a babysitter?

"What's wrong?" Kitty asked, noticing the strange look on his face. He frowned and glanced around.

"I don't know, I ..." he licked his lips and struggled to explain himself. "I think I almost remembered something, but it's gone."

"Oh no!" she gasped, then she was grabbing his hands and squeezing them in her own. "It's gone already?"

"Yeah. It was just a second, more like a feeling. Probably nothing, don't worry about it," he tried to shrug it off. Kitty was having none of it, though, and she shocked him by pulling him into a hug.

"I'm so sorry you have to go through this, Jon," she sighed as she dropped her head to his shoulder. "You're a good person. You are now, and I just know you were one before, and you don't deserve this. I wish I could give you your memories back."

"It's okay," he said, slowly wrapping his arms around her shoulders. "I'm building new ones with you, and that's almost as good."

They stood together for a long second. He didn't want to let go.

She was so warm and wonderful smelling. She eventually did pull away, but only enough so she could look him in the face. She kept her arms around his waist.

"Jon," she spoke in a slow voice. "Come spend Christmas with us?"

"What?" he asked, shocked again.

"I was gonna ask you later today anyway. I want you to come home with me for Christmas next week," she insisted.

"No, I can't, it would be weird. I'd be the random dude who showed up to Christmas. I don't want to make your family uncomfortable," he said, shifting around in her hold, trying to break free. She squeezed him tighter.

"My mother loves you, you know that, and my dad has been asking to meet you. No one will be uncomfortable."

"Kitty, I can't afford to get anyone presents, I'd have to show up empty handed."

Ten-thousand dollars really didn't stretch very far when a person had literally nothing to their name. Sloany had worked out a budget for him which would optimize the money, make it last as long as possible, but it also basically meant he was dirt poor. He had planned on splurging and getting Kitty a gift anyway, but he couldn't get stuff for her whole family.

"Do you honestly think I care about stuff like that? You're going, it's done. I want you there, and we both know you can't say no to me, so you might as well give in now," she informed him.

He stared down at her. She was so good. Like a living angel. Her brown eyes carried her smile to him and when he looked down to see if her lips were mimicking them, he couldn't help it. His head dropped down to her and he met her lips with his own, wanting to taste her wholesome smile for himself.

She seemed shocked at first and went stiff, which almost scared him into stopping. God, what had he been thinking? But then she leaned into him and kissed him back, letting out a soft sigh.

"I'm sorry," he breathed when he finally pulled away. "I didn't think, I just—"

He knew he was on the verge of babbling, but she stopped him by placing her hand over his mouth.

"You definitely don't have to worry about presents," she said. He was confused.

"Why not?"

"Because you just gave me what I wanted for Christmas."

BEFORE

"I have the best idea," Delaney gasped.

Jayson nodded, digging his fingers into her hips as he walked her backwards across her bedroom.

"You always do. Can it wait till we're finished?" he asked, pushing her shorts down her legs.

"No," she said, sucking on his bottom lip quickly before shoving his jacket to the floor. "You're gonna love it, it's awesome."

"Nothing is as awesome as fucking you," he growled, throwing her coat at the bed. In doing so, he lost his hold on her and she skipped across the room, only wearing black tights, a tiny pair of panties, and a cropped sweater top with no bra.

"There's something I've always wanted to try," she said, bending over her dresser.

He tilted his head to the side as he walked towards her. He stared at Delaney all the time. Constantly. But he hadn't realized until that moment how much weight she'd lost over the past couple weeks. She was a short girl, as small as he was lanky, but she'd always had soft curves and rounded edges. She still had her perky breasts and her full ass, but he was surprised to realize she was kind of thin now.

"Maybe we should go to dinner," he suggested, wrapping his arms around her from behind. She snorted and rubbed her butt against him.

"Oh yeah, with what money? *Ah ha!*" she exclaimed, pulling a baggie out of his drawer in her dresser.

After losing his job, he'd never been able to get another one. Between parties and Delaney and occasionally side hustling drugs, he couldn't seem to find the time to turn in applications. His roommates had kicked him out, but it was okay because he and Delaney had already been talking about moving in together. It was well into June, they were together constantly, so it just made sense. So he carried all his meager belongings to her place in a trash bag and he'd barely left her room since.

His drug bullshit brought enough money to keep him fed, and Delaney had her job. She'd quit the beauty school—"*why pay for it when you can become Instagram famous doing the same shit?*"—and had gone to work full time. She didn't get paid great, but it was enough to keep them happy.

That was a month ago. A month of heaven. A month of laughing and talking and walking absolutely *everywhere* together. Jay was pretty sure there wasn't a piece of Brooklyn left unseen. A month of fucking and making love and promising each other forever. Of getting high and dancing and laughing and being young.

I swear, I mean it. I really am going to marry her. When things settle down and I get a proper job, I'm getting her a ring.

"My stash?" he asked, running his hands up her body and cupping her breasts. She nodded and shook the little bag full of white powder.

"I want you to fuck me," she said. "And when I'm about to come—give me a little bump."

"*You're so fucking sexy,*" he groaned, biting into her shoulder. She moaned and leaned her head back on his shoulder.

"You make me this way," she sighed, pushing her ass harder against his erection.

"Okay, sex and cocaine first. Then we're getting you a hamburger," he said, then he grabbed her by the hair and forced her to bend over the dresser.

"A hamburger? Kinky," she joked, then shrieked when he slapped her across the ass.

"You need to eat, babe," he told her, smoothing away the sting.

"What are you saying?"

"I don't want you to lose your curves," he replied, grabbing her ass cheek roughly before slapping it again.

"Not possible, I've been pudgy since birth," she laughed.

"I never would've called you pudgy, but you certainly aren't now. A little less coke, a little more carbs, okay?"

"Okay, after tonight. Right now I need you to fuck me."

He started yanking at her tights, ripping a hole over her hip, when someone began pounding on the bedroom door. They both groaned and Del dropped her head to the dresser.

"What!?" she shouted. "We're *busy!*"

"Get out here, right now!" her roommate all but screamed.

"No! It can wait till later!" Delaney shouted back.

"We talked about this, Del! I'm sick of it! I want you out!"

Delaney gasped, then stomped away from Jay. He reached for her too late, trying to stop her so she could put on some clothes. He knew how she got when she was mad—her brain shut down and nothing else mattered.

"What the fuck did you say to me?" she demanded. "I pay my fucking rent."

"No, you fucking don't," her roommate snapped. "You're a week late right now, and you were two weeks late last month. And I never agreed to living with *him!*" the girl leveled an accusatory finger at Jay while she spoke.

"Hey, don't blame her for me. I can go," he said, starting for the door. Del held up her hand.

"No! Jayson is my boyfriend and my guest, he can be here as long as he fucking wants."

"No, he can't, Delaney! We signed a contract, you and I! *Not him!* I don't want to listen to your weird sex anymore, or have to smell pot, or find fucking drugs everywhere! Just get out! *Get the fuck out!*" the other girl was shrieking. Del gasped, then narrowed her eyes. Jay recognized that face.

Oh, shit. It's on.

"You want me out? Fine. Fucking fine! I'm fucking gone! Good luck finding someone else to pay these prices, and to tolerate your stupid fucking ass. I can't have my boyfriend over, yet you can parade half of Red Hook through here? Fuck you, you piece of trash. Jayson, get your shit."

There was absolutely no arguing with Delaney when she was on the war path. He now knew better than to even try. They fought just as passionately as they made love. He'd received several more slaps since the first one back in March, and he didn't feel like getting another one that afternoon. He stepped aside as she started tearing around the room, shoving her clothing into a huge duffle bag.

"C'mon," Jay groaned, heading to the door. "Don't make her leave. I'll go. I won't ever come back, I promise."

"No," the roommate shook her head. "I don't want to live with some pill popping, coke snorting, wasteoid. Just go."

If he had thought it was on before, he had been sadly mistaken. She flew across the room and it took him a solid couple minutes to tear her off the other girl. When he finally picked her up, Del was kicking and shrieking, one of her hands clutching strands of her roommate's hair.

"Stupid bitch! Say shit again, you fucking piece of trash! You stupid slut!"

Jay kicked the bedroom door shut and they listened as the

roommate crawled off to her own bedroom, sniffling and crying. Delaney was breathing heavy and a scratch mark on her cheek was faintly bleeding. He frowned and rubbed his thumb over it.

"You need to calm down," he said in a soft voice, and she nodded.

"You're right. Shit, that was bad."

"Yeah, it kinda was."

"But I can't stay here, Jay. I don't want to stay with someone like her. Fuck, what are we going to do?" she asked, staring at up at him, her big blue eyes opened as wide as they could go.

He took a deep breath and closed his own eyes, having the same old argument with himself. Delaney was too good for this lifestyle. Too good for him. He should leave her. Dump her, make her hate him, make it so she'd never take him back. Make her want to go back to Connecticut and never even think of New York again.

Just the idea of it, though, made his heart hurt. It felt like he couldn't breathe without her. So he would just have to get better. He had to become worthy of her, had to give her the kind of life she *deserved*. He smiled and cupped her face in his hands.

"We'll figure it out, babe. We've got each other."

She sighed and pressed her hand over one of his.

"I love you, Jay. I really do. So much.

"Not as much as I love you."

They spent the rest of the time packing. Jayson's stuff went back into the trash bad. Delaney was able to fit her clothing and most of her belongings into a piece of rolling luggage, the duffle bag, a backpack, and a tote bag. Jay took the backpack and the duffle and stood near her door while she got dressed to go outside.

"You sure about this?" he asked. "Maybe you could talk to her."

"Fuck that," she snorted, shouldering the tote bag. "Let's get out of here. On to the next adventure."

"Whatever you say, babe."

They strode through the living room. The roommate's door was cracked open at first, but then it slammed shut when Delaney glared at it. Jay opened the front door and went into the hallway, but Del stopped and sat down her stuff.

"Just a sec," she said, stepping back into the apartment.

He stood there, then realized he could hear the sound of something glass shattering. He poked his head back into the room. He couldn't see her, though, she was in the kitchen doing something.

"What's going on?" he yelled. The light in the kitchen went out, then there was the breaking sound again.

"Nothing! Just leaving a parting gift," she replied, hurrying back into her bedroom where there was more breaking. Next was the bathroom, which had more of the same.

"Seriously, Del, let's just get the fuck ..."

His voice trailed off when she came into the living room. She had a sock covering one of her hands, and for a moment he thought she'd gone insane. Then she shoved the sock-hand under a lamp shade. She hissed a couple times, then the light went out. She'd unscrewed the light bulb. She threw the object to the ground and it shattered. She ground the glass under her boot heel, then went to every single other light bulb and repeated the act.

"There!" she shouted. "Have a nice fucking life in the dark, you awful gross bitch!"

Jay laughed clear until they were on the next block.

"Let's go to Crash's," he suggested after he'd calmed down.

"Party?" she asked, glancing up at him.

"No, not tonight, but he's usually good for a couple nights of crashing. We'll stay there through for the rest of the week while we sort this shit out," he told her.

"Oh my god," she gasped. "I never got it before!"

"Got what?"

"*Crash*. Everyone calls him Crash, and everyone *crashes* at his place. I feel like an idiot."

"At least you're a cute idiot," he offered, hugging her to his side. The walked in silence for a couple moments, then she spoke up again.

"I'm glad you're here. I'd be lost without you," she sighed. He snorted.

"Del, if I wasn't here, you wouldn't have gotten kicked out," he pointed out. She shook her head.

"Not possible. You and I were meant to be together, so this was meant to happen. It's just a step to something bigger."

They got to Crash's house. It would always hold a soft spot in Jay's heart. Where he'd first met Delaney, where they'd first had sex. He knocked on the door, then leaned down and kissed her quickly. He smiled when he saw the same familiar blush on her cheeks.

I hope it's always like this between us. Fast hearts and rushing blood and stained in love.

They were shown to the basement, where there were a couple of questionable mattresses strewn about. Luckily, Del'd had the forethought to bring a flat sheet along, so they spread it out over a bed in the corner. Then they sat down and counted all the cash they had between them, the money she had in the bank, and looked at how much coke was left.

"It's not good, babe," she mumbled, stacking the one dollar bills together.

"It will be, though. C'mon, let's order some Domino's, they've got a special going on right now. We'll eat pizza, I'll call some guys and unload these drugs, and that should hold us for a while," he assured her, playing with her phone, looking over the pizza deals. Del nodded, then picked up the baggie and opened it. She dipped her pinkie nail into it, scooping up a small amount of the white stuff.

"Last one for the road," she sighed, then she delicately snorted it up. Afterwards she dipped her pinkie back into the powder, coating it with cocaine, and brought it back to her mouth, rubbing it along her gums.

Jay stared at her, then leaned forward and kissed her. She was startled, but she opened her mouth to his tongue. He ran it up between her teeth and her lips, sweeping up trace amounts of the coke.

"You're so fucking sexy," he breathed for the second time that night, and she rolled her eyes at him.

"Whatever, loverboy. Order the pizza."

They got the food, then decided to go out and walk around. They headed to an upscale hipster neighborhood and managed to score—a couple tourists were wandering around, and they bought the remaining coke for way more than it was worth. Jayson suggested they start heading back towards Crash's place and Del actually skipped.

"I don't understand how you can be so excited," Jay laughed, looking down at her as she bounced along. "You're technically homeless."

"For the moment," she shrugged, then she got in front of him and wrapped her arms around his waist, walking backwards. "But I've still got you, and you're honestly all that matters."

"Love don't pay the bills, Del."

"Pretty soon, I won't have any bills. The phone is the only thing left. Love is all I need."

"Ah, love," he sighed. "That age old currency. Fuck god. In *love* we trust."

She stopped moving and he almost fell over her. He wrapped his arm around her as he stumbled to the side, trying to keep her upright.

"That's beautiful, Jay. You should go back to writing," she told him. He frowned at her.

In a moment of weakness, he'd told her what he wanted to be when he grew up. An author. He used to write all the time. But he'd just turned twenty-five the week before—he was pretty sure he *was* grown up, and he hadn't ever finished writing one single book. He rubbed his right hand up and down her back, thinking about the feather quill tattooed on his thumb.

"Maybe some day," he replied. "But not today."

"Well, remember that line. '*In love we trust*', I think it's great. I want to remember it forever," she told him, stepping to the side and linking her arm through his, falling into step beside him.

"You have the memory span of hummingbird. It'll be gone tomorrow," he teased her. She frowned.

"I don't want it to be gone. I want it to be a part of me. I want—oh my god, Jay! Look!" she exclaimed.

At the end of the street was a sandwich board he couldn't quite make out. Above was a blinking neon sign, and that he was able to read no problem.

Moonlight Tattoos.

"You want to get a tattoo?" he asked.

She didn't answer, just started running and dragging him along behind her.

There was no stopping her—not even pointing out it would take a lot of their meager savings. She just ignored him and took off her jacket, showing the tattoo artist where she wanted the ink. Just minutes later, there was beautiful, small script trailing along her skin at the base of her neck. The same spot where he had a geometric, abstract tattoo of the earth on his body.

While she giggled excitedly with the female tattoo artist, Jay stood close behind her. He put his hands on either side of the tattoo, staring at it. Such black ink, practically glowing against her pale skin. His words were on her forever. He would *literally* be a part of her *forever*.

Exactly how it should be.

"Hey," he said, startling the women when he started pulling off his t-shirt. "You got time for one more?"

CHAPTER
six

Kitty's family was amazing. Of course, he knew her mother Sarah already, but he'd never met her father or sisters. Mr. Franklin Beaumont was a large gentleman with a thick white mustache and a rolling laugh. He was some kind of important judge in Manhattan and Jon was somewhat in awe of him.

The other Beaumont sisters, Virginia and Clarice, were almost as lovely as their older sister—but not quite. They were pretty and polite and kinda funny once he got to know them. It was strange, but he kept having the nagging feeling he recognized them. Or at least, he recognized something *about* them.

What is it? I couldn't have known them before, could I? They go to NYU—maybe I went to NYU?

"*Jon!* Get in here!"

When Franklin shouted, people listened, and Jon was no different. He hurried into the kitchen to see the older gentleman holding up a bottle of dessert wine. Jon hadn't gotten Kitty a present—at her urging—so he'd used the money to buy a nice bottle of wine for the Christmas dinner. It made him feel like he wasn't showing up totally empty handed.

"What do you need, sir?" he asked. Kitty's dad laughed.

"I told you, call me Frank, this ain't the military, son. Do you want to do the honors?" he asked, holding out the bottle towards Jon.

"Oh, no, your house, your present, you go ahead," he urged.

They stood around the kitchen island while Frank grabbed a corkscrew and went to work. A live-in cook moved behind them, putting away the leftovers from dinner and setting out pies for dessert.

"So. No memory, huh," Frank grunted while he twisted. Jon nodded.

"Yup. It's all just … a fog," he said, using the only description he'd found which seemed to fit.

"That's a damn shame. You might have family out there lookin' for you, and you don't even know it."

"That's true, but honestly, they must not be looking too hard," he laughed. "I was in the hospital for almost a month, newspapers ran stories on me, I was on TV once, but nothing."

"Their loss, son. So Kitty tells me you're having some legal issues?"

Jon explained about his identity situation, how he couldn't get a new social security number issued, and how at every turn, he and Mrs. Sloan were told there was nothing they could do. Most lawyers wouldn't go near the issue because of how complicated it all was, not to mention the fact that Jon couldn't afford to pay them. He didn't tell Frank how in the early days of living at the halfway house, Jon had considered trying to buy an identity. A fake I.D., fake social security card. Would solve all his problems. But between Gary Tupper's rules and Kitty's faith in him, he hadn't gone through with it. He would see it out the good and honest way, as long as he could.

"So I'm kind of stuck," he sighed. "I have some money, but it won't last forever. One newspaper guy said I should write a book about my amnesia, said there's lots of interest in that kind of stuff, but I don't even hardly like reading all, how am I supposed to write a book? I mean, I'll figure it all out, I'm sure. Sloany, er, Mrs. Sloan, my social worker, she's rabid about helping me, she'll make it happen."

He didn't want to sound like he pitied himself, or like his life was hard. He didn't want Frank, or any of the Beaumonts, pitying him.

"Well now, I don't want to make any promises, but Kitty told you what I do for a living, right?" Mr. Beaumont asked. Jon nodded.

"Yeah, she said you were a judge of some kind, downtown."

"I am, and I know a lot of very important people, and I think some of them would be able to help you."

"I'm not sure how they could, the Social Security office is really strict."

"They give new identities to people in the Witness Protection Program, don't they? You don't think those come with shiny new social security numbers? Like I said, I'm not promising anything, it may be the same proceedings can't be applied to your case at all, but I can look into it for you," he offered.

Jon was blown away. He couldn't even think of how to respond for a couple moments, he just gaped while Frank finally pulled the cork free from the wine bottle. A maid started pulling down wine glasses.

"That would be … thank you, sir. That's amazing. I … appreciate it. You don't have to do all that, you barely know me," he finally managed to stammer. Frank chuckled and slid a full wine glass to him, then picked up one of his own.

"Tell you what—stop calling me sir, and we'll consider it even," he replied, then toasted his glass.

Dessert went by in a blur. His mind was reeling over the idea Frank might possibly be able to help him. He barely even noticed Kitty mothering him, pestering him about putting a napkin in his lap, or using the correct silverware, or straightening his hair. And all her smothering was completely forgotten when they all sat down to open one present each—she sat in his lap. Just like that, as if it was the most natural thing for them to do. Then to round the night out into almost-perfection, she handed him a small gift wrapped present.

"For you, Mr. Doherty."

He waited till he was alone in the guest room before he opened it. He chuckled as he pulled a silver bracelet out of a small white box. There was a flat, shiny metal piece in the center of the chain, and he looked it over in his hands. One side read: *Jon Doherty. Harlem, New York.* The other side: *Just in case you forget again.*

An I.D. bracelet. It was so perfect, and so hilariously off color, he was almost surprised it had come from Kitty. He wrapped the chain around his wrist and locked it together, then held it out in front of him. Then he chuckled again and looked out his window.

He'd originally planned on going home right after dinner. It had taken him almost two hours to get there that afternoon, and the way the snow had started coming down, he knew it would take even longer getting back. But Kitty had laughed at him and informed he wasn't going anywhere. They'd made up the spare room before he'd even gotten there. He would be staying at the Beaumont's all night. So he'd called the Benson House and told them he wouldn't be back till tomorrow.

He was placed in a corner of the main house, in a not often used guest room that over looked the free standing garage and large back yard. Kitty technically still lived at home, but she stayed in a small apartment built onto the top of the garage. He'd glanced at it when he looked out his window, then he did a double take.

One of her windows faced his, and she had all the lights on in her place. She was perfectly visible, the window almost glowing in the dark night. She was moving slowly toward the window, her head bent down, looking off to her right. She'd already removed the heavy knit Christmas sweater she'd had on earlier, and as he watched, she slowly started to peel off her tank top, exposing inch after inch of bare flesh.

*Stop looking. Stop looking right now. You're not a pervert. Shit, what if I am!? What if this is like my thing!? Oh god, I'm a fucking peeping tom, I know I mus–, holy shit, her breasts are **amazing**.*

The tank top was gone. She was wearing a pale pink bra that pushed her surprisingly large breasts up high and tight. She always wore nice clothing, but nothing tight, and he hadn't realized exactly how impressive her figure was—she was easily a C-cup, if not more.

Then she started unbuttoning her pants and he forgot to breathe, let alone remind himself to look away. How could he? Her movements were slow, almost deliberate, as she slid the denim over her hips and then pushed it down, down, down, all the way to her feet. She bent at the waist, her hands touching the floor, her ass sticking up high. Jon started to sweat.

I wonder when the last time I had sex was? I wonder if I'm good at it?

He didn't bother wondering if he was virgin. Like some things, he just *knew* he wasn't one. It was pointless, anyway. He wasn't getting laid that night, or any night soon. No, what he was going to do was get up and close his blinds and then jerk off his uncomfortable thoughts.

When he got up to do just that, though, Kitty lifted her head. She stared straight at him, freezing him in place. He was standing in front of his window, his hands on the blind. His room was dark, she couldn't possibly see him. Could she? He watched as she slowly smiled, then she carefully pulled her curtains shut. They were white and made of a thin, gauzy material. He couldn't see through them, but he could see her silhouette and outline easily. His pulse raced as her shadow took off her bra and threw it to the side. Then, while she was reaching for her underwear, she stepped out of view.

What the fuck was that!?

Jon shut his blinds, then laid down on his bed. Stared at the ceiling. He wanted to do something, go somewhere. His blood was screaming through his veins at a million miles a minute and he almost thought of calling Gary Tupper. It was one of the things about Benson House—anyone could call Gary at any time, night or day, and he would help them with any problem they had, no matter how weird or bad or illegal it may be.

How could he help with his? "Hey, Gary, my dick is so hard I could cut a diamond with it. Oh, and I'm pretty sure I'm a pervert."

In the middle of berating himself, he became aware of his cell phone vibrating near him. He looked at the night stand, then reached over to pick it up. Who could be texting him? Only like four people on the planet had his phone number, and it was after midnight.

What are you doing?

Oh god. Kitty. What were the chances? He licked his lips and took a deep breath, then banged out a response.

Laying down. I opened your present. Thank you.

That bracelet was from my family. You haven't opened your present from me, yet.

He stared at his phone, as if the messages might disappear if he blinked.

What do you mean?

You can come over and get it if you want.

It's late, we're both tired, I don't want to bother you.

I'm not bothered, and you didn't seem tired a minute ago when you were staring at me.

Shit. She *had* seen him. He clenched his teeth together and slammed his head back against his pillows a couple times. Then he took a deep breath and went back to his phone.

I didn't mean to. Your light was on. I'm really sorry.

The minute it took her to respond felt like a life time.

I left my light on on purpose. I'm not sorry. Come over.

Jon was downstairs and out the door so fast, he forgot to put shoes on. The snow was past his ankles and he practically hopped through it, almost slipping and falling on his ass when he reached her stairs. He raced up them, then took a moment when he reached the top landing, catching his breath and running his hand through his hair. Then he softly scratched at the door.

"That was fast," she giggled when she opened it.

She wasn't naked, like he'd been hoping, but she looked pretty damn good. She was wearing a man's old dress shirt with the sleeves rolled up. The hem reached the tops of her thighs and he tried not to stare at her.

I wonder if she actually took her underwear off …

"Nice place," he managed to say something normal, stamping his frozen feet on her carpet as she shut the door behind them.

"It's okay. Jon! You didn't even put on shoes?" she laughed, moving around him.

He didn't pay attention to her, too busy taking in his surrounding. It was a loft style apartment, no real walls. A cozy kitchenette was tucked against one wall, and a comfy queen bed was in the corner, right next to the window he'd been looking through ten minutes ago. It was decorated in a quaint, country style, and a string of mini-paper lanterns hung above the stove. Those, and a small Christmas tree on the table, were the only lights left on in the apartment. She'd turned them all off during his mad dash across the driveway.

"This place is so … you," he finally commented.

"What's that supposed to mean?" she asked, grabbing his hand and leading him to her bed. Once he sat down, she went about pulling off his wet socks. She had an incredibly nurturing nature, he'd noticed. She just liked to take care of people, it's what fulfilled her.

"I don't know. Homey, warm. Nice," he described.

"Thanks. It was originally for stable hands, there were bunk beds up here. But Dad sold all the horses off a couple years ago, except for Virginia and Clarice's horses. When I left school, I thought about living downtown, but I liked being home so much, I asked if I could renovate this old place. I've been here for a year now," she told him.

"What about you?" he asked. "You don't get your own horse?"

"I had one for a while, but she got sick and died. Broke my heart, I don't have it in me to get another one yet. If you want, though, we can take out the girls' horses tomorrow and go for a ride in the snow," she offered. He went to happily accept the invitation, then stopped himself.

"I … I doubt I know how to ride. At the hospital, they said their guess was I had been born and raised in the city. Doubt there was much opportunity for horse riding," he said. She shrugged.

"Who knows? Maybe we'll get down there and you'll be a natural in the seat," she pointed out. "Maybe you're a great horse rider and you come from a family of horse farmers."

He laughed at the idea.

"Yeah, I'm not gonna put any money on that."

"Forget about horses, that's not why I invited you over," she said, waving her hand at him. The entire mood in the room changed and he took a deep breath.

"Why *did* you invite me over? Is your dad going to kill me if he finds me in here?" he asked.

"Probably, but we'll be careful. I wanted to ask you a few questions," she continued, and she grabbed his hand and held it between both of hers, then rested them on her lap.

On top of her bare thighs.

"I'll try to answer."

"So, you really don't remember anything?" she asked.

"No. Trust me, I wouldn't lie about this stuff. It's not fun," he replied. She nodded.

"So you don't know if you've got a family out there? Brothers, sisters, mom, dad?"

"Well, I assume I've got a mom and dad somewhere, unless I just spontaneously came into being."

She laughed and let go of his hand so she could playfully slap him in the chest.

"You know what I mean! I mean, gosh, who knows who's out there waiting for you. Maybe a girlfriend. Maybe a wife," she said slowly. He smiled at her.

"Would you be upset?"

"Extremely."

"Well," he sighed, looking down at his hands. "When I was admitted, they kept all my clothing and personal items for me. I got back a hemp necklace, two earrings with anarchy stars on them, and a mood ring that fits my right index finger. But no wedding ring, so I'm pretty sure I'm not married. I mean, c'mon, who would marry a dude who wears a mood ring?"

"Oh, I don't know, mood rings can be kinda sexy," she replied, looking down at his lap. He had his fingers splayed on the tops of his thighs, and she started running her index finger across the back of his hand.

"Sexy, huh?" he managed to grunt.

"Sure. Someone can be acting one way, all normal and easy going, but the mood ring can tell you how they're really feeling. Like maybe black for sad or yellow for happy or …" her voice trailed off.

"Or turned on?" he blurted out.

Real smooth, asshole.

"Mmmm, I bet they can show that, too. Maybe they turn red to show when someone's really excited," she breathed out, her head still bent.

"What color would your mood ring be right now?" he asked.

She finally looked up at him, and he realized just how close she was—he could see how sharp her cupid's bow was, how gold her hair looked in the soft lighting. She was breathing shallowly and she leaned close enough so the tips of their noses brushed against each other.

"Bright, hot, cherry red," she whispered.

Amnesia or no, he was positive he'd never heard anything hotter, and Jon didn't waste another second. He closed the gap between them and kissed her hard. She gave a soft little moan, then her hand was in his hair. Her touch was gentle, but his scar was still sensitive, and when her fingernails brushed against it, he let out a surprised hiss.

"Oh, I'm sorry," she said quickly, yanking back. He shook his head and pulled her close again.

"Don't be, I liked it," he breathed, kissing along the side of her jaw.

"But I hurt you. You like that?" she asked.

"Yes. No? I don't know, you make it hard to think straight," he replied.

That seemed to satisfy her and her hands went to wandering along his broad shoulders. He wanted to get lost in the feel and scent and taste of her, but the moment stuck in his mind for a minute. Did he like pain? Not a lot, of course—the pain from his arm and head healing had been awful. But her fingernails against his skin, he was shocked to realize he wanted her to press harder, to really dig in and rake across his skin, leave some marks behind.

And even more shocking, he kind of wanted to do the same back to her.

Just take it easy, buddy. This is basically like your first time, just go with the flow. Don't freak her out. Your brain is going haywire right now, don't pay attention to it. You've got more important things to focus on.

The top three buttons on her top were undone, just inviting someone to come inside. He gladly accepted and slipped his hand under the material, finding soft warm breasts and hard nipples.

"You feel so … incredible …" he breathed, licking a path down to her collarbone.

"Do you think you've done this before? Had sex?" she asked, letting her head fall back.

"Yes."

"How do you know?"

"Same way I knew I was left handed. It's just … there. It's in my skin, it's in my muscles," he explained as best he could. Then a thought occurred to him and he pulled away. "Are *you* a virgin?"

"No," she replied, looking up at him. A rosy blush tinted her already tan skin. "But I'm not the kind of girl who sleeps with just anybody. I … I've always wanted you. I remember seeing you on the news and thinking you were so handsome. And then when you walked into the community center, it was like someone was giving me a gift. But I swear, I don't do this with just anybody, I'm not like that. And I don't know what you're like, either. And neither do you."

"True," he said, pulling his hand away from her chest. Her mouth twitched, like it wanted to frown. "But I know who I am now. I'm the kind of man who would very much like to make you feel good. It doesn't have to be right now if you don't want it to be, but maybe some day in the future."

The frown disappeared and she practically fell against him, forcing him back onto the mattress.

"I want it to be now. *Right now,* Jon."

He unbuttoned her shirt, kissing the pathway of skin as it opened up to him. As he pulled the material apart, he rolled her onto her back before taking a nipple between his teeth. He wanted to make her moan and hiss, wanted to teasingly bite down, but he resisted.

Get to know each other first.

"You're so fucking beautiful," he breathed, and she surprised him by giggling.

"You have a dirty mouth, Mr. Doherty," she teased.

"You make me want to be dirty. Filthy," he responded, then abruptly sucked hard on the same nipple. She gasped.

"Oh, god, more. So much more, Jon," she urged.

He complied, moving so he was on top of her. He pulled his own shirt off and let it drop to the floor. Her eyes went wide for a second, then he felt her fingertips against his rib cage.

"What does this mean?" she asked. He glanced down at what she was touching, then remembered he had tattoos.

"I have no idea," he was honest, tilting his head to the side.

It was script, maybe an inch tall, traveling along a rib—maybe four inches in length, total. It was in Latin, and a doctor had told him it read "In Love We Trust". He explained all that to Kitty.

"See? You must have been a good man to get something so romantic," she sighed sitting up and kissing along the tattoo. He frowned and looked away.

"I don't know," he mumbled.

"What about the other ones? They don't mean anything?" she asked, touching the tattoo on his forearm. It was a sparrow, done old school style in heavy black ink that was a little faded.

"Not a thing."

Under the bottom joint of his left thumb, stretching down to his wrist, was a detailed tattoo of a feather. The last tattoo was on his back, right below the base of his neck. Invisible when he was dressed, but the biggest of his tattoos. It was circle with a lot of smaller, geometric circles inside of it. He had no clue what it meant, but for some reason when he looked at in the mirror, he thought of the world. As best anyone could guess, the tattoo on his chest was his newest. The one on his forearm was his oldest. None of them got him any closer to figuring out who he was.

"I don't have any tattoos," she said, picking up his right hand and lifting it to her face. "I've never been with anyone who had them."

"I think if I could do it over, I wouldn't have gotten them at all," he said, then sighed when she ran her tongue over the feather tattoo.

"I'm glad you have them. They're sexy," she told him, then she started unbuttoning his pants.

"See? There you go again. You're just a bad ... naughty, naughty girl," he informed her, faltering on the term. He didn't want a repeat of how he'd felt in the community center, when he'd called her a bad girl.

"I think a guy like you could teach me what being naughty really is," she whispered, laying back again.

He took the hint and slowly peeled her panties away from her body. They were pink and had the word Wednesday on them. He laughed as he dropped them to the floor, then he went to take off his own pants. He didn't get very far before she suddenly folded her arms across her chest and looked away from him.

"What's wrong?" he asked, freezing for a second.

"It's probably silly to someone like you, but could you ... will you turn out the lights?" she asked. He smiled and leaned down to kiss her quickly.

"It's not silly. Maybe I don't like the lights on, either, who knows?"

He traipsed across her apartment and unplugged everything. He had to feel his way back—the only light now was coming from the main house, and it just barely provided a soft glow which was concentrated on the corner of the bed.

"Thank you," she breathed when he was back in front of her.

"No, thank you. Merry Christmas, Kitty," he whispered, shoving his pants and boxers down before stepping out of them. He immediately moved to kneel over her.

They learned about each other in the dark, bodies like braille to their souls. She whined and mewled and sighed, still delicate even in a moment like that. Jon found it was getting harder and harder to hold himself in check. He wanted to dive into her and make sure his muscle memory wasn't lying about how good sex was going to feel. But he didn't want to rush her, so he took his time.

"So pretty," he sighed into her ear before slowly moving down her body.

"*You're* pretty," she replied, writhing around as he went back and forth, kissing the tip of each breast. "Your eyes. I feel like they look right through me."

"Maybe they can," he whispered, kissing his way across her stomach.

He only wanted to make her feel good. That was number one in his mind. And while his brain didn't have any actual memories to back up his feelings, he was pretty positive going down on a woman was one of the top most ways to make her feel amazing. That's what he had in mind as he sucked and licked and nipped his way along her hip, but then she stopped him.

"No. Not that, not right now," she said, pulling at his shoulders, urging him higher.

"Oh, sorry," he said quickly, pulling away from her.

"Don't be sorry. *I'm* sorry. I just … it's really intimate, don't you think?"

He didn't think it was any more intimate than him putting one of his appendages *inside* of her anatomy, but he wasn't going to argue over something like that. Not when she was naked underneath him.

"It's okay. We can do whatever you want. This is fine, too. We don't have to do anything else," he told her, laying his weight down on top of her and kissing her face.

"I want to do more," she assured him. "Please. I want to feel you. I want to have sex with you."

He certainly wanted to have sex, too, but now it was a little awkward. He didn't want to scare her or hurt her, but he was pretty sure with her disposition, it couldn't be avoided.

So he bit down on his bottom lip and tread carefully. She opened her legs for him and he laid down between them, ran his hand down to her center. He didn't dare tiptoe a finger inside of her, though, and when he felt how warm and wet she was, he figured that was good enough.

"Are you sure?" he whispered, bracing himself over her. She stared up at him, moonlight and lamplight catching her eyes, and she smiled at him. He smiled back, gently rubbing his hand up and down her thigh.

"I'm positive," she whispered back.

She was so tight, he almost wondered if she was lying about being a virgin. He had to go inch by painful inch. Her back arched up and she would whimper, then her body would turn into one giant muscle spasm, locking him out. So he laid down with his chest on hers and he whispered in her ear.

"God, you feel so good, Kitty," he breathed. "Just *relax*. I would never hurt you."

"I know," she panted. "I know you wouldn't. You're just so … so …"

"It's okay, you don't have to—"

"*Big,*" she finally finished, then she cried out when he gained another inch. He chuckled and bit down on her earlobe.

"That's a handy fact to know about myself," he joked. She laughed as well, relaxing for a second, and he seized the moment. He thrust his hips forward and that was it. She was as full with him as she could possibly get.

"Oh god, oh god, oh god," she said over and over again, pushing at his chest.

"Too much?" he asked, starting to back off. Her arms wrapped around his neck and locked him in place.

"*Not enough,*" she said, licking her lips. "This is amazing, Jon. *Thank you.*"

He began pumping in and out of her. Gently at first, but then faster. He could feel her stretching more, accommodating his girth. Getting wetter, making it easier to move within her. The sensation was incredible—better than anything his brain stem had stored, that was for damn sure. He propped himself and began thrusting harder, clutching one of her breasts in his hand.

"Holy shit, Kitty," he groaned, rolling his head back.

"Please, Jon. Please," she whimpered, smoothing her hands across his chest.

"What? What do you want?" he asked, looking down at her. Her head was thrust back, her silky blonde hair a halo around her face, and her eyes were squeezed shut.

"This. Just this," she replied, clawing her hands down her thighs.

"Oh no, a naughty girl like you? I think you want more," he said, moving his hand and grabbing her right leg behind the knee, forcing it higher. Wider.

"I'm a naughty girl," she repeated after him, her hands now on her breasts, pinching her nipples.

"I think you like this," he grunted, pushing harder still. The sounds of their pelvises slapping together filled the room.

"I do, Jon. God, I love it," she cried.

"Of course you fucking do," he growled, and began really pounding into her in earnest. The whole bed started creaking and squeaking. "You love getting fucked, you dirty fucking girl."

That caused her to lift her head, but he didn't notice.

"Jon, maybe we should—" she started to say, but he put his hand down in the center of her chest, anchoring her to the bed so he could thrust even harder. She let out a startled shriek, followed by a moan.

"You like this? Like how I'm fucking you hard? How I'm fucking you like a dirty slut?"

"*Stop.*"

The word registered instantly, and it was like cold water was thrown on him. Like being yanked out of a dream. He stopped moving and looked around, trying to catch his breath. Fuck, what had just happened? It was like he hadn't even been there. The things he'd been doing to her, the words coming out of his mouth, it had been reflex. Just like he'd said—*muscle memory*. It was as if he'd gone into a trance, his body acting on autopilot.

Jesus, my autopilot has a dirty fucking mouth.

"Oh god," he gasped, letting her go. "I'm sorry. I don't know … I didn't know I was going to do that."

"It's okay," she whispered, petting his sides. "Really, it's okay, Jon."

"No, it's not. Fuck, did I hurt you?" he asked, starting to pull away. She stopped him by leaning up a little and grabbing his arms, holding him in place.

"No, not really," she assured him. "I guess whoever you were before, he was a little too intense for a simple girl like me. It's okay."

"It's *not* okay," he snapped, wishing she'd stop saying those words. "I don't want to be *too intense*. I want to be the kind of guy who makes love to you, not the kind who calls you names and tries to break your bed."

She started pulling on his arms, forcing him to lay down on top of her. It was an awkward position—his dick was still hard, twitching inside of her, begging for release. Pleading him to finish what he'd been starting.

"You can be that kind of guy," she whispered. "We can teach you how to be gentle. And who knows? Maybe you can teach me something. Maybe breaking my bed once in a while won't be such a bad thing."

God, she was too good for him. He should go back to his room. But she was so soft and supple, and he was still so very hard.

It was gentle. He supposed they really were making love. She held him close and pumped her hips against him, meeting him thrust for thrust as he pumped, as well. He kept everything slow and steady, kissing her softly the whole time.

It took him a long time to come doing it that way, but it seemed to make her happy. She had her orgasm first, then was halfway to another one before he was done. Then they took a shower together and he finished off her second orgasm with his fingers.

They got dressed in the dark, laughing and giggling. At the door, she pointed out the mistletoe hanging above them and he kissed her. He pressed her against the door jam, letting his tongue do an in depth exploration of her mouth.

"You better stop, or we'll be out here all night," she breathed.

"I'm okay with that," he replied, then he kissed her again, rocking his pelvis hard against hers, letting her feel just how okay with it he was.

"I'm serious. My dad gets up in a couple hours, and if he finds out you're not in your room, you'll be looking down the barrel of his shot gun," she laughed, pushing him away gently.

"But this was okay?" he asked, holding onto her hips. She nodded and kissed the base of his throat.

"More than okay. This was fantastic. Best Christmas ever," she told him.

"Can I see you again?"

"You'll see me tomorrow at breakfast, Jon."

"I mean outside. Away from family and the community center."

"You can see me anywhere you want," she told him.

A statement like that deserved another kiss, and he had his hand in her panties and was rubbing his crotch against her thigh when she became the voice of reason again. She shooed him down the stairs and watched after him till he was back inside the house.

Back in the guest room, he laid in bed for a long time, trying to think his erection away. Before he realized it was happening, though, his hand had wandered down his body and was rubbing at the hard on through the sheets. He ground his teeth together and hissed as he stroked himself. But he wasn't fantasizing about his shower with Kitty, and he wasn't fantasizing about the beautiful sex they'd just finished having, either.

No, he was fantasizing about how they'd started. About holding her down and fucking her hard and saying whatever the fuck he wanted.

When he was done, his arms fell limply to the bed. He stared at the ceiling for a second, breathing hard, when he realized something. He was on the right side of the bed. Not the center, but distinctly off to the right.

He looked over to his left side, to the empty mattress next to him. Then he stretched his arm out, laying his hand palm down in the space.

"Who were you?" he whispered. "And where are you now?"

BEFORE

A ugust was great. A crazy heat wave was blanketing the city, which was a good thing at night.

They'd found an apartment building to squat in. A good location as far as abandoned buildings went, and full of lots of other squatters. For whatever reason, the electricity was still on. No heat and no water, but they could plug things in, and that was good enough for the two of them. Crash let them have one of his mattresses and they hauled it across town, laughing hard when they crammed it onto the subway.

"I think me getting kicked out of my apartment was a good thing," Delaney commented one day. Jayson glanced at her.

She was sitting on the edge of the mattress, completely naked. He zeroed in on her tattoo first and smiled. It had healed well, and so had his own. Then his eyes wandered down her back and side, looking at her tiny waist and thin arms. He reached out a hand and scratched at her back.

"How so?" he asked, rolling onto his side.

"Look at this. Spacious apartment with a decent view, rent free! No utilities, no maintenance, quiet neighbors. *It's awesome.*"

"Except we can't shower and we'll freeze to death in the winter— *if* the cops don't bust the place first."

"Such a negative nancy!" she laughed, looking over her shoulder at him. Then she grabbed his t-shirt off the floor and slipped it on. "We'll be out of here before it starts to get cold. I'm gonna get a raise, and you'll find a job."

So optimistic. She may had had a fiery temper, but depression was completely unknown to Delaney. She was always happy, and she always made the most out of anything. He loved that about her.

I love her so much.

They got up and shuffled around the kitchen. They'd somewhat furnished the place, using what they found for free on street corners and a couple Goodwill finds. A large chipped table with a loose leg was in the center of the kitchen, two mismatched chairs on either side. An old mini-fridge was on a kitchen counter, with a scratched up hot plate next to it. A futon mattress minus the frame served as their couch. Del had a laptop and in the evenings, they would set it on top of a milk crate and watch old movies and cartoons.

They were some of the best days of his whole life.

She got them bowls of cereal while he loaded his bong. In his opinion, waking and baking was highly underrated. After they'd both taken a couple hits, they settled in on the futon and laughed at more cartoons. Afterwards Del got ready for work, humming along to a tune in her head, then she headed out the door.

Jay laid around for a couple hours, letting the high wear off. Using a jug of water, he took a hobo shower in the tub, then got dressed in a clean pair of jeans and a button down shirt. He tied his dreads back, forcing them into some semblance of order, then stared at himself in the mirror. His eyes were clear—the high from the morning was long gone, which was good. He needed to be sober that day. He smiled at his reflection, then headed off to a job interview.

He was a smart guy, he almost never had a problem getting hired. Showing up to interviews and actually keeping said job, though, was where the problems started. Del didn't seem to have a problem getting up in the morning after a hard night of partying, but maybe that's because she'd only turned twenty-two in May. He'd turned twenty-five in July, he didn't recover as fast anymore.

He was offered a stocking position at a liquor wholesaler. He thanked the man profusely, then ran all the way to Del's work. He opened the door to the diner and didn't even wait to be seated, he just made his way to her section. A minute later she came bustling over.

"What can I get—hey, you!" she exclaimed when she realized it was him. "What are you doing here?"

Jay put down the menu he'd been looking at and clasped his hands together.

"Hello, ma'am," he said, using his professional voice. "I'd like to order the country fried steak with two eggs, and also the club sandwich with fries. A bowl of soup to start, a side of onion rings, and you might as well go ahead and write down my dessert. I want the ice cream sandwich."

"Are you insane?" she laughed, not writing anything down. "We can barely afford off-brand lunch meat. Your 'breakfast' would cost like fifty bucks."

"Well then, it's a good thing *someone* got a job this morning, so I can pay for—"

Her scream cut him off and he let out a startled shout when she leapt on top of him. He fell back in the booth, knocking over a bunch of shakers and condiments.

"I can't believe it! Oh god, Jay, I'm *so proud* of you! Didn't I tell you it would happen? I knew you could it, I had faith in you," she said, hugging him tightly.

"I couldn't have done it without," he replied.

He vaguely became aware that people around them were

snickering, then someone was clearing their throat. Jay opened his eyes and her manager was standing at the end of the booth. His face was bright red.

"Delaney!" the man hissed. "Delaney, stop it, *right now!*"

Jay realized her short skirt had ridden up and the entire restaurant was getting an intimate look at her amazing ass. She laughed and slowly crawled off him, straightening herself out as she went.

"I'm sorry, Mr. Feens," she chuckled. "It's just my boyfriend here is celebrating because he got a—"

"I'm sorry, Delaney, but I cannot tolerate any more of this," Mr. Feens said, holding up his hand. Del's smile froze on her face.

"What are you talking about?"

"You come in every day a mess, smelling like weed and looking hung over."

Del blushed a little, but Jay could see her steeling her nerves.

"Well, I may come in like that, but I'm professional on the floor," she insisted.

"Practically having sex in a booth is hardly professional."

"*Sex!?* I was *hugging* him!"

"I'm sorry. After your appearance as of late, and the *doobie* incident in the bathroom last week, and now this, I just can't allow it anymore. I'm sorry, Delaney, but you're fired."

A pin drop could've been heard. The entire restaurant was dead silent. Del gasped, glanced around, then shut her mouth.

"Okay, fine. Fine! Fire me. I'm sorry I showed up to work *every day* on time. I'm sorry I was nice to any and every single customer, even the ones who don't tip and the ones who touch inappropriately. I'm sorry I've smiled through all your bullshit. But most of all, I'm sorry I can't blow you to save my job like Jorge did."

Every employee in the joint shifted their gaze to a waiter standing in a corner. Jorge's jaw dropped and Mr. Feens looked like he was going to explode.

"Get out of my establishment, right now!" he bellowed.

"*Your* establishment? Please, your wife is the real boss and everyone knows it! You hear that, *Mrs. Feens!?*" Del was shouting as she ripped off her apron and threw it to the floor. "Your husband fucks any cute piece of ass that walks in this place, so long as it's under twenty-five and male!"

A frumpy looking woman appeared in the doorway to the kitchen, looking shocked. Another waitress rushed out from behind her, carrying a large purse and jacket in her arms.

"Del," Jay hissed, sliding out of his booth. "Let's just *go.*"

"Oh, I'm going," Del growled, stomping forward and taking the items from the other waitress. She struggled with her jacket as she walked towards the exit. "I'm sorry if my outburst upset anybody. I didn't realize a quick flash of panties with hearts on them would get me fired."

"I'm sorry," Jay murmured as he hurried after her. He got around her and held the door open, but she whirled around before she left.

"But since you've all seen it already, *suck on this!*"

With that, she lifted her skirt and flashed them the front of her underwear. A huge kiss print was directly over her crotch. A man sitting at the bar started clapping, and a disgruntled woman covered her son's eyes.

They made it halfway down the block before they both dissolved into laughter. Jay leaned against a building and she fell into him.

"Suck on this!?" he gasped for air. She snorted and coughed and tried to breathe.

"I don't know. I go into black out mode. Shit, just when something goes good, something else goes bad," she sighed, her laughter finally falling away. He grabbed her hand and squeezed it.

"No. Don't let this ruin today—it's a good day. Like you said, there's other jobs, you'll find another one. And mine pays better than yours did, so we're still better off than we were before," he told her. She smiled up at him.

"You see?" she said softly, then she reached up and stroked her fingers across his forehead. "We're two parts of a whole, always making up for the other one. We couldn't survive without each other."

"I know," he replied. "Let me take you out. Let's have some fun."

"But—"

"Don't worry, nothing crazy expensive. I have some ideas."

"Okay."

They took the train to Coney Island. He bought them hot dogs and beer, then they rode around on some rides. Delaney had never been before—she hadn't been to a lot of New York. She'd met Jay pretty soon after she'd moved there, and he wasn't into the touristy stuff. She'd never even gone to Central Park or Times Square, or any of Manhattan at all, really. She screamed and clung to him and laughed harder than he'd ever heard.

This is better than any high. She's sober right now. I'm sober right now. This is it. This is a moment. Seize it.

While she stopped at a booth to get some henna tattoos, Jay was able to slip away. He hurried down the boardwalk and finally worked his way underneath it. He wanted to go while it was still daylight out. He'd seen a lot of shit during his time in New York, but even he didn't want to mess with the Coney Island underworld at night.

After he found what he was looking for, he hightailed it back to the shinier side of the boardwalk. Del was done with her tattoo and looking around for him. He snuck up behind her and squeezed her sides, making her jump and yell.

"You scared me!" she laughed, slapping him in the arm. "Where did you go?"

"Just around. C'mon, let's go play a game," he said dragging her to the nearest booth.

It was an old school dart toss. Hit X amount of balloons, get a prize. Simple enough. Jay had pretty decent aim, and had been coming to Coney Island long enough to know the way things worked. He hit enough balloons to get a low level prize and called it good.

"Can I pick?" Del asked, hovering next to him.

"No. I know exactly what I want," he replied, digging through a bunch of trinkets. When he found what he was looking for, he glanced at the guy running the game. The dude was flirting with some super young looking chick, so Jay took a chance. He grabbed two of the same prize and slipped them into his pocket before hurrying away.

"Did you just do what I think you did?" Del asked, hurrying behind him, holding a ridiculously huge cloud of cotton candy.

"Yup. C'mon, hurry," he urged, grabbing her elbow and pulling her along. Her short legs struggled to keep up with his and she wound breaking into a light run.

"What was it? What did you pick?" she asked, trying to eat the cotton candy while they moved.

This wasn't how he'd pictured it. Not once. Delaney deserved roses and diamonds. A small house with a white picket fence. He couldn't give her those things, and chances were, he never could. But he'd already given her his heart and soul—all he had left to offer was promises. So he pulled her between two buildings and stood her against a wall.

"How long have we been going out?" he asked, his fist in his pocket. He felt sweat start to break out along his hair line.

"Hmmm," she thought to herself, curling her tongue deftly around another piece of the sugary confection. "Like … five months. Almost six."

"It feels like forever," he told her, and she nodded in agreement.

"Like the best time ever," she said, smiling big at him.

"I still … shit, Del. You know you could do better than me. You're gorgeous, you're funny, you're so goddamn caring, and you're the best fucking sex I've ever had in my life," he said. She frowned.

"Thanks, but I think I did pretty good with you. Have you looked at yourself lately? So sexy it hurts me sometimes. Those green eyes of yours? I have to watch girls drooling over you all the time, and the only thing that gets me through it is knowing I'm the one who gets to be in bed with you at night. Not to mention you're incredibly talented and smart and so sensitive," she pointed out.

"Still not anywhere near good enough for you, babe."

"Jay, just stop—"

He put a finger against her lips.

"And also not strong enough to let that stop me. I fucking love you, Delaney. You are the first thing I think about in the morning and the last thing I think about before I go to bed. I want to be inside you forever. Want to lay with you and love you and make you laugh until we're old and gray," he babbled. He wasn't sure if he was making sense, but he didn't care. He was winging it, and he knew Delaney loved it when he winged it. *He knew her.* So as she stared at him with wide eyes, he pulled his hand out of his pocket and opened his fist. "Delaney Carter, will you marry me?"

She gasped and two large tears immediately spilled over onto her cheeks. She put her hand over his, delicately touching the rings he'd been clutching.

"I know it's not a lot," he said softly, taking her hand and slipping one of the rings onto her finger. It was too big and slid around, so he adjusted the cheap metal band to fit better. "And I can't even promise you that someday I'll do better. But it's for you, and only you."

She was still crying as she held up her hand, and for the first time ever in their relationship, Jay got nervous. Her eyes wandered over the large ring on her finger, at the seemingly opaque black crystal that was on top of it. Then, while they both stared at the ring, it started changing color. It slowly swirled to a deep, deep blue, with a tinge of pink at the edges.

"It's a mood ring," she whispered. He nodded.

"It is, but I don't know what the colors mean," he replied. She sniffled and laughed, then cried some more.

"Blue means love," she said, then took a deep breath. "Pink means happy."

"It does?" he asked, his voice equally as soft. She finally looked at him again,

"It does. Oh my god, Jay. Yes. To everything. To always. To you and me, forever," she sobbed, dropping her cotton candy and throwing her arms around him. He picked her up off her feet and crushed her to his chest, burying his face in her hair.

"Forever and ever and ever," he whispered, holding back tears, as well.

After he set her down, she put the matching mood ring on his finger and they watched as it turned to a milky soft pink.

They ran back to the subway, laughing loudly and wildly. The train was mostly empty, but it wouldn't have mattered if it was full. He held her against a pole and shoved his tongue into her mouth, ran his hands under shirt. She returned the favor, moving her hands under his dreadlocks and scratching down his back. Then they walked home glued together and basically fell into bed, leaving behind a trail of clothes which led back to the front door.

Hours later they called a truce. Jay felt like he was gonna pass out, and he still had more gifts to offer. They were both naked and sitting on the mattress. Del was on his lap, her legs wrapped around his waist, and she was tightening his dreads for him. The rubbing sensation was soothing, but he didn't let it distract him.

"I got us something to celebrate," he whispered, bending forward and kissing her chest.

"Before you proposed?" she asked.

"Mmm hmmm."

"Awfully confident."

"Just really in love," he replied. "So while you were getting your henna tattoo, I went and got some party supplies."

Holding her tight to him, he leaned back and grabbed for his jacket. She laughed as they rocked and almost tipped over, but he finally got them back upright. He held up the piece of clothing and she dug through the pockets. When she felt what was in there, she gasped.

"You didn't!"

"I did."

She pulled out a small baggie of coke. Since the night she'd gotten kicked out of her apartment, they hadn't done the drug. It was too expensive—pot and alcohol were cheaper and easier to get, so they made a deal to stick to those for a while. But he felt like a proposal deserved a proper celebration, and he knew how much she loved the drug. And that wasn't even all.

"What are these?" she asked, pulling out another baggie which was full of small square shaped pills.

"These are a lot of fun," he replied, taking the bag and pulling the zip lock apart. He took out one of the pills and held it out to her. Without a question, without hesitation, she opened her mouth and held out her tongue. Absolute trust.

Goddamn, if this isn't love, I don't know what is.

He placed the small tablet on her tongue.

"Are you going to tell me, or do I just wait for it to take effect?" she asked, picking up the baggie of coke again and smelling it.

"*That* was premium ecstasy," he informed her. She squealed and wiggled around on top of him.

"Babe! I've always wanted to try it!"

"I know, that's why I got it for you."

"Can I do them both?"

"Wait for the E to start wearing off," he urged her, popping a pill into his own own mouth. "When the roll starts to end, we'll bang out a couple rails, surge right back up. You'll see stars."

"I already do," she whispered, staring into his eyes as she leaned forward to kiss him. "That's what you are to me. An entire galaxy."

"We're going to have so much fun together," he groaned, smoothing his hands down her back.

"For the rest of our lives," she agreed, arching into him.

The rest of our lives. Sounds like the best time ever.

CHAPTER
seven

Jon saw Mrs. Sloan several times in early December, but then not at all during Christmas break. They were almost halfway through January before they were able to meet up with each other again. He was surprised by how much he'd missed her. The guys at the halfway house and Gary Tupper were fun, but Sloany was the O.G.

"My god, you're so tan!" he exclaimed, sitting down across from her at the little cafe she'd picked out. She smiled and preened, smoothing her hand over her hair.

"Costa Rica is awesome. How were your holidays?" she asked. He grinned.

"*Amazing.* I have so much to tell you."

"And I want to hear every word of it."

He started off slow, giving her the more official stuff. Life at the halfway house, how good he was doing there. What was going on at the community center, how he'd been transferred to recreations. Now he and Kitty spent most of their time organizing games for underprivileged kids and teens. Playing basketball and badminton. Hiding in the locker rooms and sneaking showers together.

"Sounds like things are going good, Jon!" Sloany said happily.

"They really are. And I spent Christmas with the Beaumonts," he added casually. She blinked in surprise.

"The ... you mean Katherine's family?" she checked.

"Yeah, Kitty's family."

"Well, that was certainly nice of her! I hope you had a great time."

"Oh, I had a *really* good time."

Mrs. Sloan lost her smile.

"You look like the cat who ate the canary. You obviously want to brag about something, so just spit it out," she urged.

"It's just that Kitty and I have spending a lot of time together. Outside of the community center," he told her.

"As in dating?"

"As in dating."

"That's ... nice, Jon. I told you working with people your own age would be fun," she said. But it didn't sound right. Normally she was playful and teasing with him, but her voice now was controlled and professional.

"I thought you'd be happy for me," he said. She nodded.

"And I am. I'm happy if you're happy, Jon. It's literally in my job description."

Suddenly, he was angry. Almost irrationally so.

"I hate it when you say bullshit like that," he snapped. "You make me feel like I'm just another case to you. Some fucking file number. We're friends, Sloany, so whatever it is you really wanna say, fucking say it."

His outburst didn't ruffle her at all. He'd had enough of them in front of her, and he was sure she'd seen worse. She stared at him for a second, then sighed and put her hands on the table, leaning towards him.

"I think it's a bad idea," she stated simply.

"Why!?"

"Because it is."

"What, because she's rich and educated, and I'm literally a no-body?" he asked. She snorted.

"There's that self-pity I missed so much. Of course not—if anyone is speaking bullshit here, it's you. It has nothing to do with your status. It's just ..." her voice trailed off and she looked away.

"Just what? What, Sloan?" he demanded.

"I want you to be careful," she started again, speaking low. "I've dealt with a lot of women like Katherine. *Kitty.* The most helpful souls you'll ever meet. In fact, you could almost say they're addicted to helping. They want to save everyone. Drag them out of the ditches and clean them up and make them new again."

"So she wants to help me, how is that bad?" he asked.

"It's not bad. But ask yourself this, Jon—if she's addicted to helping, and you really need help, what happens to the relationship when you don't need help anymore?" she told him.

God, he was angry. So fucking angry. He wanted to rant and rail and throw things. Smash their coffee cups and flip the table. Tell her what he had with Kitty was real and honest and the only good thing in his life. Scream that she didn't know what the fuck she was talking about.

Tell her I've been having the same thoughts.

"We don't know that's true about her," he said in a low voice as his hands gripped the table edges.

"No, we don't," Mrs. Sloan agreed. "And she is a really sweet girl, Jon. She genuinely cares about you, that's a fact no matter what. I'm glad you've got such a good friend."

"Yeah, you're just not glad I'm fucking her."

"No, I'm not glad that eventually you'll *stop* fucking each other, and then I'll have to pick up the broken pieces."

"Saint Sloan," he whispered, and he was rewarded with a laugh.

"Just tread carefully, Jon. I could be wrong, but I've seen it before.

With men *and* women. The adrenaline rush that comes from helping someone truly in need is amazing—better than any drug. The come down, though, is not so great. Suddenly a person you thought was amazing is kinda boring. Plain, or just not your type," she warned him.

"Is that what's gonna happen to us, Sloany? I get all better and you drop me like a bad habit?" he asked.

The idea actually upset him more than losing Kitty.

"Nah. Kid, what you and I got defies logic and reasoning. I'm afraid I'm stuck with your whiny ass for the rest of my life," she teased him.

"Her father is helping me," he blurted out.

"Excuse me?"

"Kitty's father—Frank Beaumont. He's a big judge downtown, and he had some ideas about getting me an identity. He's working on it now," he said.

"Oh, Jon, do really think that's a good idea? I just know—"

"What is your problem?" he suddenly snapped, his voice so loud several tables looked over at them. Mrs. Sloan shut her mouth. "You don't want me dating, you don't want me having sex, you don't want me getting help. What, you want the glory? You want to help the forgotten guy!?"

"No, Jon, that's not it at all. If Mr. Beaumont can help you, that's wonderful, I hope—"

"Then what? What is the problem?" he threw his hands up.

"It's only … you have to be careful. You're dating his daughter. What happens if your relationship ends?" Mrs. Sloan asked.

"So what if it ends?"

"Kitty is his daughter, Jon. Whose side do you think the judge will take? And dating his daughter or not, it's rare thing that people help others for nothing. Can you be sure he won't ask for something in return? That you won't owe him anything later?" she checked.

Jon clenched his teeth together. He didn't want to hear this, not one bit. Mr. Beaumont working on his identity issues was probably the best thing going on in Jon's life. He couldn't bear the thought of letting it go.

I need a name. A **real** *name. I need to be somebody, Sloany. If I have to pay whatever, I'll do it!*

"You don't understand anything!" he snapped, climbing to his feet and grabbing his jacket. "You're just angry because these people could help me when you couldn't. They could save me when you didn't have a fucking clue."

"You know that's not true, Jon," she argued.

"Fuck you, Sloany. A real friend would've been happy for me."

He went to storm out, but she grabbed him by the wrist.

"Don't do this, Jon," she urged, staring up at him. "I'm the realest friend you've got. Sit down. *Talk to me.*"

He knew he should. It was the right thing to do. She *was* his friend, he knew that, he was just angry. And the anger boiled and bubbled up inside him, blocking everything else out. He yanked his arm free and stormed out the door.

He walked for blocks. Blocks and blocks, not even paying attention to where he was going or what time it was. He was in the middle of some random park when his phone started vibrating in his back pocket. Figuring it was Sloany, he took out the phone and answered it without looking at the screen.

"I'm sorry," he said. "I don't know why I freaked, I—"

"Jon?"

He stopped walking. It wasn't Mrs. Sloan, it was Kitty. Shit, he'd forgotten he was supposed to meet up with her. He glanced at his watch. He was hours past when he should've been there.

"I'm so sorry," he groaned.

"Jon," she sighed. "This was a big deal. I really wanted you to meet these people."

"I know, I know. Something happened, I totally spaced it," he said.

"What could possibly happen that could make you forget

meeting me?"

"I had my meeting with Mrs. Sloan. She … we got into a big fight. I wound up yelling at her and storming out of the cafe. I've just been walking around ever since," he explained.

"Oh, sweetie, I'm so sorry. I know how close you two are. It must be hard for her, now that you've got other people to take care of you," she said. He frowned.

"I'm not a Labrador, Kitty," he said. "I don't *need* to be taken care of. I generally manage to dress and bathe and feed myself."

"That's not what I meant. Stop being so sensitive, silly. I'll reschedule for tomorrow."

She didn't ask, she *told* him. Jon knew he was still in a bad mood from his fight, and of course Sloany's words were still rattling around in his brain. He took a deep breath and closed his eyes.

"Okay. Okay, fine, yeah. Tomorrow, I'll be there for sure."

"Promise?"

"Promise."

"Good. Now to make up for it, you have to do me a favor," she said, but her voice was full of teasing.

"What?" he asked, instantly on guard.

"You have to come to dinner tonight with my parents," she told him.

"Oh. Okay, where at?" he asked, glancing at his watch. He hoped not in Westchester. He had to get approval from Gary Tupper to stay out of the halfway house overnight, which was always granted, but it was getting late. Gary preferred advance notice, liked knowing where all his wards were at any given time.

"Mid town," she replied. Okay. That was a little easier for him. "This great little place near the park."

"Sounds good. What time?"

"We're meeting at five for drinks. And Jon," her voice took on an edge, and he knew it meant work for him. "Wear something nice, okay?"

"Why?" he asked, dragging the word out.

"Because my dad is bringing some of his lawyer friends, he wants you to meet them."

Jon groaned. Mid town dinner with a bunch of Manhattan lawyers? Meeting people in general made him nervous. How could you introduce yourself if you didn't even know yourself? And meeting smart, successful people? *The worst.*

"Please, Kitty," he grumbled. "I had a really tough day today. I don't think I'm up for schmoozing."

"It's not 'schmoozing', what an awful word! You're making new friends, and very important people, I might add! I mean, don't you *want* their help? You have to make a little bit of effort, Jon. How do you think they'll feel if you can't even be bothered to show up to dinner? Do you think they'd still want to help you?" she told him.

He wanted to argue. Wanted to inform her that he wasn't some circus sideshow she could parade around for all her Upper East Side friends. That if they were the kind of people who expected everyone around them to drop all their plans to have last minute dinner with them, than no, he didn't want their help.

He was being stupid. Irrational. He did need help. He also *needed* a nap and a stiff cocktail and … something. He couldn't define what, exactly. He'd go home and get ready and by the time he got downtown, he'd be in a better mood. The Beaumonts had done so much for him, he could at least show up to dinner.

Trained monkey, here at your disposal!

"You're right," he sighed, heading back onto the street. "I *do* want their help. I'll go home and get cleaned up, then I'll message when I'm on my way."

"See? That's wasn't so hard. And don't worry, I have a big surprise planned for you. If things go well tonight, I'll tell you all about it," she promised.

A crowd of people poured out of a building in front of him and he almost ran someone over. He side stepped and mumbled apologies and tried to push his way through, when suddenly the smell hit him. Like a punch to the chest. He stopped moving and gasped.

There it was again. That sinking feeling in his chest. Like he was nervous or scared, but really, it was because he was *remembering*. Not literally, no memories came with the sensation. But he knew that's what it was—it was his body remembering, even if his brain couldn't.

Kitty was squawking on the other end of the phone, but he didn't listen. He closed his eyes and took a long, deep breath though his nose. Just kept inhaling the scent. It was awful, really. Coarse and even a little painful to his lungs. He let out the breath on a sigh.

Cigarette smoke. *Holy shit, I used to be a smoker.*

"Oh my god," he gasped into the phone.

"Where did you? I thought you'd had an accident!" she yelled at him. He shook his head and jogged through the group of people, then leaned against a lamp post.

"Kitty, holy shit! I used to smoke!"

"Wait, what?"

"Smoke!" he exclaimed. "I was walking and this group of people got in front of me, and they were all smoking, and it was like … jesus, it was like I just *knew*. I could feel the smoke in my lungs, taste it on my tongue! Feel the cigarette between my fingertips!"

"Ew. That's gross, Jon. Smoking is a disgusting habit," she told him. He pulled back and stared at the phone for a second like she was insane, then put it back to his ear.

"Kitty, I don't give a shit about bad habits—*I remembered something.* I mean, it's not much, but it's something! I used to be a smoker! I can *remember* smoking!" he exclaimed. She sighed down the line.

"Well, I'm happy you remember something, but I wish it wasn't a bad habit. Do you really think you smoked? God, I hope you don't take it up again," she said.

"No. I mean, I don't plan on it. You don't think this is huge?" he asked.

"Of course I do! It's a baby step back to your memories, it's great.

Remember to be there tonight at five o'clock sharp, okay?" she reminded him.

He muttered something agreeable into the phone, then listened as she made kissy noises and hung up. He dropped his arm and just stood there, staring across the street at a corner shop.

I used to smoke. I used to buy ... something. What brand? God, I can see it in my mind, why can't I say it!? I used to smoke. Not a lot, maybe once or twice a day. Sometimes not at all.

It was a dirty disgusting habit. Awful. Unhealthy. Made people smell bad. Made their teeth yellow. Wasted their money. Kitty found it repulsive, and didn't want him to do it.

Jon walked into the corner shop and didn't stop to guess at what brand, just bought a pack of Camel 99's like he'd been doing it all his life. He smoked five back to back on the walk home, not coughing even once. Every breath, every puff of smoke, was like being transported to somewhere else. To another time.

Baby steps, Jon. Baby steps back into the past.

BEFORE

Jayson leaned against a wall, staring across the street. Delaney was over there, window shopping. The late September day was rainy and wet and miserable, putting him in a difficult mood. Shouldn't the sun always be shining on him? He was in love, after all. Forever and ever.

In love with someone who can do so much better than me.

"You're not gonna get it?" he asked when she jogged back to him. She hadn't even gone into the costume shop.

"Nah. Too expensive. We can go to Goodwill and I can probably jerry-rig something," she told him. He frowned, but she kept smiling and grabbed his hand, leading him down the street.

Jay had only lasted a couple weeks in his job. Luckily, Del got a new one before Jay could get fired, so they weren't destitute. But it was a shitty job waitressing at some run down titty bar. He didn't like it at all, but Del pointed out how much he liked eating, and how they both liked doing drugs, so someone had to bring in some money. The tips were also pretty okay, so that made it slightly more bearable.

They were still squatting. Still living on the fringe. Del never once complained. She went to bed with a smile and she woke up with smile. Jay lived for her smiles, so he tried to trust her when she said everything was okay. She also *never* took off her ring. She wore it with pride, no longer introducing him as her boyfriend, but as her fiancé. He just about wanted to die, she made him so happy.

Then why can't you do better for her?

"I'm sorry, Del," he sighed as they turned into a residential neighborhood.

"For what? Oh god, did you leave the milk out again?" she groaned.

"No. I'm sorry we're not in a house like these people. That I can't get my shit together," he said, gesturing to the buildings around them. She burst out laughing.

"Jay, this is a shitty neighborhood. Most of these houses are abandoned. I wouldn't want to live like these people. I like our life. It has you and I in it," she told him, wiggling their arms.

"Still. I just … I can never quite shake this feeling I'm bad for you. Like if we'd never met that night, you wouldn't have done coke with me, and we wouldn't have gone out. I never would've introduced you to gravity bongs or wake-and-bake or ecstasy or oxy. You'd probably be with some nice guy right now. Not an asshole like me," he said.

"Stop it, right now," she snapped, moving in front of him and coming to a halt. "Newsflash, Jayson Fairbanks, I wasn't some princess living in an iceberg before you came along. You think that was the first night I'd ever gotten stoned? That I'd ever done coke? *No.* I would have done it regardless of whether or not it was with you. Think of it that way, *asshole*. If you *hadn't* been there, I would've wound up doing it with Crash. Or worse, one of his nasty friends. Then where would I be?"

He'd never thought of it that way before, and he had to admit, he didn't like it.

"You can do better than me, babe. So much better. Sometimes, I think you should."

She went completely still.

"Are you breaking up with me?" she whispered.

"No, Del. I just think maybe you should think—"

"This is you breaking up with me!" she yelled, startling some birds out of the tree next to them. "Well, guess what!? *NO!* You can't! I don't accept your break up! You said forever, so it's goddamn forever. You *promised.* So sucks to be you, but we are in love, and that's just the way it's going to be, *so deal with it.*"

He was shocked by her outburst, then flat out stunned when she turned and started running. She had a solid block on him before he came to his senses and started chasing after her.

"Delaney, stop!" he yelled, pumping his legs.

She wasn't listening, but it didn't matter. He was a natural runner, had been doing it all his life, and his legs were so much longer than hers. He caught up to her in no time. She had veered off the sidewalk and was dashing into the bike line when he reached her. She shrieked and kicked as he wrapped his arms around her from behind.

"You don't get to do this!" she cried, and he realized she was sobbing. "You can't just leave me. I love you, Jayson! *I love you.*"

"Shhh," he breathed in her ear as he carried her back to the sidewalk. "Calm down. We can talk about this."

"Calm down? Fuck you, *you* calm down! How would you feel if I tried to dump you and make it seem like it was for your benefit? Don't touch me. *Don't you fucking touch me!*" she shrieked.

And that broke him. The idea of not being allowed to touch Delaney, it was completely foreign to him. It would be like telling him he wasn't allowed to breathe or eat or sleep. He might as well be asked not to touch his own body. *No one* had that kind of authority. Not him, and not even her. She *belonged* to him.

"Don't ever say that," he said, sinking down till he was sitting on the curb. She was a ball of elbows and knees, still struggling against his hold. "Don't you *ever* say that to me again."

"How could you want to leave me? For any reason? I can't live without you, Jay," she sobbed, finally curling into him and gripping onto his jacket. He held onto her tightly.

"I can't live without you, either," he said, struggling to breathe. "I'm just afraid of doing the wrong thing, Del. I love you so much, I just wanted to do what was best."

"Well, I love you so much I can't even stand the thought of letting you go. *That's* real love. *That's* what's best," she said, her voice full of anger and tears. Another wave of shame and guilt passed over him.

She thinks I don't love her as much as she loves me.

"I'm sorry," he whispered. "I'm so sorry. I'll never do something like this again."

"You have to trust us," she hiccuped and gasped. "It's real. *Real* love. And it will find a way. We'll get through all the bullshit, no matter what, because we always have each other."

"I'm sorry. You're right. I should trust us," he sighed, pressing his lips against her head.

"In love we trust, remember?" she reminded him.

"I remember. I remember everything about you."

"Don't ever leave me," she whispered, shaking in his arms.

"Never. I will *never* leave you," he promised.

They sat on the curb like that for a long time, just crying and holding each other. Love was such a strange thing. He'd thought he'd known what it was when he was younger, when he'd loved his sisters and his parents. He'd thought he'd understood better when he was older, when he'd met Jenny Horowitz and she'd taken his virginity. And of course the end all be all—drugs. When he'd first discovered getting high, he'd been sure *that's* what true love felt like, no other loves needed.

Now he knew he'd had *no idea*. Not the faintest clue. All other kinds of love were obliterated in the presence of Delaney. How could it be possible to love another human being so much? She hadn't even existed in his world six months ago. Now she *was* his world.

And my heart and my soul and my everything.

"Where have you been all my life?" he whispered. She hugged him tight for a second, then sat back. Her face and eyes were puffy, red. She looked miserable, he'd never seen her like that before. They fought all the time, but she never cried, not actual sobbing. Never. Not even once.

"I don't want to feel this way anymore," she sniffled, holding onto the edges of his jacket. "Please, Jay. Let's go somewhere, do something. Let's be happy."

He nodded and stood up, then gently set her back down on the sidewalk. They held hands and resumed walking.

And that was the night he introduced Delaney to speed.

CHAPTER
eight

Things were great.

Things were awful.

Things were fun.

Things were boring.

Anymore, it was like Jon's moods changed with the weather. Some days he was glad to be alive and thankful for all the gifts he'd been given. He'd high five Gary Tupper in the morning, help Ms. Gaines make breakfast, put in a solid three hours at the community center, then go out with Kitty. Life was *good*.

Other days, though, were the complete opposite. He could barely pull himself out of bed in time to go to work, let alone help with anything around the house. He half assed his chores, and lost his door privileges more than once. Life was *annoying*.

And he cared about Kitty, he honestly did. She was gorgeous and lovely. She really did take care of him, and most importantly, she cared *about* him. She was funny and energetic and bright. They went out to the movies and dinner, took in shows and went shopping. It was a lot of fun.

Sometimes they spent the weekend in Westchester, with him sneaking over to the garage apartment every night, and even a few times during the day. Other times, she'd surprise him by renting a hotel room and staying downtown. It was awesome, and yet something was missing. He could feel it. Like it all wasn't enough.

They had sex all the time, and it was … sex. Sex is awesome. She'd come, he'd come, bing bang boom, *done*. She'd gotten over some of her shyness, allowing the lights to be left on once in a while, or lighting a candle. She even let him go down on her a couple times. On Valentine's Day, he got a blow job. He couldn't remember ever having one before, but he was pretty sure he could tell she wasn't experienced at it. It didn't matter, it was still awesome, and it was a very sweet gesture.

That right there was the issue, though. *A sweet gesture. Everything* they did was sweet. They held hands and they kissed while walking into the sunset. He laid down on top of her and they made love. He was pretty sure she'd even said *"I love you"* to him once, while in the throes of passion. He didn't mention it afterward, and neither did she, and he was glad. He wasn't ready to say it back and he didn't want things to be awkward.

It all should have been more than enough, but sweetness just wasn't, at least not for him. It was like he'd been eating ice cream all his life, and then someone handed him fat free frozen yogurt and claimed it was just as good. No it fucking wasn't—it wasn't even close.

Technically, he couldn't remember ever having had "ice cream", so he supposed there was no guarantee he ever actually had experienced it. He could just *feel* it, though, and somehow knew Kitty wasn't quite what he looked for in a lover. And once you've tasted something amazing, you just can't go back to bland.

He tried to spice it up. She may not have been a very sexually open person, but she always encouraged him to be honest with her.

To tell her anything. He'd ask her to try different positions, and sometimes she'd be willing, but other times not. He tried easing her into dirty talk, but it was always a hard no.

One time, he'd gotten his hand under her skirt while they'd been out at dinner. Watching her come at the table had gotten him so turned on, he'd been ready to drag her to the bathroom and fuck her over a sink. She wouldn't hear of it, though, and she was too embarrassed to jack him off under the table. He had to wait until they left, and by then, he was too annoyed to be interested anymore.

It's just sex—a relationship isn't built solely on sex. You two have lots of other things.

That was true. They joked a lot, and talked for hours. She encouraged him in all things, even if she could be a bit condescending at times. She took him everywhere, showed him everything, introduced him to all her friends. It was nice.

*Nice. Nice and **sweet.***

"How are we doing today, Jon?"

Sloany sat down across from him and immediately took out her binder. It had been over a month since their fight, but she wouldn't let it go. Their meetings were strictly professional anymore. No more banter, no more playfulness. She would go over his finances with him, give him his allowance, listen to any issues he had with the halfway house, and then she would just go.

He hated it. He couldn't control his memory or his love life, apparently, but he could take control of *this* situation. Starting right now.

"Not so good," he sighed, rubbing at the back of his neck.

"Oh? An issue at Benson House?" she asked, clicking her pen and taking out her notepad.

"No. It's something else."

"The community center?"

"No."

"Have you heard about your hearing?" she asked, referring to Mr. Beaumont's court case to help get Jon a social security number.

"That's all fine."

"If you don't want to talk about whatever is bothering you, I understand," she said, unclicking her pen and starting to put things away. "We can meet up next week."

"It's this guy," he blurted out. She raised her eyebrows.

"At the halfway house?"

"Yeah. Yeah, he stays there."

"Alright. Have you spoken to Mr. Tupper about him?"

"No, I can't really go to Gary with this one."

"Then what's the issue? Maybe I can broach it with Mr. Tupper," she offered. Jon took a deep breath.

"You see, this guy, he's a real asshole. Emotional, too. Like a teenage girl, just all over the place," he said. She kept staring at him. "And you know, people do a lot of nice things for him, and he's still a dick. Even this one time, his best friend was just trying to look out for him, and he was such a bastard to her. She told him how she honestly felt, and he just lashed out at her. Mostly because he thought she was right, and that made him angry."

"Wow. This guy *does* seem like a real asshole," she agreed.

"Believe me, you have no idea. You should try living with him."

"Thanks, but I've lived in a place with a pest problem. I'm good for a while."

He smiled at her.

"Even worse, though, is this guy is awful with words. He's too stupid to know how to apologize right, and he's really bad at asking for help, even though he needs it all the time. I was thinking maybe you could help him?" he asked. She took a deep breath and let it out in a dramatic sigh.

"I don't know, Jon. I have such a heavy case load, and this guy sounds like a real problem child."

"He is. But I think he's worth it."

She was silent for a second, her eyes appraising him. He hoped she didn't find him wanting.

"Yeah. Yeah, I think he is, too," she said slowly. He tentatively reached across the table for her.

"Friends again?" he asked as she reached out to shake his hand.

"Huh uh, you said *best* friends. Don't puss out on me now," she said. He barked out a laugh and let her go.

"God, I missed you, Sloany."

"Good. I knew if I held out long enough, you'd break down."

"You're evil."

"To the core, kiddo. Now tell me about life."

And he did. He told her all about his and Kitty's relationship, how it was great and yet not great. He didn't go into detail about the sex, but he did broadly explain how it just didn't do it for him. How it was weird, but he just somehow knew he liked something else.

"And there's nothing wrong with that," she assured him. "Relationships wax and wane, even for people with amnesia, Jon. Maybe it's just running its course. Or maybe you just need to get over this hump and then you two will be better than ever."

"Yeah … maybe. Hey, I meant to tell you something. I used to smoke," he said casually. Her jaw dropped.

"I'm sorry—what? Explain yourself," she demanded. He smiled. That was the reaction he'd been hoping for from Kitty when he'd told her.

"I was walking down the street and wound up in this group of smokers and it hit me like sledgehammer. I've never craved anything so bad in my entire li-, well, you get the idea. I went to a store and bought a pack, smoked half the thing like it was nothing. I haven't smoked any since, but I tell you, I was *definitely* a smoker," he told her the story. She leaned forward over the table.

"I think that's *amazing*, Jon. I mean, don't smoke anymore, for christ's sake, but still. Wow! You remembered something!" she exclaimed. He grinned at her, then just had to say it.

"You know, Sloany, I think I love you," he blurted out. She blinked a couple times, then waved him away.

111

"They all say that to me, you know. Every single one of you sad cases," she teased him.

"Yeah, but the difference is, you love me back," he pointed out. She snorted.

"That makes absolutely *no* difference. My undying love for you is kept completely separate from our professional relationship," she informed him. He burst out laughing.

"Oh, Mrs. Sloan. In another life, I think I would have married you."

"Hey, you never know. Maybe you did."

BEFORE

Halloween.

Jay had always loved Halloween. Acting silly, going to parties, scary shit. All of it was awesome in his opinion.

Delaney loved it even more than him. He refused to dress up, but she'd created a gypsy type of costume for herself. Her bright red lipstick was tempting him all night, just begging to be smeared across her mouth with his own lips. Or other body parts. Her skirt was made out of a bunch of scarves and gave up tantalizing glimpses of thighs and hips. More than once throughout the night, he was able to sneak a hand inside the billowy fabric.

She'd lost her job that morning. She'd come home and they'd both taken ecstasy to make her feel better. Then they'd fucked until they'd started coming down, after which they'd done a couple lines each. Afterwards she'd been buzzing around their shitty apartment, putting together her costume and chattering away.

Jay didn't have any job at all, except occasionally running weed and coke in exchange for more drugs. While Del got ready, he packed them doggy bags of goodies. Portable fun.

They went from party to party. Some they were invited to, and some they crashed. They took straight shots of Everclear and smoked weed which had been mixed with oxy. She'd blown smoke rings into his face, and he'd laughed and laughed.

They ended the night at Crash's, stumbling around and trying virtually anything that was put into their hands. More ecstasy, more coke. Crushed up codeine was snorted with vigor, and even more grain alcohol was drunk. They'd been ready to go when good ol' Crash had popped up with a hypodermic needle. Del had already been outside, laughing and cackling with some of the other girls, so Jay had followed Crash into the back of the house.

"Thought you'd be interested, my man," the other guy creaked out. Jay nodded and slipped off his jacket.

It had been a long, long time since he'd injected anything into his body. He'd left all that behind in Iowa when he'd moved. But somewhere along the line during the night, a sort of funk had fallen over him. Watching Delaney smile and be happy. So poor and so skinny. All his fault. But forever was forever, as she liked to say, so he just had to deal with a moment of depression and trust they'd be okay. He knew the speed would help. Would bring back the happy.

"Been a while," he mumbled, fumbling with the tourniquet

"You wanna wait, do this with Del?"

It was a natural question. Everyone knew there was no Jay, and there was no Del—there was just Jayson-and-Delaney. Where one was, the other was right with them. Normally, it would be the same right then. She'd probably want to tie it on for him.

But then she'd want to try, and that he could not allow.

"No. Fix me up."

A cotton dunked in Everclear was smeared on the inside of his elbow. He slapped at his arm, making the veins bulge, while Crash mixed the amphetamine in a baggy. Then Jay closed his eyes and didn't move until he felt a pin prick on his skin.

"You ready, man?"

"Do it."

A quick stab. Pressure. A moment of silence, and then … a rush. Moving through his entire body. He gasped and dropped his arm, then let his head fall back. He stared at the ceiling as goosebumps broke out all over his skin.

"Yeah," Crash chuckled. "That's the good shit right there. Happy Halloween, fucker."

Jay sat still for as long as he could, then he put his jacket back on. Crash handed him a baggie of crushed up speed, which Jay took before going outside. Del was still talking to her friends, but he wrapped an arm around her waist and literally dragged her away.

"Sorry, girls, but I gotta take this little lady trick or treating!" he called out, then he picked her up and tossed her over his shoulder.

"Jay!" she squealed and laughed, clinging to his jacket while he carried her down the street. "What has gotten into you?"

"Only you, babe. Only you," he laughed as well, then he smacked her on the ass.

"C'mon, put me down, or I'll puke down your back," she threatened, then made convincing retching noises. He sat her down.

"God, you look amazing tonight, Del. But didn't everybody? What a good time. Crash was really on point tonight. How long do you think he can keep going?" Jay asked, walking so fast she had trouble keeping up. Their subway stop was a couple blocks ahead and he felt like he was walking in slow motion. He wanted to jog, run, sprint, *go into hyper drive.* "He's been throwing these crazy parties for over a year now, the cops are gonna shut him down soon. Will suck when it happens. You ever been arrested, Del? I can't believe I've never asked you that! Jesus, what else don't I know about you?"

She abruptly grabbed his arm and pulled him around so he was facing her.

"What did you take in there?" she asked, staring him in the face. He swallowed thickly and glanced around.

"What all did *you* take in there?" he asked back. She punched him in the shoulder.

"I'm serious, Jay."

"Me, too, because I'm not gonna share if I don't know what other drugs you've got in your system."

She looked surprised, then she thought about it.

"I don't know, whatever I took with you. Some oxy, some coke. A bunch of E," she prattled stuff off. Jay nodded and pulled the baggie out of his pocket.

"You should be fine."

"What do you have?"

"The most incredible speed I've ever had."

He'd been very careful with Delaney and speed. He didn't want to become addicted again, and he *did not* want her using it a lot. It was a fun party drug, but nothing more, and he was determined to keep it that way for her. It was a rare treat, and she could barely contain her smile.

"Jesus, it must be. Your pupils look like marbles," she told him. He shrugged and managed to pinch out a healthy amount of the powdered drug onto the back of his hand.

"C'mon, get this over with quick so we can go home and ride it out," he urged. She leaned over his hand and carefully snorted it all up.

"Good to go, babe."

At Crash's, it had been like electricity boiling through his veins. Lightning in his body. Fucking amazing. By the time he got to the bottom of the subway platform, though, he knew something wasn't right. He felt murky, like he was wading through mud. He blinked his eyes and tried to clear his head. He was practically a professional drug do-er, he could figure out what was going on.

*You took a massive hit of stimulant from an unknown source, **on top of** drinking your weight in a depressant, numb nuts. Shit, how much alcohol has Del had!?*

She was laughing at something. Leaning against him and laughing and laughing. That sound he loved so dearly. It took him two tries, but he managed to capture her chin in his hand and bring her head around to face him. They fell into a wall and he kissed her, his tongue all over the place.

"I wanna do it," she whispered against him, pulling at his t-shirt. "Right now."

"Home," he managed to mumble. "At home."

"No, now," she whined, rubbing her body on his.

"You're so fucking amazing," he sighed, sliding to the floor. She groaned.

"No, no, no," she complained, pulling at his wrists. "You can't black out! I need various parts of your anatomy right now!"

He managed to climb to his feet, but he almost immediately fell over again. Del took the full brunt of his weight and they stumbled clear across the platform. She was a tiny girl. So much smaller than him— that she was even managing to keep him off the ground was amazing.

"I love you, babe," he said to the top of her head. "I love you more than air."

"I love you, too," she replied through gritted teeth. "But I need you to stand up right now."

"I don't have to stand. When I'm with you, I can fly," he told her.

"No flying. Standing is good. Please, Jay," she begged, starting to pant.

"Watch me," he whispered.

"Babe, I just need you to—*BABE!*"

He'd jerked upright abruptly, flinging his arms out to his sides. He could feel his feet leaving the ground, knew it was happening. Delaney's voice was loud. She must have been cheering, and he could just barely see her reaching out for him. He grabbed onto her hand as he started to fly.

"*Come with me,*" he breathed, pulling her along.

And then they were flying over the edge of the subway platform, soaring up, up, and away.

CHAPTER
nine

Something about New York in March.

Jon couldn't put his finger on it, but it felt … *special.* Maybe it was because the weather was occasionally nice. Sometimes the chill was almost out of the air. Or maybe it was knowing spring was right around the corner. He couldn't put his finger on it, but he could *feel* it. He'd been able to feel it way back in February, when he'd been anticipating March. He'd told Kitty about it, and unbeknownst to him, she'd held onto the info and ran with it.

"*Surprise!*"

John Doe didn't have a birthday, but Kitty didn't see why Jon Doherty couldn't have one. He'd said March felt special—maybe it was because he'd been born in that month.

She'd gotten them tickets to a Yankees game. They went with a large group of people, a bunch of her friends he could usually tolerate pretty well. They had great seats and it was really an awesome day. They drank beer and ate hot dogs and yelled at the teams.

"*Enjoying yourself?*" she'd asked him during the seventh inning stretch.

"*So much. Thank you, babe,*" he'd replied, and she'd scrunched up her nose.

"*Babe? Ew, I don't like that, makes me feel like a doll.*"

"*Sorry. Force of habit.*"

"*How? You've never called me babe before.*"

Then a batter had struck a home run and he hadn't wasted too much thought on the word. He supposed it was strange—how could saying "babe" be a habit, when he'd never said it? Oh well, he'd just make sure not to say it again.

After the game they all separated. Normally, he spent 99% of his social time with Kitty, and only her. She'd been kind enough to realize maybe a little male bonding would be good for him. So the girls went on their own adventure, and the men were left to their own devices.

Since Jon couldn't remember if he'd ever been to Times Square or not, they all thought it would fun to go down there. Celebrate his kinda-birthday and go be tourists. He could even drink as much as he'd wanted, Kitty had gotten them a hotel room for the night, so he wouldn't have to go back to the halfway house.

They took over a high top table at the back of some large chain restaurant. Everything was over priced because, hello, Times Square, but none of the other guys cared. They all came from a lot of money, made a lot of money, *had* a lot of money. Since it was Jon's psue-do-birthday, they were all treating. The wings kept coming out of the kitchen and the beers kept flowing, and it was really a pretty good time

"Wild, man," one guy was chuckling. "No memory at all. I still can't believe it."

"Believe it," Jon laughed. "Wanna see the scar?"

"Nah, I'm too drunk for that shit."

The guy wasn't lying, he could barely stay on his stool. It wasn't quite seven o'clock, but Jon thought maybe it was time to start calling it a night. He kept glancing at his phone, wondering when Kitty would text him, or if he should text her.

"So, you and Kitty have been together a while now, huh?" one guy asked as several others carted Drunky off to the bathroom.

"Huh? Oh, uh, maybe? What's a while? Since late December," he answered, trying to think back.

"Three months, not bad, not bad. Real nice girl," the guy commented, and Jon nodded.

"She's a sweetheart. Too sweet, you know? I'm not half good enough for her," he replied. The dude shrugged.

"Don't sell yourself short, man. This time in three years, you'll be at a Hollywood premiere for a movie about your life."

"Wouldn't that be awesome?" Jon laughed. Before they could keep bullshitting, though, the rest of their party returned. Well, all but one guy.

"Shit, we need to bounce. Reggie's puking his guts out."

"I'll go hail a cab," the guy he'd been talking to sighed, then he pulled a credit card out of his wallet and handed it to Jon. "Go take care of the tab, will you?"

Jon glanced around for a nearby waiter or waitress, but the restaurant was packed. There was a large, round bar in the center of the room. He figured if he headed up there, they could look up his ticket and take care of it. So after the other guys had hauled drunk-Reggie outside, Jon started making his way across the room.

The bar was slammed, and there seemed to be only one bartender behind it. Jon frowned. It would be forever before he got his attention. But while he was still half the room away, a waitress swooped in, hurrying up to the P.O.S. station on the end of the bar. He started walking faster, hoping to catch her, but it was already to late. She moved away from the register and started walking towards him, but on the opposite side of the room. Her head was down as she looked at an order in her hand.

Oh, well. Bartender it is.

He took four more steps when she lifted her head. He didn't know why it caught his attention, but it did. She lifted, and he looked. Their eyes caught each other and they both stopped moving.

That jolt. That sinking feeling, only times a million. Times *infinity*.

I know this woman.

She was staring back at him with the biggest, brightest blue eyes he'd ever seen. Pools, threatening to drown him. She lifted a hand and pressed it to her chest.

I know this woman.

Time stopped. There was no one else in the room but them. He kept staring and struggling to breathe and trying so hard to find his way back to her. Her? Her who?

Who are you?

She seemed to be having the same problem. She was breathing fast, her hand still on her chest, clutching the front of her shirt. She looked stunned, as if she were looking at a ghost. Then she opened her mouth, and even before she spoke, he knew what her voice sounded like.

"Jay?"

He didn't recognize the name, but he recognized her soul. They took a couple of halting steps towards each other, and then he was striding. And then she was running. And then they were crashing into each other, holding each other. He was shocked to realize he was crying.

"Where have you been?" she was sobbing. "I looked everywhere! *Everywhere!* God, I thought you were dead! *I missed you.*"

"I …" he didn't know how to talk anymore. His throat had turned to ashes. He choked on words he couldn't remember how to speak. "I …"

"Are you okay?" she asked, pulling away so she could look up at him. He missed her instantly.

You don't even know her.

"I don't know," he whispered. She lifted a hand and gently swiped her fingers across his brow. A tender, intimate gesture. Familiar, yet completely alien.

"Jay, I can't believe it's you. You look so different!" she gasped, clinging to his arms. "Where have you been all this time? Did you … Jay? *Jayson!*"

I don't know any Jason.

The edges of his vision had started turning black. The more she said, the worse it got, and when she said that name, that name he didn't know at all, he couldn't take it anymore. His eyes rolled up in his head and he started to fall backwards. She held onto him, but he knew it was pointless.

She's so tiny. How could she possibly stop me from falling?

CHAPTER
ten

God, he fucking hated hospitals.

When he'd first woken up, he'd been positive he was in some version of hell and that he was waking up from the accident all over again.

But he'd quickly realized he wasn't in Lenox Hill, and his accident had been months ago. He was all better, yup yup yup! Well, all except for his pesky missing memory. Darn that brain of his!

"I'm really touched, you know."

The voice startled him out of his pity party and he jerked his head to the side. He was scared he'd see more ghosts, but it was just Mrs. Sloan.

"What?" he croaked out. His voice was hoarse, his throat dry.

"You have me listed as your emergency contact. They called me the minute you got here," she explained, walking into his room and taking a seat near the bed.

"Well, you are like my mom," he chuckled. She smiled, then

reached out and grabbed his hand.

"Actually, your mother is forty-seven. Her name is Claudia Fairbanks," she told him. He just stared at her, and when he didn't say anything, she kept speaking. "Your father's name is Lucas Fairbanks and he's fifty-eight. They live in Cedar Rapids, Iowa. She had you when she was just twenty-two."

Jon took a deep breath and did some quick math.

"So I'm twenty-five?" he asked. She squeezed his fingers.

"Yes. You'll be twenty-six on July eighteenth," she informed him. He laughed, but stopped before it could turn into a sob.

"Twenty-six," he whispered. Then he looked around him, suddenly frantic. "How long have I been here? Did anyone call Gary Tupper? And where's Kitty? Someone should've called her, she should be here. And where's …"

His voice died somewhere just past his lips.

You can't remember her name because you're not worthy of her.

"Kitty was here, but we sent her home. She wanted to stay, but both her mother and I felt she needed to get some rest," Mrs. Sloan explained, her soothing voice working full throttle.

"I don't want her to worry," he said, laying back down. He kept convulsively clenching his fists.

"Don't even think about it, Jon. I mean, of course she's worried, but she just wants you to feel better."

"What happened?"

"You fainted. Hit your head pretty good on the side of a table, you've been out for about three hours," she said, and he glanced at a clock. It was just after eleven at night. "The doctors were concerned, considering your history, so they wanted to let you wake up naturally. They're keeping you tonight and tomorrow for observation, but they did a lot of scans, and everything seems fine."

He laughed at her statement.

"Yeah, totally fine, except I don't remember any of the things you just told me about."

"How are you feeling?" she asked. He took a deep breath and stared straight up.

"Like I got hit with a semi truck," he answered truthfully.

"You look like it," she responded honestly, and he barked out a laugh. Good ol' Sloany, making him feel better even when he felt like death. It was just what he needed to get up the courage to ask his next question.

"Is she here?"

He didn't need to elaborate.

"Yes," Mrs. Sloan responded. "She's been waiting this whole time. Both the doctor and I explained to her how it might be difficult for you, and how you might not want to see her. She said she understood, and she just wants to make sure you're okay. Do you want me to tell her to go home?"

I want you to tell her to not exist. Life was less scary when it was all a blank.

"No. I want to meet her."

"Jon, I really think you should rest. It's been—"

"*Send her in.*"

Sloany pressed her lips together and he could tell she thought about arguing, but then she let out a sigh and stood up. She held onto his hand for a little longer.

"We told her your medical history. What happened to you, your condition. She understands you don't remember, but Jon … it'll be upsetting for her, too. Please keep that in mind," she urged, squeezing his fingers tightly.

"I'll try. I *will*," he insisted.

"Okay. Do you want me to be here?"

"No, thank you."

"Okay. I'll be down by the nurse's station. Just press the buzzer if you need us."

"I will. And Sloany … *thank you*. I'm glad you're here. There's no one else I'd want more," he said, squeezing her back. She smiled and patted the back of his hand.

"You're just trying to tempt me. I know you're wearing one of those hospital gowns without a back. Keep it in your pants," she teased him, then she dropped his hand and walked out of the room.

A panic attack began to descend on him immediately. He gripped his blankets and struggled to breathe. Then he thought of Mrs. Sloan's voice, let it wash over him and calm him down. Pictured Kitty's smile and her soft touches.

Imagine blue eyes worshiping you, and skin so pristine you shouldn't be allowed to touch it.

There was a soft knock on the door jam, then light footsteps walking across the tiled floor. They came to a stop at the foot of his mattress and he finally lifted his head.

She was small, he remembered that much from the restaurant. Slight of build, too, but sort of rounded. *Soft.* She was wearing a uniform, black dress pants and a button down shirt with the restaurant's logo on it. She even still had on an apron with her receipt book in it. She had unruly dark hair, a thick mass of it. She'd swept it all to the side in an intricate, messy braid of some sort and left it to trail over her shoulder. She wasn't wearing any makeup, but she didn't need to—with eyes like hers, she could pierce right into his soul.

"Hi," she said in a soft voice that hurt his heart. "How are you feeling?"

"Okay," he replied, then cleared his throat. "Head hurts a little."

"Yeah, you hit it pretty hard on the way down. I tried to stop you, but ..."

"I was too heavy," he finished for her. She managed a smile.

"Yeah."

There was a heavy, awkward silence. Jon couldn't take it.

"Please," he said, gesturing to the chair Sloany had left empty. "Sit down."

She did as she was told, crossing her feet at the ankles and sliding them under the chair. Then she placed her hands in her lap and looked everywhere around the room but at him.

"Your friend, Mrs. Sloan," she finally spoke. "She seems really nice."

"She is really nice," he agreed. Then he decided it would be best to just get it over with. "I'm really sorry, you know."

She finally looked at him.

"For what?"

"For not remembering," he said simply. "For disappearing. I don't know what kind of person I was before, but I hope … I like to think I wouldn't have done that to you on purpose."

She smiled at him, and it broke his heart.

"You would never have done something like that, I never thought it for a moment," she assured him. He took several deep breaths and had to look away from her. He rested his head back on the pillow and looked at the ceiling.

"Really? What was he … I. What was *I* like?" he asked. She was silent for a very long time. A large tear escaped his eye and rolled down the side of his face. Then he felt her hand curling into his.

"You were … life," she said simply. "You were funny and you were generous. You had a smart mouth and a hot temper. A great laugh, and an even better smile. Anyone who met you, liked you. You could make friends just by walking into a room."

"Is that true?" he whispered, and without looking, he knew she nodded.

"It is."

"Then why didn't anyone look for me!?" he burst out, crushing her fingers in his grip. She didn't move a muscle.

"Our friends … I'm not gonna lie. They weren't the best people. Maybe *we* weren't the best people, I don't know. But *I* looked, Jay. That's all I've been doing since October," she told him. He couldn't control himself. All the emotions from the past five months came boiling out of him and he turned to glare at her.

"Oh, really? *All* you've been doing? Then how come you couldn't fucking find me? I was in the papers, on the news! You didn't check hospitals? Where were you when it happened? Why was I alone?" he demanded.

She took it all in stride. Didn't look scared or upset or offended. Just clung to his hand and kept that simple, sweet smile on her face. It made him feel like dying. If anything ever deserved to be remembered, it was her smile.

"I didn't know about the amnesia," she said simply. "We lived way out in Brooklyn. That's where you fell, so that's where I looked. I looked in every single emergency room in Brooklyn, I swear to you. I've been kicked out of more than a few."

"And not one of them knew where I was?"

"I don't know," she sighed. "I wasn't ... I wasn't in a good place then. I don't know if I didn't know the right questions to ask, or what. Maybe I didn't know where to look. I always asked for you by name, but of course, no one knew your name. I feel stupid now. But I looked for you, I swear. I never stopped looking."

He looked away from her again.

"Tell me about the accident."

She took a deep breath and let it out slowly, then slipped her hand free from him.

"It was Halloween," she started.

"I know that's when I was admitted," he said.

"We had been to a bunch of parties. You were sort of like the king of parties," she told him. "We just ... we drank way too much, and we got way too high on way too many different kinds of drugs. We were trying to go home, and I couldn't ... I couldn't hold on to you. You kept saying you could fly, and I kept trying to hold you, but Jay, you're so much bigger than me. I held on, but you just kept falling."

She was crying into her hands. He was crying silently while he stared straight up.

"My name is Jon," he whispered, and she cried even harder.

"You fell and you pulled me down with you," she managed to

pant out. "We both hit the tracks. I broke my ankle, but you, oh my god. There was so much blood. I thought you were dead and I started screaming. A man jumped down and picked me up, carried me back to the platform, but they were scared to move you. Thought maybe you'd broken your neck. So instead, they closed the lines and called an ambulance. Someone carried me back up to the street, but I couldn't stop screaming. Paramedics showed up and finally sedated me. I was taken into surgery for my ankle, and when I woke up, I wasn't even in New York anymore. My parents had been called, they had me transferred back to Connecticut, where I'm from.

"God, I wanted to come find you. They had to strap me into my bed. Then I was taken to my parents' house, with my foot in a cast, and I wasn't allowed to do *anything*. They were so scared, they'd had no idea how I'd been living. Hadn't known about the drugs and partying. They made me detox for *weeks* in their fucking house. Afterwards, I wasn't in any shape to do anything. I had to wait until they could take off my cast. You made the local news in New York, but I guess not in Connecticut, so I had no idea what had happened to you. Now I almost wonder … maybe my parents kept the news from me, too. My phone had been shut off right before the accident because we couldn't pay, so I just didn't … didn't know. But the moment I got fitted for a boot, I took the first train to New York, and I spent days going to *every* hospital in Brooklyn, even called a couple police stations, but I was scared. You'd had drugs on you when you fell, and if they didn't already know, I didn't want to get you in trouble. It didn't matter, anyway. No one could, or really wanted, to help me. It was like you'd disappeared. Like you were just *gone*."

She was still crying, her shoulders heaving with the act, but he didn't know what to do. Part of him wanted to hold her, but another part of him knew it wouldn't be okay. Could possibly scare them both beyond repair. So he stayed still.

"I wonder," he said, wiping at his face. "You said I had drugs on me?"

"Yeah," she said, then hiccuped. "Yeah, you did."

"I wonder what happened to them, because they weren't with any of the stuff I got back when I left the hospital."

There was silence for a moment.

"Some nurse must have had a great time."

He laughed first, which set her off, and then they were both in hysterics. Her laugh was gorgeous, like notes on a scale, and her face was meant to smile.

"It's weird, but I don't remember being a drug addict at all," he finally started speaking. "They said I detoxed while I was unconscious."

"You're lucky," she sighed, leaning forward and crossing her arms on top of his mattress, then resting her chin on top of them. "It's not pleasant."

"Were we both speed addicts?" he asked casually, trying to play it cool. She made a face.

"What? No. I'd only ever used it maybe twice before that night," she replied. He glanced down at his arm, at the now faded scar from a needle mark.

"Seems like injecting is pretty serious. I figured I was an addict," he said.

"Injecting? What are you talking about?"

He showed her the scar and told her what the doctors had all said. She examined the spot, holding his arm in her hands. Little bolts of electricity fired off under his skin.

"That's got to be what that is," he said. She nodded, a frown causing a crease in her forehead.

"Crash," she sighed. "The last party on Halloween, you stayed inside after I'd gone outside. When you finally did come out, you were like a live wire. He must have shot you up."

"Sounds like a charming guy. The doctors said there was a whole cocktail of drugs in my system," he said. She nodded.

"Yeah. We were ... we were pretty crazy."

"Were?"

"I haven't touched anything since that night," she said in a solemn voice. "No drugs, no alcohol, nothing. I never even took anything stronger than Tylenol for my ankle."

"I've had a couple drinks since then," he admitted. "Smoked a couple cigarettes, but that's it. I don't even have any desire to use."

"Good. That is *so good* to hear," she breathed. There was another long silence, then she gave an awkward cough. "I saw your … *girlfriend*. She's very pretty."

The subject he'd been at once dreading, yet also dying to cover.

"Kitty?" he asked. She nodded.

"I guess—Katherine? That's what Mrs. Sloan said."

"Yeah, Katherine. Everyone calls her Kitty for short. We volunteer at a community center together."

"Volunteering, wow. That's amazing. I'm so … I'm so proud of you. And she seems like a great girl for your life now."

He took a deep breath.

"And what about you?"

"What about me?"

"Were you once a great girl in my life?"

Another silence, so long he wondered if she'd fallen asleep. But she hadn't. She was staring down at her hands in her lap, taking deep breaths.

"I think …" she whispered, and he could see a tear falling from her face. "I think I really was. One of the greatest."

He tilted his head forward and realized what she was staring at—a huge mood ring was on her left hand. Identical to the one he owned. He belatedly realized he must have given it to her, or they must have exchanged them. They meant something important to the two of them.

One of the greatest.

"Stop crying," he urged in a soft voice. She laughed and finally lifted her head, wiping at her cheeks as she moved.

"I'm sorry," she wept. "I told myself I wouldn't get upset, and that if I did, I'd leave so I wouldn't upset *you*."

"Stop," he stated, then he didn't even think about what he did next. He just scooted over to the right, as much as the tiny hospital bed would allow, and held his arm aloft over the left side. "Come lay down."

She stared at him for a second, her bottom lip trembling. He stared back. He didn't know what was right or what was wrong, but he needed this moment. And he thought maybe she did, too.

She stood up out of her chair and climbed into the bed. Rolled onto her side and curled up against his chest.

"God, I missed this," she whispered, pressing her face into his hospital gown.

"I think ..." he started to whisper back, and he gently rested his hand on her head. "I think I missed it, too."

CHAPTER
eleven

"Her name is *what?*"

Jon rolled his eyes at Kitty, then continued pacing back and forth.

"I told you, Delaney. Delaney Carter."

"What kind of name is that?"

"I don't know, the kind of name people in Connecticut give."

"And you really recognized her?" Kitty asked. She was sitting at the foot of the hotel bed, watching him wear out the carpet.

"Yes. I don't know, maybe. It's so hard to explain. It's like … you know when you have a dream?" he asked, finally stopping and turning to face her. She nodded.

"Yeah, sure. Are you saying this girl is your dream?" she asked.

"No, jesus. Look—sometimes you have a dream. And you can see it in your head, but when you go to describe it, there are just no words. It's bizarre and frustrating and you can't figure it out. The feeling and the tone and the emotions, they're all there, but you just can't *say it*. This is just like that. It's like … I've never seen her before in my life, yet I know her, but I just can't explain why. I can't find the words," he broke it down. Kitty was silent for a second, then she crossed her arms.

"I don't like this," she sniffled. He was blown away.

"Don't like what? Me getting my real identity back? My family? Are you crazy?" he snapped. Her face fell and he instantly felt bad.

"I sound like a monster when you put it that way. No, I want all those things for you, but this girl … I just know she was a girlfriend. Someone special. Are you going to leave me for her?" she demanded, wiping at her eyes.

"Kitty," he sighed, and he squatted down in front of her. "I know you. Right now, I don't know her. And I really don't know what to-morrow brings. But I know I care about you and I would never do anything to hurt you."

His words seemed to pacify her, which was good. They only had fifteen minutes. Jon changed his shirt for the hundredth time and Kitty went into the bathroom to clean up her face. She'd just shut off the water when there was a light knock at the door. Jon walked across the room and opened it.

"Hello, hello!" Mrs. Sloan sang out as she brushed past him Delaney followed behind her, holding a box in her hands. "It's a *mad house* down there! Have you seen it?"

The press *really* wanted Jon/Jay's story. Kitty's family had put him up in a hotel, figuring it would be better than staying at the halfway house, and would allow him a little more privacy. It was nice, having a gorgeous suite all to himself which Kitty had twenty-four access to, but he also kind of missed living with the guys. Missed his shitty little room.

"Yeah, I made the mistake of going for water earlier," he chuck-led, then he turned his attention to Delaney. "How are you?"

She smiled back at him and hurried to a sofa across the room. They'd spent the whole night wrapped around each other in the hospital, and they hadn't touched since then.

"I'm fine. I brought some of your stuff."

Sloany and him sat on either side of the tiny girl. Kitty hovered for a moment, then sat on the armrest next to Jon.

A laptop was pulled out first, which Delaney deposited on the cushions behind her. Next was a leather bound journal, which she handed over to him. He glanced in the box and saw several just like it.

"You liked to write," she explained. "These are all your personal journals, filled with stories and observations, everything."

"You've read them?" he asked, turning the small book around in his hands.

"Yeah. We didn't have a tv, no cable, so most nights we would just lay around and you would read to me from them," she explained.

"Wow. I thought journals were supposed to be private," he chuckled. She shrugged.

"It seemed natural, we always told each other everything. We didn't really keep secrets, not from each other."

She said it so simply, yet it landed in the room like a grenade. He could feel her tense up on one side of him, and Kitty tense up on the other. He awkwardly cleared his throat and looked down at the feather tattoo on his hand.

"So, I was a writer, huh? I guess that's what this is for," he said, wiggling his thumb around, making the tattoo bend and move. She nodded.

"Yes."

"What about the one on his chest?" Kitty interrupted. "He's got some Latin script there, a doctor translated it for us. But we don't know what it *really* means, like why he would get something so random?"

Delaney dropped her head and started scrounging through the box, but Jon could see the blush on her cheeks.

"He never explained it to me," she said quickly. "Oh, look—one of your dreadlocks!"

She was a real good sport, Delaney. She handled everyone's questions well, never cracking or getting upset. Jon absentmindedly wrapped his arm around Kitty's hips at one point, then instantly felt guilty. Delaney was looking at them, but she just smiled and passed around some more stuff.

Once the box was empty, the laptop was brought back out. She'd uploaded all the pictures from her phone and his old phone onto it so they could see what his life had been like before. As the machine booted up, Sloany suddenly jumped to her feet.

"Well! I am *thirsty*. C'mon, Kitty, let's go get some drinks down at the bar."

"What?" Kitty's jaw dropped. "No, I want to see what Jon—"

"Kitty, maybe it's for the best, you and I can—" Jon started to pipe up.

"Really, it's fine," Delaney spoke above them all. "I didn't … the pictures are separated into folders. It's okay."

Kitty finally caught on to why Jon and Sloany didn't want her there. Pictures of Jayson Fairbanks and Delaney Carter together might be awkward to look at. She shut her mouth and walked out of the room, grabbing her purse along the way.

"Half an hour okay? I'm not sure I can hold her longer," Mrs. Sloan said as she hurried after the blonde. The door slammed shut behind them.

"We don't have to—" Del started speaking when he interrupted her.

"Show me all of them."

The man in the pictures was completely alien. She'd organized them chronologically and was starting with when they'd first started dating, almost exactly one year ago. He hadn't had dreadlocks then, but his hair had been shaggy. Long and unkempt.

"Wow," he breathed, leaning close the the screen. She smiled and clicked to the next picture.

"Yeah. You are so different now. You were always so skinny before, but now you've kind of filled out. And your hair! You look so clean cut, I'm afraid I'll get you dirty," she teased. It was the same kind of joke he often made at Kitty's expense. He didn't like it when the joke was on him, though.

After the two month mark, there were a lot more pictures. He could tell it was hard for her to look at them, but she continued on. Smiling away and answering any of his questions.

"I can't believe you dated this guy," he mumbled, gently touching the screen.

It was a photo of them together, outside of some nightclub. Delaney looked great in a cute outfit, with her hair up in a bun on top of her head. The guy with her, though, this Jayson character, looked completely untrustworthy. He wore a long olive green jacket with a black knit sweater underneath, a pair of jeans with holes in them, and a large pair of boots. He'd just gotten his hair dreaded, and he stared dead eyed into the camera, not even a hint of a smile.

They weren't all like that, though. There were lots of them smiling together. Being silly together. At parties, at stores, at restaurants. One of them playing Guitar Hero together made him laugh, and she informed him he sucked at the game.

They were almost through all the pictures when he realized he hadn't seen any with them kissing. Lots with their arms around each other, but nothing truly intimate.

"Wait, wait, wait," he said. "I said I wanted to see all of them."

"These are all of them," she insisted, tilting the screen towards him. He shook his head.

"No, Delaney. *All* of them."

She stared at him for a second, her lips in a hard line. Then she sighed and opened a different folder.

"I didn't want to upset your girlfriend," she said in a soft voice. The thumbnails were too small for him to see clearly.

"My girlfriend isn't here, so I'd like to see them."

"I ... I don't know if I can," she whispered, and he glanced at her. "It was hard enough separating them. I'm sorry, Ja-, I mean, *Jon*."

"It's okay. Do you mind if I look?"

"No, I saved them for you."

She got up and walked to the bathroom. He shifted to the center of the sofa and balanced the laptop on his knees, then he clicked on the first picture.

They were standing next to the entrance to a subway stop. He had her face in his hands and he was kissing her. Even through the pixels, he could feel the passion. Her mouth was parted, her bottom lip caught between both of his. It sent a shiver down his back and caused his stomach to sink.

You wanted to see these pictures, you asked for this.

There were so many. Most of the selfie variety, but there were a bunch obviously taken by friends and then sent to them. Kissing in restaurants, bars, taxis, trains. Everywhere. Anywhere. Holding each other, touching each other. There was one of her straddling his lap while they were in a booth at some bar. She was standing on her knees and he had his hands up the back of her shirt, and they were staring at each other so intensely, it took his breath away a little.

How could I possibly forget something like that?

But if he thought that was intense, the next batch were even more so. Taken in a dark room, the flash had lit them up like beacons, leaving everything else in the shot to be drowned in blackness. They were on a mattress which was flat on the floor, if he wasn't mistaken. All at awkward angles, yet still beautiful in odd ways. He'd been the one taking the photos—Delaney's mouth was in the top of one shot, her bright red bottom lip trapped between her teeth. Her arms were raised, disappearing out of frame. She'd been wearing some sort of tight, lightweight, gold knit sweater, no bra, and a pair of black underwear. She was again straddling his lap, and his free hand was under her shirt, cupping her breast.

He stared down at his right hand, at his palm. Could feel it tingle.

Could swear he remembered the softness of her skin.

In the next shot she was bending over and his hand was on her ass, and the next she had switched positions entirely. She was between his legs, her back against his chest. His arm was snaking down the front of her body, his hand inside those black panties.

The tingling sensation grew.

She wasn't wearing a top in a couple of the pics, and it gave him weird feelings. Like he was violating her privacy by seeing her in such a state, yet also like he *deserved* to see it. Like her breasts belonged to him every bit as much as they belonged to her. He ran his fingers down the screen, then instantly felt guilty.

His favorite picture, though, was surprisingly tame in comparison.

They were in a men's bathroom somewhere—it was very clear they'd had no shame whenever they'd been together. Delaney was holding up her phone, taking a picture of their reflection in a full length mirror.

She was against a wall, arching her body away from it and pressing herself to him. He was leaning over her, such a tall imposing presence compared to her tiny one. He had a hand in the hair at the base of her skull, and he was pulling. Quite hard by the looks of it. His other hand was on her hip, holding her pelvis flush with his. Her mouth was open in a gasp and he had her bottom lip trapped between his teeth, pulling it slightly away from her.

No nudity. No sex. Yet still. It was like the picture held in it everything he'd been missing for the past five months. Sensuality, aggression, pleasure, passion, dirty, raw, naughty, nasty, *love*.

I loved this woman.

Jon's pulse was pounding in his ears. The pictures weren't bringing anything back, not in any literal sense. He didn't know where the shot had been taken, couldn't remember that bathroom, and had no idea why they'd been in there.

But *something* was happening.

He slowly stood up and started walking across the suite. Delaney had left the bathroom door open and he could hear the faucet running. When he got to the doorway, he looked down at her.

She had her hands on the vanity top and was bent over the sink. Hot water was flowing out of the faucet, causing the mirror to fog up at the bottom and steam to rise. It was curling around her bowed head. She was taking deep, steadying breath, and though he couldn't see her face, he knew her eyes were closed. She didn't seem to realize he was there.

He let his eyes wander over her, committing everything to memory. *Again.* She was familiar to him in a strange, indefinable way. Her hair was up in a messy bun. Despite the fact it was cold outside, she was wearing a loose brown tank top over a black sports bra, black skinny jeans, and she'd taken off a pair of black ankle boots while they'd been going through the pictures. As she stood in front of him barefoot, he was surprised at how small she really was—she could practically fit inside him.

That wasn't the most surprising thing about her, though. When she'd first arrived at the hotel room, she'd been wearing some sort of sports jacket, with the zipper pulled all the way up to her chin. She'd taken it off in the bathroom, he could see it on the floor at her feet. The tank top exposed a lot of her smooth, pale skin, and his eyes zeroed in on a tattoo on her back, sitting right at the base of her neck.

He didn't question what he was doing, didn't stop to think if it was appropriate or not. Didn't think about *anything*. He stepped forward so he was right behind her and he laid his palm against her back, right next to the black ink. Delaney didn't move, didn't even flinch. She must have known he was standing there the whole time.

"You lied," he breathed, reading the scrawling script.

"I know," she whispered back.

In Love We Trust

Delaney's tattoo was in English and Jon's was in Latin, but they were the same words. The same font, even. He stepped closer to her, staring down at the tattoo like it could give him all the answers.

Tell me who this girl is. Remind me.

"Why?" he asked, and she let out a chuckle, then lifted her head enough to look at their reflection.

"I'm trying really hard here, Jay—, I mean, *Jon*," she said. "But it's not easy for me. Some things are sacred, you know? And that you don't remember … it makes it seem not as special. Some things I guess I want to keep sacred."

He was silent for a long time, still looking at the ink on her skin. She was wrong—it *was* sacred. Maybe even more so now. It was like an icon. A *relic*. One of the only things tying him to a way of life he didn't remember.

She abruptly let out a shuddering breath and her head fell back. She wasn't looking at him, just the ceiling, and she was rapidly blinking her eyes. Her gorgeous blue eyes were shiny and bright with unshed tears, and it made him sad. That he was the one making her cry, it caused his soul to ache. He didn't know how or why, but he wanted to comfort her. Wanted to take all her pains and fears away.

He turned his gaze to their reflection and his body once again went on autopilot. The hand he had on her back slid over her shoulder slowly, and then went across her chest. While he watched in the mirror, her eyelids fluttered shut. His hand kept moving over her skin, sliding under her tank top and bra strap, then hooking around her side, his fingers under her arm.

She sighed softly and almost imperceptibly started to lean towards him. When her back came into contact with his chest, he looked down at her. His arm was stretched lengthwise across her chest, bracing her against him. He let out a shaky breath and tilted his head down, moving closer to her ear.

"*You can call me Jay,*" he whispered.

He didn't know what he was doing, didn't know what was going on. His mind didn't remember her at all, but his body seemed to know every inch of her. All he knew was her skin felt like home and that when she breathed, he was the one taking in oxygen.

He also didn't know what would have happened next or how far things would have gone between them in that small bathroom. She had just met his gaze in the mirror when there was a sound from outside. People in the hallway, talking. Kitty and Mrs. Sloan.

Whatever magic had been happening, those voices broke the spell. While they stared at each other, he slowly pulled his arm free of her and she took a step forward. She was the first to look away, sticking her hands under the running water and rinsing them. Jon stepped backwards out of the bathroom, but couldn't stop staring at her. Not even when the front door opened and the other women walked in.

"Sorry, sweetie," Kitty sighed. "There's all these reporters hanging out down there and they recognized us. Mrs. Sloan didn't think it was a good idea to talk to them without your permission, so I figured we should just come back up."

Jon didn't say anything, just kept staring in the bathroom. Kitty's gaze shifted between him and the small girl in the other room. Mrs. Sloan started chattering away, trying to kill the awkward silence. Meanwhile, Delaney finished washing her hands and she turned towards the group, her perfect smile back in place, her eyes bright and clear.

"Ready to see what Jon looked like with dreads?" she asked Kitty, then she lead the way back into the suite. The other two women followed her happily, laughing at the idea of clean cut Jon Doherty with dreadlocks.

Meanwhile, Jon stayed rooted in place, staring at an empty space where she used to exist.

CHAPTER
twelve

Delaney Marie Carter had been born in the suburbs of Hartford, Connecticut. Her first name was actually her mother's maiden name. She was an only child, born after many years of fertility treatments, and was adored by her parents.

She grew up in a nice neighborhood and went to good schools. She was raised in a caring and loving and encouraging environment. She had been taught to treat others as she wished to be treated. Made to understand that every day was a gift. Always told that somewhere out there, someone had it worse than her, so she should always be thankful.

As a result, she had an exceptionally positive outlook on life. A spirit which was almost impossible to crush. Whenever anything bad happened, she could almost always find a silver lining. Find a way around it or through it, or a way to laugh at it and learn from it.

But even Delaney Carter had her limits.

She looked over the PG-13 pictures with Kitty and Mrs. Sloan.

They laughed and gasped and even got a little teary eyed, looking at their friend Jon in his former life. He had been so different, they kept pointing out. A different person entirely.

He really was, too. The entire time she'd known Jayson, she'd probably only seen him clean shaven a handful of times, and never with short hair. Always in loose clothing, second hand threads, and worn shoes. Always bohemian, he fit in wherever they went in Brooklyn.

Jon was the opposite. He had clean cut hair which she had to admit looked good on him. He was a soft brunette, and the sides had been cut short, with the top thick. Just begging to have fingers run through it. And both times she'd seen him, he'd been wearing nice jeans, expensive looking shoes, and polo shirts that stretched across his broad chest. He'd looked right at home in Midtown.

He looked good, she could admit it. Great, even. Healthier than she'd ever seen him. His eyes were bright and alert, his wit sharper than ever. And he seemed to be surrounded by good people—Delaney genuinely liked Mrs. Sloan, and she supposed Kitty was a very nice person. A chipper Upper East Side type of blonde, who fussed and fawned over Jon. Had been there since almost the beginning of his ordeal.

After Del had closed down her laptop, she'd made excuses to leave. Said goodbye to Kitty and hugged Mrs. Sloan. Jon hadn't spoken once since the other women had come back into the room, so Del just smiled comfortingly at him, not wanting to cause him anymore undo stress. Then she'd collected her stuff and left.

She'd been escorted out of the hotel via a back door, to avoid reporters. Jon's story was big news, and both Delaney and Kitty were a part of his story—she'd been getting phone calls from newspapers asking for interviews. She turned them all down.

Once outside, she'd hailed a taxi and had it take her to her apartment in the heart of the Flower District. It was walking distance, but she didn't feel like going out in the rain or getting chased by reporters.

She smiled and said hello to all of her roommates. Renting anywhere in New York was expensive, but so close to Midtown, it was virtually impossible to even live. She'd answered a Craigslist ad for a "spacious, sunny, affordable apartment! Completely furnished, have your own room! Utilities divided."

Spacious and sunny were being generous, but it was affordable, and technically, she did have her own room. She had her suspicions it was actually a very large broom closet, but she didn't care. She had a bed, she had a small desk, and she'd managed to cram a tall dresser into the space at the end of the room. That's all she needed. She barely saw the other people who lived there—two couples occupied the other two rooms, and occasionally, they rented out their sofa on Airbnb. That was all fine with her. She locked her door when she was gone and she kept her space clean and she paid her rent on time.

She went into her room and put her messenger bag on top of the desk. Then she hung up her jacket to dry—she'd gotten soaked during the short jog from the cab to her building. After that, she took off her boots and carefully placed them at the foot of the bed, so she wouldn't trip over them later. Then she sat down and took a deep breath.

And started to cry.

Why!? Why, god, why, this is almost worse …

She curled into the fetal position and sobbed. She didn't want to be nice or sunny or positive. She *hated* Kitty, with her perfect blonde hair and her money. She even wanted to hate Mrs. Sloan, for being the perfect best friend. And most of all she wanted to *despise* Jay. *Jon.* God, *fuck him.* Forever meant for-goddamn-ever, and he'd gone and forgotten.

How was she supposed to live like this? She was still in love, as much as she'd ever been before the accident. Jayson was alive and real and present every single day, deep inside her heart. He was still the second half to her whole. What she was supposed to do if she was only half a person?

When he'd touched her in the bathroom, it had almost broken her. She'd wanted to jump out the window. Make it all end. *Demand* that he leave the stupid blonde girl. Beg him to just love *her*, Delaney. Just pretend to love her, please, and maybe ... maybe he'd learn to *really* love her again.

This is so much worse.

She gagged and wanted to throw up, but she held herself in check. She rolled onto her back and put her hands over her face, trying to breathe while sobs continued ripping through her chest. Jealousy and anger and self-loathing kept crashing over her. A rip tide of hatred, threatening to pull her under and drown her.

I don't want to feel this way anymore.

Bad thoughts. Dangerous thoughts. Delaney had been telling the truth, she hadn't used drugs since the accident, but that didn't mean she hadn't wanted to. She never showed it, but there were some dark places in her mind. Since she'd lost him, she'd spent a lot of time in those places. Wishing she could use. Wishing she could escape.

Wishing I could just end it all ... what am I without him?

She dropped her hands and stared at the ceiling. No. She wouldn't think those kind of thoughts, she wasn't that kind of person. She still had her parents, who had been very supportive throughout everything. She had friends, some old ones, and a lot of new ones, all of whom cared about her.

And she had Jayson back. He may not have been himself. Maybe Jon would never be as close to her as Jay had, but he was *alive*. That was enough. She would learn to live off that knowledge. That's what love did. It *survived*.

He was out there breathing and living and happy. God, seeing him happy, it made her heart want to burst. So she focused on that feeling. It would be her new purpose. If she couldn't be the love of his life anymore, she would help him *love* life. She would make him smile and laugh, she would encourage him and share with him. She would be nice to Kitty, and if it came down to it, she would organize their wedding some day, and then she would babysit their children.

Because that's what *real* love did—in all things, it strove for the complete and utter happiness of its counterpart.

It wasn't jealousy or anger or malice.

It was happiness.

So she would work on helping Jon find true happiness.

And then, maybe, she could think about what it at all meant for her.

CHAPTER
thirteen

Meeting his parents again was by far one of the strangest moments in Jon's short memory, which he felt was really saying something. He didn't recognize them *at all*. Not one pang of remembrance, not one thrill of recollection.

Sloany had brought them to the hotel and let them into the suite. Jon had looked up from his laptop to find a woman slowly walking towards him. Older, yet still youthful in her face. She was very dark, some kind of Hispanic, with thick, coarse brown hair much like his own, only darker.

Behind her was a ridiculously tall man, taller even than Jon. He was older than the woman, and unlike her, his face showed it. He had blonde hair that was graying, and wore glasses with thin silver rims. He was very trim and tone, with a body type much like Jon's.

"Hello, Jayson," the woman said in a slow voice. He'd plastered a smile onto his face and stood up.

"Hello, Mother."

He wasn't sure what he'd been expecting when he'd been told his parents were flying to meet him. Maybe a similar reaction to the one he'd had with Delaney. That had been like a freight train of emotion hitting him. But there was nothing like that with his parents. He felt like he was sitting in the room with two strangers.

They talked for a long time, with Mrs. Sloan sitting silently with them, watching Jon carefully to make sure he didn't get upset. His parents said a lot of things he didn't like hearing, but they didn't really bother him too much because he didn't remember any of it. It was like they were talking about another person. He apologized for everything Jayson Fairbanks had done to them, but he knew it sounded hollow.

"I know this sounds awful," his mother started, and she rested her hand on top of his. "But in a way, I'm … I'm glad you had the accident."

"Claudia!" his father burst out. Sloany leaned forward, ready to intervene.

"You are?" Jon asked, keeping his voice level, even though he was a little shocked.

"It's like getting our little boy back," she cried. "You've been lost to us for so long! We haven't spoken in four years, Jayson. Everyday, I kept expecting to get a call that you'd overdosed. Everyday, I waited to hear that you were dead. But now you get a chance to start over! To try again! And you're surrounded by such good people, Katherine is such a good girl. I'm so happy for you."

Kitty had been there when they'd come in, and then she'd left. She'd of course been the perfect girlfriend, saying all the right words, smiling that smile of hers that he'd loved so much when he'd first met her. And yet he couldn't help asking himself …

I wonder what they'd think of Delaney.

"She doesn't mean that, Son," his dad spoke quickly. "We're just happy that maybe we can *all* start over again. We can all have a chance to be better."

Jon looked at his father. Realized their eyes were identical. He'd gotten his size and shape and eyes from his father. His coloring and hair and laugh from his mother.

We? We can what? Be a happy family? I don't even know these people.

They showed him pictures of his sisters, two young women aged twenty-two and twenty. They'd even sent a video along, and he laughed as he watched them on his mother's phone. All the Fairbanks kids looked just alike, with their gray-green eyes shining against their tan skin. The girls also seemed to share his sense of humor. There wasn't much crying, a lot of laughing, and they said they hoped to see him soon.

I don't know them, either.

His parents would be in the city for the rest of the week. He made plans to go to dinner with them, and to bring Kitty along. Maybe before they left, he could introduce them to her parents.

More strangers meeting more strangers.

When he shut the door behind them, Sloany let out a big sigh.

"Well, that wasn't awkward at all."

He turned around to find her slumped back in her chair, her arms hanging limply at her sides.

"You should feel it from my end," he suggested, walking over and collapsing into the chair next to her. "I feel more comfortable calling *you* mom than that woman."

"Watch it," she snapped, smacking him in the arm. "I really am just ten years older than you."

"Awfully young to be having kids, Sloany."

"Shut up. Have you heard from Delaney?"

He glanced over at the social worker. She'd sat upright and was messing about on her cell phone, not looking at him.

"Not today, no," he replied.

"Yesterday?"

"Why do you ask?" he questioned, going on guard. She shrugged and finally looked at him.

"I like her. I think she's good for you."

"Don't play matchmaker," he said quickly. "It's already weird enough as it is."

She held up her hands.

"Who said anything about matchmaking? It's just that ..."

He knew she was goading him. She wanted to tell him something she knew he didn't want to hear, but she *also* knew he couldn't resist knowing, so she made him ask for it.

Well not this time, Sloany, HA!

A few seconds passed.

"It's just *what?*" he demanded with a groan.

"It's like your whole presence changes when she's around, Jon," she explained, sitting on the edge of her seat. "I can't explain it. I mean, I thought I knew you, but when the two of you are together, it's like I'm finally seeing the *real* you."

"Then the *real* me is awkward as fuck, because she kinda makes my skin crawl."

What he didn't explain was how Delaney made his skin crawl in such a way that he wanted to climb out of it and into her. Like he belonged inside of her.

"Don't be rude!" Mrs. Sloan snapped. "Do you have any idea what that poor girl has gone through? What she's *going* through? She comes here, rain or shine, whenever you call. At the drop of a hat. She answers all of your questions, all of my questions, and all of Kitty's. The love of her life doesn't even remember her, and she has to watch him parading around with another woman, and she does it all with a smile. *With a smile,* Jon. A genuine goddamn smile. So you better treat her with respect, or so help me god, I will put you back in that hospital."

He was shocked. Sloany rarely spoke so passionately about anything. Even when they'd had their fight, she hadn't gotten so worked up. But she looked seriously mad. Like she wanted to hit him.

"Jesus. You really like her, don't you?" he asked. She glared at him for a second, then turned away.

"Yes, I do," she replied. He took a deep breath and stared at his lap.

"Yeah. Yeah, I think I do, too," he whispered.

"I like her a whole hell of a lot more than Kitty," she started. He didn't voice his agreement, but they could both feel it. "And honestly, Jon. I like her better *for you.*"

"Stop it, right now," he said in a low voice. "We're friends, and I want to stay friends, but this is some personal shit. I don't need anyone else messing with my head right now. You don't know her, Sloany, and neither do I. Neither do *any* of us. We used to do drugs together. She said we were homeless! How can she possibly be good for me? We almost killed each other. I'd probably be doing us both a favor if I told I never wanted to see her again."

"If you say that to her, then you'd better be prepared to say it to me."

He clenched his teeth together and balled his hands into fists. No, he wasn't going to say that to Delaney. He *needed* her, and not just because she held all his memories. Not just because she was the only link to his past. He needed her because … because …

Because for better or for worse, she's the biggest part of you.

Almost two weeks after he'd bumped into his past, he and Kitty tried to have sex again. He initiated. He had to do something. Ghosts had taken up residence in his brain, and they were getting worse. Torturing him. He needed her to burn them out of him with her heat and passion.

He could tell she was feeling the tension, too. She was a lot more timid around him than she'd ever been. Very compliant. He was pretty sure if he'd asked her to clean the bathroom floor with her tongue, she would have done it. She'd never been like that before, it was strange.

Because she's afraid of losing you.

They went to dinner and a movie. Buzz about him had died down and the reporters were leaving him alone. There was one persistent journalist from the Times who called all the time, the same one who'd talked to him in the hospital, right after his accident. The man encouraged Jon to write a book, but that was it. So Jon and Kitty were free to roam around again.

When they got back to the hotel, he held her hand during the elevator ride up. He kissed her in the hallway, pushing her against the wall by their door. She moaned and pressed her breasts again him, and he realized for the first time she hadn't worn a bra all evening. Shocking behavior for Kitty.

They stumbled into the room, kicking off their shoes. He pushed her onto the bed, then started undressing them. She was moaning and writhing around under him, but it almost seemed … orchestrated. He'd barely touched her, and she was acting like she was about to come. Normally a boost to any man's ego, but not for him. Not that night. Not anymore.

"I'm sorry," he sighed, laying flat on top of her. They were both down to just their underwear.

"Sorry for what?" she panted. He slid off her, then sat up on the edge of the mattress.

"I can't do this," he breathed, putting his head in his hands.

"What?" she asked, and he listened as she sat up. "What do you mean? I thought things were going good."

"No, yeah, they are," he stammered, glancing over his shoulder at her. She was kneeling behind him, the moonlight splashing on her toasty tan and pink nipples.

I'm insane. How am I turning this down!?

"If they are, then why are you stopping? Don't you want me?"

she asked, her voice full of tears as she crawled to his side.

"Of course," he said, looking over at her. "It's just ... it's been a rough couple weeks, okay? I'm tired and I'm stressed out and I'm just really sorry."

"It's her, isn't it?" Kitty stated in a dead voice.

"No," he replied.

"It is," she shook her head. "You've been different ever since she found you. Do you still love her!?"

"Kitty, I don't even *know* her. Not any better than you do," he lied. "How can I love someone I don't know?"

"I can be like her," Kitty breathed, moving off the bed and standing in front of him. "I know you like ... other stuff. Dirty stuff. I can be dirty."

"Kitty, stop," he urged, holding up his hand, wanting to stop this embarrassment train from leaving the station.

"Why don't you *make me* stop, you ... you bad boy," she snapped, then she lightly slapped him on the side of his face. She could've pulled out a gun and he would've been less shocked.

"What did you just say?"

"You heard me."

"Kitty, please, let's just—"

She slapped him again, then grabbed his hand and placed it against one of her breasts.

"Kitty," she purred her name, "has been a very naughty girl. She needs to be punished." She started dragging his hand down her body, awkwardly pushing it down the front of her panties.

"This can't be real life," he whispered.

"That's right, stroke the Kitty. She's been a bad, bad ... *pussy.*"

He couldn't help it, he burst out laughing. He knew it was wrong and he would probably scar her for life and it would send him to hell, but he couldn't help it. It was so ridiculous, and so not her. So not them.

"Stop laughing at me!" she yelled, stamping her feet. He had tears in his eyes as he stared up at her.

"Stroke the Kitty!?" he gasped for air.

He knew he should stop laughing, but he couldn't, so he was extremely grateful when she started laughing, too. He took his hand out of her panties and she bent at the waist, laughing so loud, she couldn't breathe.

When their laughter calmed down to just chuckling, he groped around for some clothing and wound up handing her his shirt. Kitty was pretty tall, almost five foot ten, but it was still big on her. She pulled it into place, then sat down next to him.

"I'm sorry," she sighed, grabbing his hand. "I tried."

"I know. Thank you. Can I be honest?"

"Sure."

"Please don't ever try that again."

They both laughed again for a minute.

"I just," she sighed when they fell silent. "I don't want to lose you, Jon. You've been like my purpose these past couple months. I don't know what I'd do with myself without you."

He frowned in the darkness, but squeezed her hand. He didn't want to be someone's purpose. That made him sound like a job. Was that how Kitty viewed him? He knew she was trying to express her feelings, though, so he let it go.

"You're not losing me," he assured her.

"It feels like I am," she whispered.

Jon got off the bed and knelt in front of her. He wouldn't lie to her—he may have been some drugged out loser in his last life, but in this one, he was a straight up guy. He held her hands in his and looked her straight in the eye.

"I'm not going anywhere," he promised. "I'm gonna tell you the truth—I don't know what the future holds for us. I can't predict that, and you're right, things *have* changed. She *is* someone special to me. I don't really know how or why, but she is, I can't deny it. But Kitty, *you're special, too.* No one can ever take your place. You gave me a family when I didn't even have an identity. You accepted me from the first moment you met me, that's a big deal. I won't ever forget that, no matter what happens to the two of us. No matter how many memories I get back, nothing can take that away from us."

She looked down at him, her eyes so big and wide and full of love that he wasn't shocked by what she said next.

"I love you, Jon Doherty," she breathed. He smiled sadly at her and squeezed her hands.

"That's because you've got the biggest heart of anyone I've ever known," he whispered back. "You can't help but love everyone around you, and I'm so thankful for that. Thank you for loving me, Kitty. Thank you for taking care of me."

They crawled into bed together and he wrapped his arms around her and held her tightly to his chest. She smiled and told him funny stories about her first impressions of him. He apologized for not being able to make love, and she said it was okay, that she hadn't really wanted to, either. Another time, maybe.

Maybe ...

Long after she fell asleep and rolled onto her back, Jon stared down at her. He was sitting up with his back against the headboard, and he reached down to brush some hair away from her face. She really was a beautiful girl. He wondered if she'd ever tried to model, with her long legs and stunning good looks. Wondered why someone hadn't snatched her up yet—they'd discovered she was actually a year and a half older than Jon. She was too special, she didn't deserve to be alone.

"I'm sorry, Kitty," he whispered to her.

How could she expect him to love her, when he didn't even know what love was?

Liar. *You saw love once. In a steamy bathroom mirror with a stranger you used to know.*

CHAPTER
fourteen

Katherine Beaumont wasn't typically a nervous person. She'd gone to great finishing schools and generally knew how to handle herself in any situation.

Not that day, though. She sat in a bar a couple blocks down from Jon's hotel, and her feet were tapping out a nervous rhythm against her bar stool. She had even started chewing on her thumbnail, ruining a ninety dollar manicure. Then the cause for her nerves entered the room and she took a deep breath. Put on her best smile and stood up.

"Hi! I'm so glad you could make it," she said as Delaney Carter hurried up to her.

"Oh god, I'm sorry I'm late," the other girl breathed, holding still while Kitty leaned down to air kiss her cheeks. "The other waitress at work was late, they held me over."

"No problem, no problem. Please, sit. I ordered some appetizers."

Kitty watched while Delaney shrugged out of her jacket. She felt awkward being around someone so short. In her heels, Kitty was over six foot, and normally it made her feel like a supermodel to be so tall. But Delaney was maybe five-foot-three, at most, and her plain black waitressing shoes didn't boost her height at all. She was petite and cute with a cherubic face, and all at once Kitty felt like a hunchbacked ogre, clomping around some beautiful fairy.

I hate you, I hate you, I hate you.

"Oh, thanks! What is that?" Delaney asked, gesturing to Kitty's drink.

"Oh, blood orange martini, to die for. You should totally get one."

"Sounds delicious, but I don't drink anymore. I'll just have some tea."

A waiter appeared and took Delaney's order, then he left them in an awkward silence. The tiny girl glanced around the room, then quickly flicked her gaze over Kitty.

"I like your necklace," she complimented her. Good manners dictated that Kitty return the compliment, but the first piece of jewelry her eyes landed on was a large mood ring on Delaney's left hand. Jon owned a mood ring, he'd been wearing it before his accident. Cold, bitter jealousy raged in Kitty's chest and she pressed her hand to the simple gold locket hanging from her neck.

"Thank you, Jon got it for me. For Valentine's Day," she said, then instantly regretted it. She wasn't a nasty person, she didn't want to hurt Delaney. Much.

"Well, it's really nice. He has good taste," she replied, her serene smile still in place.

It killed Kitty. How could Delaney be so cool all the time!? Kitty had seen the pictures. She'd come to the hotel early one morning and Jon had been in the shower. He'd left his laptop open. Some word document had been open, filled with what looked like notes about his accident and his life with amnesia, but that wasn't what interested Kitty.

She'd gone immediately to the pictures folder, then to the

subfolder labeled "*Jayson. Private*" and she'd opened it.

Oh, it had been rough. Thank god Jon took long showers, because Kitty had broken down while looking at the photos. Sobbed as she saw her boyfriend more in love with some girl, *some stranger*, than he had ever been with her.

How can she look at me? I hate her for loving him, and I get to sleep with him at night. Does she secretly want to murder me?

"I know things have been awkward," Kitty sighed, toying with a breadstick.

"I think that's an understatement," Delaney said, but she laughed, so Kitty laughed, too.

"Yeah. Yeah, it is. I just … I know how special Jon is to you. *Jayson*, whatever. And really, I'm happy you've found each other," she insisted, babbling a little.

She didn't really know what she was going to say, just knew she had to do something to keep Jon. Everyday, she could feel him slipping further and further away from her. She had put too much work into him to lose him now.

"Thanks," Delaney said slowly. "I'm glad, too. And I want you to know, Kitty, I'm genuinely happy for the two of you. I would never, ever try to come between you. The two of us … that ended on those train tracks. I know that. He's *your* boyfriend. I just want him to be happy. That's all. Just … happy."

She was smiling and she certainly sounded genuine, but there was a sadness behind her voice. It really did make Kitty feel bad, because she could imagine how Delaney had felt when she'd lost Jayson. They both loved the same man, the hurt would feel the same, she was sure. But she knew in the end, her hurt would be greater, because Delaney would have lost him and then got him back—*after* Kitty had fixed him. Kitty, however, would just lose him forever. And she couldn't handle that.

"Can I be honest with you?" she asked, dropping the breadstick to the floor. Delaney glanced at it, then looked back at Kitty.

"Of course. Please, always. I appreciate honesty," she replied.

"If you want Jon to be happy, then you should ..." Kitty took a deep breath. "You should leave him alone"

The comment seemed to startle Delaney. She blinked rapidly a couple times, jerking back in her seat.

"Leave him alone?"

"Yes," Kitty nodded. "It's hard for him, seeing you. He feels so guilty because ... because he just doesn't remember you. It kills him to think he hurt you, and now he can't even remember you."

"Really?" Delaney breathed, her face going even paler than usual. Kitty knew she was on the right track.

"Yes. It's ripping him apart. He stresses about it, tries to remember. It gives him headaches, nightmares," she explained, and that was the complete truth. "After you leave, every time, he's just so upset he can barely function. *It's killing him.*"

Delaney's eyes welled up with tears, surprising Kitty a little.

"I never wanted to hurt him," she sniffled. "I just wanted ... I wanted to help him. Make him happy. And yeah, be near him. But never hurt him."

"Well, you are, Delaney. You're hurting him every time you go see him."

"I don't want that," the other girl cried, wiping at her cheeks as the tears fell down.

"He was happy before, you know. I have pictures, too. Folders full of them. We spent Christmas and New Year's together, he's practically a part of my family now. I mean, *we're in love,*" she said.

Of course, Jon had never once said that to her. It drove her nuts. She'd said it the other night. She'd been desperate, willing to do anything to keep him. He hadn't said it back. He'd given her a very beautiful speech which had made her happy in the moment, but when she'd thought back on it, it had sounded a little like he'd been breaking up with her.

*And that **cannot** happen.*

"I just want him to be happy," Delaney whispered.

"Then let him *be* happy," Kitty whispered back. "Let him live his life in the *present*. Stop trying to make him live in the *past*."

Delaney took a deep breath, then looked around, as if realizing where she was for the first time. She practically fell off her stool and her hands were shaking as she put her jacket back on.

"I'm so sorry," she breathed. "I had no idea. I'm just ... I'm so sorry. Tell Jay—*Jon* that I'm so incredibly sorry. I never ever meant to cause him any pain."

"Of course you didn't," Kitty said, standing up as well and helping the other girl with the coat.

"Tell him if he ever needs me, I'll always be there for him. And will you ... I'm sorry, but will you send him my love?" Delaney asked, staring up at her.

Kitty stared right back. Into big eyes so full of love and hurt and heartbreak, she couldn't stand it. Her own eyes started to fill with tears.

Not a chance in hell.

"Of course," she whispered.

She was shocked when Delaney hugged her.

"Take care of him. Make sure he's happy, okay?"

"Of course."

And then she was leaving. Once a happy fairy, her shine now a little duller. Kitty felt a pang of regret. A wave of guilt. But an even bigger wall of resistance went up.

I love him. I know I do. And I know he'll love me, too.

CHAPTER
fifteen

Jon felt like he was going crazy.

It had been two weeks since the failed dirty-talking-sex. They hadn't tried again, though Kitty seemed more than willing and eager. While out at dinner one night, with her parents no less, she'd slid his hand up under her skirt, revealing the fact that she wasn't wearing any underwear. Once upon a time, that would've been sexy. Right now, though … he'd just squeezed her thigh and winked at her, then put his hand back on top of the table.

He almost never left the hotel room. He'd decided to take the journalist up on his idea to write a book, and the guy made himself available to Jon for any questions he had, and Jon had a lot. What kind of program to use, what he should he write, how he should start, did he need an agent, everything.

Once he got started, though, he found it hard to stop. He would type late into the night. New York was the city that never slept, but sometimes he felt like he was the only person in the world who was awake. He would stare down at the street, at the random taxis crawling by, then he'd go back to typing. Only one thing was ruining his concentration. Was keeping him from finishing.

Delaney.

He hadn't spoken to her in over two weeks. It was like she'd disappeared again. She didn't respond to phone calls or texts or messages. He'd gone down to her work more than a couple times, on days when he knew she should be there, but she was always busy in the kitchen, or she'd called in sick.

He was kicking himself for never getting her address.

He didn't understand it. What had happened? They'd been meeting up about every other day, just talking and going through his journals, or the pictures. She would tell him stories Jayson had once told her about himself, filling in the little details of his life. Had it been too much for her? Was seeing him too difficult?

Didn't matter. Even if it was, she owed him an explanation. *He* was the one who'd gotten left behind. *He* was the one who couldn't remember. She was his memory, and how *dare she* take that away.

"Where the fuck is she!?" he raged one day to Sloany. She held up her hands.

"I don't know, Jon. She doesn't answer my messages, either."

"You could go down there, you know!"

"Contrary to what you might think, my life does not revolve around you, Jon. I don't have time to be constantly running back and forth from Harlem to Midtown, searching for your ex-girlfriend!"

Ex? But when did we break up? When were we together?

"Sweetie, maybe you just need to let her go," Kitty urged during another day when he'd been pouting.

"Why should I? She's my only link to my past, Kitty," he'd snapped. She'd started massaging him.

"That's not true. You have your parents, and she gave you the numbers for some of your old friends."

Right. A pair of strangers he happened to share DNA with, and a bunch of people who hadn't been very excited to hear from him. They'd just wanted to know if he could help them score.

"It's not fair," he'd breathed. "I *need* her. I need her to remember for me. Without her it's like … like I'm starting all over again." At that statement, Kitty's hands had gone still.

"You know, this has probably been hard for her, too, Jon. Seeing you again, still being in love with you, then seeing us together. You can't ask her to subject herself to that kind of pain. I mean, if I had to watch you with another woman, I'd want to die."

A very valid point, but still not good enough for Jon. No excuse was good enough, and he didn't know why. Couldn't understand why he felt like she shouldn't be allowed to walk away. After all, he technically didn't remember her, so she didn't owe him anything. He was nothing but pain and heartache for her.

And yet still, even recognizing all that, he just could not accept her disappearing on him.

We promised each other, and she's going back on it … what did we promise?

He finally went full blown crazy. He waited until it was late at night on a Tuesday. It was pouring down rain and it was cold, Times Square would be dead. He'd had dinner with Kitty's family earlier in the night. She'd tried to invite herself in, had been as provocative as she'd known how to be, but he hadn't taken the bait. The mood he was in, if they did have sex, he'd probably scare her for life. He wanted to *hurt* something.

So shortly after he got rid of Kitty, a little after midnight, he took off his suit jacket and put on a long trench coat. He didn't have an umbrella, but he didn't care. He turned up his collar and walked out into the rain.

Times Square was only a few short blocks away. Her restaurant was at one end of it, sandwiched between Broadway and 7ᵗʰ Avenue. It was a popular chain and featured cheap drinks, so normally it was packed with tourists and local workers. Lucky for him, the cold snap and the rain were driving everyone away. So he settled in across the street from the restaurant, and he waited.

It took about an hour. They closed up shop early. All the lights flickered out, one by one, then workers started pouring out a side entrance on 7th. He stood there for a while, but when the crowd thinned out and still no Delaney, he moved so he was facing up Broadway, where the front door was located.

Ten minutes later, she came outside. She was wearing an over sized olive green jacket that he recognized as his, based on the pictures she'd shown him. She had an umbrella tucked under her arm and she was wrapping a scarf around her neck while she came to stand at the curb, almost directly across from Jon's hiding spot.

A man came out after her, laughing at something she'd said. He locked the door in several places, then turned to Delaney. Pressed his hand to the small of her back, urging her down the cross street, and they started walking together.

Jealousy swooped down on Jon with a startling ferocity. Who was this guy, and what the fuck did he think he was doing, touching Jon's property!? He clenched his fists and ground his teeth together.

Then he realized what an absolute asshat he was being. Property!? Sometimes he had trouble remember her last name. Besides, he and Kitty had kissed in front of Delaney, so what business did he have being jealous of her walking home with a coworker?

With his jealousy successfully handled, crazy came back into full effect. He glanced around, then dashed across the street and started following them.

He kept about a block between them for what felt like forever. They walked a straight line, thankfully, but the rain didn't let up once. After about ten minutes, he was surprised to find they were in Hell's Kitchen, heading towards the water. *Hell's Kitchen,* he'd followed them to a completely different neighborhood. Jon fully realized how insane he was being. Tailing these two people, two coworkers, in the middle of the night. *Ridiculous.*

He didn't want to let her go, though. Not now that he had her in his sights. He wanted her to give him a reason for her disappearance, wanted to hear it from her lips. So he started speeding up, lengthening his stride to catch up with them.

That stretch of street was pretty dead. They were surrounded by crowded apartment buildings, but no one seemed to want to be outside. Only an adventurous raccoon was braving the night, stopping to sniff at some trash before scampering into a community garden. He watched the animal for a moment, then Delaney's voice caught his attention.

"*Stop it.*"

Jon stopped walking. He was pretty sure his heart even stopped for a second. She had her umbrella up and its rod balanced on her shoulder. The wide black circle covered her body clear down to her butt, so he hadn't noticed before, not when he'd been so far away. But now he could see how the guy kept trying to put his arm around her waist.

Forget jealous. Cold, hard rage filled his veins and flooded his vision.

"I said *stop!*" she suddenly yelled, turning on the guy and holding her umbrella in front of herself. "I agreed to come with you to your friends' house—*not* fuck you."

"You're such a tease, Del," the guy laughed, reaching for her again. She jabbed the point of the umbrella into his chest.

"Try and touch me one more time, see what happens," she growled, closing the ribs of the accessory and twisting the black material shut around it.

"What the fuck, Del? When I invited you tonight, I thought you knew what was going on!?" the guy snapped.

"Yeah—I knew I'd been invited to a chill movie night with your friends! That's it, bro! Nowhere in that invitation did you mention sex was required!" she shouted at him.

"What year are you living in? Why would I invite you if I

thought you wouldn't sleep with me? Get the fuck outta here. C'mon, we can have a good time together. I promise," he said, his words coated in slime as he slid his hands onto her hips.

Even from a couple doors down, Jon saw the look that crossed over her face. Somehow, he knew what it meant. Knew her coworker should probably start running. Things were about to get ugly. He started walking again.

"*You* get the fuck out of here!" she shouted, swinging the umbrella and hitting him in the arm. "And don't you ever"—she punctuated each pause with a swing—"fucking touch me … *again!*"

"Are you crazy!? Stop, you stupid bitch!" the guy shouted, then he shoved Delaney. So hard, she went reeling back into some wrought iron fencing that surrounded the garden.

Jon's vision went red and he was on the guy in a second. No announcement, no shouting. He led with his right fist, slamming it across her coworker's face and sending him to the ground.

"You don't fucking touch her!" he started screaming, grabbing the guy by the collar. This time he was at the right angle, and it was his left hand that threw the next punch. His dominant hand. All those workouts in the basement of the halfway house came into play, and the guy groaned in pain, spitting out blood as his head flew back.

"*Jayson!*" Delaney gasped from behind him. He felt her grabbing at his shoulders, but he shook her off and got in another left hook.

Her second attempt at stopping him worked. She was on her knees, wiggling her body between him and the other man. She forced him to his feet, then wrapped her arms around his waist. Behind her, her coworker slowly stood up, wiping blood from his chin.

"You're fucking insane. You never said you had a boyfriend, Del! Who the fuck is this guy?" the man yelled at her.

"This is the guy who's gonna rip your fucking head off!" Jon yelled back, pulling at Delaney's arms, trying to break free. Wanting to finish what he'd started.

"Just stop! Let it go," she hissed. He stared down at her for a second.

"Let it go? *He fucking touched you.*"

"Whatever. She's just a fucking bitch-tease, anyway," her coworker swore.

There was no stopping Jon after that—he surged forward, dragging Delaney along with him like she was nothing more than a weight belt. The other man gave a shout, then started running down the street.

"He's gone. *He's gone!* Please, *stop*," Delaney begged, trying to get her feet back under her.

Jon finally stopped moving and she pulled herself upright, stepping away from him at the same time. Her umbrella had fallen to the ground in the struggle and her scarf was loose, most of it hanging down her back.

"Who the fuck was he?" Jon asked, gasping for air.

"He's a bartender at work. What are you doing here?"

"Has he ever tried shit like that before?"

"Jon."

"I'll fucking kill him if he has."

"*Jon!*" she shouted his name. "What the fuck are you doing here?"

He blinked at her outburst, then glanced around. What *was* he doing? Jesus, what had just happened? He looked down at his knuckles and hissed.

"Shit," he grumbled, looking at the scratches and bleeding. How was he going to hide that from Kitty?

"Were you following me?" Delaney demanded. He looked over at her.

"Yeah, I was," he answered honestly. Her jaw dropped.

"How dare you! Why?" she asked.

"Why? *Why?* Because you won't speak to me, *that's* why! What the fuck is going on? You can't just do that!" he yelled at her. Now it was her turn to look startled.

"I …" she seemed to be searching for words. "I've been busy."

"*Bullshit*. What happened? Last time I saw you, everything was fine."

And it had been. He'd asked her to come over to look at the stuff he'd had on him when he'd gone to the hospital. The hemp necklace, she'd explained, had been a gift from a guy named Crash. The earrings were a pair he'd always worn, she'd never seen him without them. And the mood ring? She'd looked down at the matching one she wore, stared at it for a long time. Then she'd calmly told him it was one of those sacred memories she wasn't prepared to share yet. Someday she would, but not that day. Then they'd watched TV, with her reminding him what his favorite shows had been, and she'd left with a promise to have coffee the next day.

*We were **fine**. What happened to us?*

"It was fine," she agreed, nervously tucking some loose strands of hair behind her ears. "And then … it wasn't. I'm sorry."

"You're sorry?" he gaped at her. "*Sorry!?* You were just *gone!* My only link to real life, and you just disappeared! Do you have any idea what that feels like?"

She shocked him by bursting out laughing.

"Is that a fucking joke? Yes, *JON,* I know exactly what that feels like! Only unlike *you,* my person disappeared and I have to see a copy of him every single day! *So imagine what that fucking feels like!*" she was shrieking by the end, shaking with anger.

"A copy?" he shouted. The rain was coming down in sheets now, soaking them, but he barely even noticed. "Do you know what *that* feels like? To not be a real person? To not be whole?"

"Yes, *Jon.* Yes, I know what it feels like to not be *whole.*"

Now he was really angry. He made slashing motions with his arms.

"You have *no idea* what this feels like! What it's been like for me!

I have nothing!" he shouted, pounding on the side of his head. "Not a goddamn thing, except a scar and fog! Months and months of fog, wondering if anyone cared about me!"

She moaned and stepped closer to him.

"I cared about you," she cried. "I swear, I did."

"Not enough to fucking find me! To stay with me! *I was all alone!*" he kept yelling. She grabbed onto his jacket.

"You were never alone," she promised. "Every day you were scared, I was scared, too. Every day you felt alone, I was alone, too."

"Not the same," he growled, pulling away from her. "And then you do show up, and everything is so fucked up, because I can't re-member you, but I can *feel you*, and what were we, even?"

"We were perfect," she whispered, starting to shiver. He barked out a laugh.

"Perfect? We were fucking homeless drug addicts! A couple more months, and one of us would've probably overdosed! And look at us now," he said. She shook her head.

"Please, don't do this," she begged.

"You have a good job, you live in a nice place, you look great. And people actually think I'm a good guy, that I'm productive and smart. We were *horrible* together."

"Don't say that," she cried, bringing her hands to her face.

It was then he noticed it. She wasn't wearing the mood ring any-more. A tidal wave of sadness and loneliness crashed over him.

I wish I could forget all over again.

"We're fucking better off without each other," he informed her, raking his hands through his wet hair. "We were toxic. We just made each other worse. I probably saved both our lives when I fell on those train tracks. *I'm glad I forgot us.*"

The biggest lie I've ever told in my whole life.

Delaney's hands dropped from her face and anger flashed in her eyes. She was soaked from the rain, but he was pretty sure most of the dampness on her face was from tears.

"How *dare you* say that to me," she said, trembling all over. "You know what? You can just forget me all over again, because you aren't half the man Jayson Fairbanks was. You go back to your ivory towers and your blonde princesses. You go back to your fog. Because you know what? I was wrong, you're *not* him. He was never afraid of *any-thing*, and all I see when I look at you is a scared little boy. *I hate you! You killed him, and I hate you!*"

"Oh, get fucked! How can you hate someone you don't even know? And you're right, I'm *not* him, so stop fucking comparing me to him! He's *gone! Get over it!*" he shouted.

She slapped him across the face, hard, then whirled around, losing her scarf in the process. She started walking away, holding up her middle finger in the air as she went.

"*Suck on that!*"

For some reason, for just a split second, he wanted to laugh. It was somehow so her to end a fight like that, and yet … he didn't know what was "so" her.

Then the anger was back and he let out an enraged shout, kicking over a trash can. He hurried away from her in the opposite direction, almost jogging.

Fuck her. You don't even know her. She was just someone you used to do drugs with, disgusting. It was probably nothing. How could it be anything? She sits there and smiles while you hold hands with Kitty. How could anyone who is something sit through that with a smile?

He got to the next intersection and kicked the light post. A couple walking by gave him a strange look and he was tempted to shout at them. What did they know, anyway? What right had they to look so happy when everything in the world was shit? It wasn't fair. *It wasn't fair.* What right did she have to take away his memories? It wasn't his fault he couldn't remember her. He'd tried, he'd *really* tried. How could she hold that against him?

He started running back down the way he'd come. Delaney hadn't gotten very far—he watched as she picked up her umbrella and fought with it. It didn't seem to be opening, so she let out a shriek and threw it at a wall before continuing walking.

"Wait!" he shouted when he was a couple buildings down from her. She increased her pace.

"Fuck off!" she yelled back.

"I said *stop!*"

She whirled around, walking backwards.

"What do you want!?" she screamed. "*Stop haunting me!*"

He ran right into her, almost bowling her over. He grabbed at her jacket, holding her in place before she could run away. She struggled against his grip, pushing and slapping at him.

"Stop it!" he growled, finally wrapping his arms around her and picking her up. She squirmed while he hauled her around.

"Don't touch me!" she shouted, getting an arm free and hitting him in the shoulder. "You don't ever get to touch me again!"

Those words. They cut a slice right through his soul. Not touch Delaney? *Not possible.* So while she struggled and slapped and cried, he did the only thing that made sense.

He kissed her.

"No," she sobbed against his mouth. "Please. *Don't do this to me.* Stop."

"I can't," he breathed back, thrusting his fingers into her hair.

They fell back against a wall, damp bodies pressed together. He felt her hands on his back, inside his jacket. Warm palms against wet fabric. Setting him on fire. They stumbled to the side, into a sliver of an alley. A rain gutter dumped a torrent of water next to them, soaking his pant leg, but he didn't care.

This is what it feels like to be whole again.

He tilted her face straight up and feasted on her mouth. God, it felt like coming home. She moaned around his tongue and her fingernails dug into his back. It sent shock waves of recognition up and down his spine.

I know this woman.

She was gasping and pulling at his shirt, untucking it from his pants. He was shoving at her jacket, forcing it off her shoulders. Then his hands were over breasts that were made to fit his palms. He was kissing lips that had been sculpted to match his own. Everything in his body was telling him exactly how right this moment was, how he was finally, *finally*, out of the fog.

I don't want to let this moment go. Please, just let me remember for a little while longer.

They moved out of the alley and kissed on the side of the street while he flagged down a taxi. They pawed at each other while in the backseat, shedding their jackets as they rode to his hotel. He picked her up and pressed her against the wall in the elevator, and her legs wrapped around him like that's where they belonged.

They crashed into his hotel room, the door banging off the wall behind it. He didn't even lift his mouth from hers, just kicked the door shut behind them and immediately started unbuttoning his soaked dress shirt. She dropped to the floor and helped him along, yanking at the wet material till it fell from his arms.

"I didn't mean it," he breathed. "Any of it. I'm not glad. I wish … I wish I could remember everything. I want to. *I'm so sorry.*"

"It's okay, I know you didn't mean it," she assured him. "And I don't hate you. You didn't kill anyone. *You're right here.*"

"It's not okay," he replied, finally yanking his undershirt free of his head and letting it drop to the ground. "And I know you don't hate me. You'd have to hate him, too, because we're the same."

"You're so different," she whispered in the darkness, her fingertips trailing up his abs.

"You feel exactly the same," he whispered back, running his hand up her smooth back.

"You don't remember."

"No, but I remember *this.*"

He lightly pressed his lips to hers, savoring the moment. She sighed against him, then the moment was over. Her tongue was between his lips, touching all the right spots, and her hands were on his belt.

When his slacks fell to his feet, she hurried away from him, struggling to pull off her own pants. She was fighting to kick the soaked material away from her feet when he came up behind her. She had one hand on the bed, to steady herself, and she was looking down. He gently ran his hand over her tattoo, dragged his fingers down between her shoulder blades to her ass, then back up again. Thought about all the things he wanted to do to her, then how he shouldn't. He *couldn't*. He would be too much. Too intense. Too fast.

This is Delaney. Nothing is too much for her.

He abruptly shoved her forward, keeping his palm flat on her back. She landed on the mattress, bent over the edge of it. She moaned and arched her hips back towards him, then stretched her arms above her head.

"God, I missed this," she sighed. He dragged his fingers down to her underwear and started pulling the material over her hips.

"How do I know you?" he whispered, palming her ass cheek. "How do I know *this?*"

"Because … some things are forever," she whispered back.

He grabbed her hips and rolled her over. Finished yanking her panties off her body, then he laid down on top of her. She was so small and smooth and curvy and *perfect*. Absolute fucking perfection. Like a symphony, and his body was humming along.

"You're so beautiful," he sighed into her cleavage while he walked his fingertips up her outstretched arms.

"Not half as much as you. Turn the lights on," she urged.

"What?" he asked, a little surprised. He lifted his head to see if she was teasing.

"Please," she moaned, rubbing her body against him. "I want to see you. I want us to see each other. It's been so long."

He practically fell off the mattress in his rush to reach the lamp. When he'd gotten it turned on, he whirled back to the bed. Delaney had her back to him and had moved so she was sitting on her knees, her legs spread wide. While he watched, she took her hair out of its ponytail. All those gorgeous tresses went cascading down her back and he crawled up behind her, burying his face in the side of her neck.

"I want to get lost like this," he breathed, wrapping his arms around her.

"Me, too," she sighed, dropping her head back.

Holding her tightly, he stood up on his knees, forcing her to do the same. Then with one hand he unclasped her bra and helped her slide the material away from her arms. After she'd thrown it to the floor, he cupped her bare breasts in his hands and they both moaned.

"I can't …" he struggled to speak, and she went still at his words. "I don't know if this right, Delaney. I can't promise you anything."

"I'm not asking for anything," she replied.

"I don't remember you. I didn't before, and I won't after," he warned her. "But I swear to you, I remember *this*. I remember *us*."

"Then let's remember together. Even if it's just for tonight."

"I don't want to hurt you," he said in a shaky voice, and was surprised to hear her chuckle.

"You died on me once. Nothing can hurt worse than that."

"I don't want to scare you."

"I've seen you at your absolute worse, Jay. Jon. *Whoever*. And I've seen you at your absolute best. And you could never, *never*, scare me."

She knew him better than anyone else. Really, she was technically the *only* person who knew him, so he figured she also knew how to read between the lines. He didn't want to lay her down gently and make sweet love to her, then hold her afterwards while they both cried.

No, he wanted to sink his teeth into her and rip her apart and pull all her memories out of her, one by one. Wanted to find out if anything could feel as good as his muscles kept promising him. *It will*, they always whispered to him. *In time*, they kept telling him. His patience had run out, he was done with waiting.

I've waited my whole life for her.

They fell to the mattress together, rolled around until she was on top of him. He sat upright, holding her close with one arm and shoving his other hand into her thick hair. He balled it into a fist and yanked back. She let out a cry as her head was forced back, then she groaned when he bit down hard on her bottom lip.

"Were we always like this?" he whispered, kissing his way to her breasts.

"Yes," she moaned, then she shrieked when he bit down on a nipple.

"Not possible. Nothing can feel this good for too long."

"*We did.*"

"Was I always rough?" he asked, shifting his arm and slapping her on the ass. She smiled, but still couldn't look at him because he kept pulling her hair.

"As rough as I could make you be," she purred.

"It was you," he suddenly whispered, staring up at her. He let her go so she could look him in the eye.

"What was me?" she asked, panting lightly.

"I had this moment ... maybe a month after I got out of the hospital. I was at my volunteer job and I called ... called someone a bad girl, and it was like ... I *knew* those words. Like I'd said them before, to someone," he told her. She pressed her forehead to his, her damp hair becoming a curtain around them.

"Mmm, you always said I was a *good* girl," she told him, tracing her tongue along his bottom lip. He laughed and squeezed her butt.

"I highly fucking doubt that."

"I wasn't, no. God, I was always so bad for you," she groaned, rocking her hips against his, trapping his erection between them.

"I want you to be bad again," he breathed, scratching his fingernails across her ass.

In response, she wrapped her hand around his cock and started stroking it. He started to moan, but was cut off by her lips. Her tongue slid in and out of his mouth in time to her strokes. She grabbed one of his hands and placed it over her breast, forcing him to squeeze, making him pinch her nipple.

"*Jay*," she breathed into him, and he didn't even correct her about his name.

"What? Anything," he sighed, wrapping his free hand around hers and making her pump faster.

"Please," she gasped, wiggling her hips closer so his hand brushed against her core with every up and down sweep. "Please, I want you fuck me. Right now. So much."

He just about exploded in her hand. Fuck, that was *hot*. Hotter than anything he could've imagined. He growled and let go of her hand, hugging her close for a second. Then he lifted her up, forcing her up on her knees again.

She held onto his dick as he lowered her onto him. Stared him straight in the eyes as he slid inside of her. Her mouth fell open and her brow creased with the effort she was exerting to accommodate him, but she didn't stop. No, not until she was fully sitting on his lap and his dick was where it belonged.

"God, you feel so … fucking … good," he groaned, holding still so he wouldn't come right then and there.

"I lied," she whispered. "You aren't different. You haven't changed a bit."

She pumped her hips slowly against him once, reacquainting them with each other. Then she picked up speed. She put her hands on the bed behind her and leaned back so she could pump faster. Jon grabbed her by the hips and held her up so they could both thrust harder. She moaned and he watched her head drop back. Stared at her breasts as they bounced up and down.

"*Fuck*," he swore when a tremor caused her pussy to clamp down on him. "Fuck, we have to stop. It's too much, I'm gonna lose it."

"No," she moaned, running her hand down her stomach. "We

just got started."

When she started touching herself, he almost lost his fucking mind. She was going to make him come, and it was way too soon for that. He didn't want the night to end any time soon, wanted to be inside her forever. But that wasn't possible, so he leaned forward and wrapped his arms around her, then spun them around. She shrieked as she was rolled onto her back, clawing at her hair and trying to push it out of her face.

"When I say something," he breathed, kissing his way down her breastbone. "Maybe you should fucking listen."

"Maybe you should fucking make me," she panted. He twisted her nipple in response, making her cry out.

Then he continued kissing and licking his way down her stomach. He wondered if she'd stop him. If it was "too intimate" for their first time back together. But then her hand was in his hair, twisting and pulling at the thick strands, then gently pushing him further down her body.

He needed no further encouragement. He roughly gripped her thighs and spread them wide, forcing her legs high up. Then he went down on her like her pussy was his favorite dessert.

Probably because it is.

She actually screamed, then both her hands were in his hair. Pulling and pushing and stroking. She started shaking and babbling, her mouth seeming to run independently from her brain.

"Oh my god … yeah … right there … holy fuck, I'd forgotten what your tongue can do … faster … faster … *faster* … fuck, just like that, just like that … right there … just like that …"

When he started thrusting two fingers inside of her at the same time his tongue was drawing circles, the babbling turned to incoherent shrieks. She pounded one hand on the mattress and alternately yelled both his names. He moved his mouth for a second to bite down on the inside of her thigh, and that did it. She came in a series of shrieks and sobs. She pressed her hands over her face while her whole body seemed to fall apart.

"God, just like that?" he whispered, sitting up but still pumping his fingers in her. "You came for me just like that."

"Always," she panted when her orgasm had tapered off. "Always like that for you."

He felt like his duty had been done, and now it was really and fully his turn. He fell on top of her, kissing her hard and then making her suck on his dewy fingers. She did so happily, all the while stroking his cock again. When he got his knees back underneath him, she didn't even wait for direction. She lined him up and he drove it home, making her scream again with how hard he pounded into her.

"Fuck, how do I know all this!?" he shouted, sitting up and grabbing her by her calves, holding her legs wide apart while he fucked her.

"Because you've always known me," she groaned, her hands on her breasts as she stared up at him.

"I know you love it hard," he panted. "I know you love it rough. I know you'll let me do anything I want."

"*Anything you want.*"

"I know you like it when I call you my dirty slut."

No words that time, she just moaned as her eyes fell shut and he felt her clamp down around him again. He dropped her legs and lowered himself so his face was next to hers, his lips against her ear. He felt her heels on his ass, urging him faster.

"I know you *love it* when I fuck you," he hissed in her ear, and he was rewarded with sharp fingernails dragging down his back. "And that you love it the most when I come inside you."

"Yes," she sobbed. "God, I love you. Please, please come for me. Make me come again. Anything, just don't ever stop. *I love you.*"

He leaned away and grabbed onto the headboard, then he didn't hold back. He was shouting as he pummeled her, his hips forcing her up the mattress and into the pillows. She was shrieking and gripping his waist with her hands, her thighs squeezing his hips tightly.

He was going to burst. Any second. Sweat was pouring over him, dripping off of him. He couldn't hold it back for much longer. He reached down and grabbed one of her hands, pried it off his body. Then he shoved it between them, forcing both their fingers in and around her wetness.

"You have to come for me, babe," he was gasping for air. "Fucking let me see that perfection again. Do this with me. *Oh, fuck, I'm coming.*"

His entire body felt like it was bursting. Like a guitar sting that had been wound too tight, he finally snapped. He came with a roar, his hand going back to the headboard. He dug his fingers in so hard, he was pretty sure he was going to break off a chunk.

He could feel his dick growing and pulsing and throbbing inside of her. Her fingers were working against herself and him, and then she was coming, too. She screamed again and her pussy went into lock down mode, almost goddamn killing him. He felt faint as his orgasm just kept going. He didn't think he'd ever come so much in his entire life.

*Well, really, **she** would know if that was true or not.*

When he was finally done and his body had no more left to give, he groaned and collapsed on top of her. He didn't care that he was a lot bigger and heavier than her. He just needed to die for a second.

She didn't seem to mind, though. Her arms were out at her sides and she was trying to catch her breath. When he turned his head to face her, he almost laughed. Her eyes were closed, her hair was everywhere, and she was covered in a fine sheen of sweat. But she was smiling. Almost grinning, really. He mustered up enough energy to scoot closer and kiss her.

"That was, without a doubt, the best sex I've ever had," he panted. She snorted.

"Considering your memory is only six months long, there's not a lot of basis for comparison," she replied, but she was teasing.

"Alright, Miss Know-It-All. I'm assuming we used to have a lot of sex," he said. She licked her lips and nodded, and he felt her hips moving in a circle underneath him.

"Mmm hmmm, we did. Lots and lots and lots …"

"So what do you think? Was that at least 'okay' in comparison to all the awesome sex we apparently used to have?" he asked. Her grin got even better.

"It was fucking amazing," she sighed in a dreamy voice. "*The best.*"

"Told you so," he whispered, dragging his tongue along the edge of her ear.

"Well," she began, and her hips started moving again. "The best *yet.*"

He groaned and bit down on her earlobe.

"You know what? I like the way you think."

"You always did."

CHAPTER
sixteen

Jon was pacing again. He didn't know if it had been a habit in his former life, but it was certainly a habit now.

Sloany was sitting at the little table in his hotel suite, her hands clasped together in her lap. She wasn't saying anything. She knew he'd speak when he was ready.

Fuck, what am I supposed to say?

"What am I supposed to say?" he blurted out, turning to face her.

"Well, for starters, you could tell me what's got you so on edge," she suggested. He groaned and started pacing again. He couldn't tell her that.

Delaney had stayed all that night and clear through the next afternoon. They talked and they had sex and they watched cartoons and they fucked and they ordered room service and they made love. Everything. Anything. All of it.

They took a shower together and nearly broke off the shower head. He pressed her against a window and she wrapped her legs around his waist, and he now knew what it felt like to orgasm while staring down forty flights. He sat on the sofa and she showed off her impressive deep throating skills. He couldn't remember ever coming down someone's throat before, but he assumed it was just as epic every time.

While laying in bed, they'd whispered to each other. She told him what the mood rings meant, and he'd cried with her, then kissed her tears away. Apologized for not being that man anymore, and the fact that he didn't know if he could ever be him. It wasn't fair, and not only for him, but even more so for her. Delaney was a truly good person, she deserved her happily ever after.

She'd also told him that she'd taken the ring off after she'd had a talk with Kitty. She wouldn't say what exactly the conversation had been about—just that it was private, and it had made her realize she might have been doing more harm than good by holding onto a memory. She only wanted him to be happy, she told him. That was it. Even at her own expense. And if happiness meant being with Kitty, then she would walk away in order for him to have it.

During one of the few times she'd slept, he'd sat up with his hands in his hair. *Fuck*, Kitty. What the fuck was he going to do? He'd just cheated on his girlfriend. His kind, sweet, nurturing girlfriend who had never done anything but try to help him. He thought of the night a couple weeks ago, when she'd offered to be bad for him. Offered to do all the things for him she'd thought Delaney would do. He'd turned her down, then gone out and gotten what she was offering from somebody else.

This is hell. I fell onto those tracks and died and this hell.

He said all that to Delaney when they finally got dressed the next day. He explained how Kitty was a good person, and said she'd done so much for him. Told her how he knew he owed something to Delaney, something to his past, but he also owed something to Kitty, to his present. How everything was confusing, and no amount of sex would ever change that for him. He just didn't know how he felt. *He didn't know anything.*

He was positive any other woman would've gotten upset. Would've asked him to make a choice. Would've accused of him of trying to have his cake and eat it, too.

But not Delaney. She smiled sweetly at him, then gave him a long, slow kiss. It got his heart pounding in that odd familiar-yet-scary way. Like he was doing something he'd done all his life, the most right thing he could possibly ever do, and yet he had no memory of doing it before that moment. It was the same feeling he got when they had sex. When she made a certain sound, or laughed in the right way.

I know this woman.

She told him not to worry about it. That she understood. That they were more like two ships passing in the night. Two lovers finding each other again and getting lost for a moment. She would never ask for more than he could give. She would never be the cause for his pain. She was in love with him, she admitted. She had always been in love with him, and would always be—his accident had proven that would never change.

But it was okay. She'd kissed him once more. He'd asked if it would be alright to see each other again sometime. She'd said it depended on how he felt. Then she'd wished him luck on the book he'd written.

"I always knew you had it in you."

And she was gone. Smiling at him as the elevator doors slid shut and separated them.

Is this forever now?

Of course, what he would never know was how she'd sobbed all the way home and didn't go to work for the rest of the week.

"Jon," Sloany snapped, bringing him back to the present. "You're gonna wear a hole in the carpet. Either start talking or sit down."

"Can you be in love with two people at the same time?" he asked. She surprised him by bursting out laughing.

"You are not in love with Katherine Beaumont," she snorted. He

184

noted she didn't say anything about who the other person was in his mind.

"I could be," he insisted. "She's amazing, and thoughtless, and selfless, and … and … amazing."

"You said that one already."

"Shut up," he snarled, finally dropping into a seat.

"Do you think you're in love with her?" Sloany asked, leaning towards him.

"Maybe? Fuck, *no*. But I think I could be, some day," he offered. She shook her head.

"Just what every girl wants to here. 'I love you, Jon!', 'And I could be in love with you, too, some day,'" she mocked him.

"Well, I'm not in love with Delaney," he stated. Her eyebrows shot up.

"Oh? Did you finally get into contact with her?"

I've been in contact with every single inch of her.

"Yeah, we made contact."

"And if you're not even sure if you could love Kitty, than how can you be so sure you don't love Delaney?" Mrs. Sloan asked.

"How could I be in love with someone I don't know? As much as you'd all like to think I do, I really, really don't. Sometimes I forget her last name. I don't know what kind of music she likes, what her favorite food is, where she went to school. I didn't even remember the tattoo!" he exclaimed.

Don't even remember my own words on her body. Don't remember promising her my heart and soul.

"You're awfully passionate about someone you don't care about," she pointed out. He groaned again and surged to his feet.

"I never said I don't care about her," he replied. "I just … I can't explain it."

"Explain what?"

"How I feel about her."

"Try," Mrs. Sloan suggested.

"It's like … I don't know her, but I can feel her. Good god, Sloany, I can *feel her*. When I wake up, when I go to sleep. On top of me, around me, inside of me," he explained, pressing his hands to his chest. "I don't know her, but she's in my blood and in my bones and in my body. I wake up reaching for her, but can't remember her ever being there. I turn around to look for her, then realize she was never with me. She's my ghost, she *haunts* me. I don't remember her, but *I know her.*"

There was a long silence after that. Jon was breathing hard, staring directly at Sloany. She was staring back at him wide eyes. After a few moments, she finally licked her lips and leaned back in her seat.

"Well," she said in a thick voice. "Sounds to me like you can explain it pretty well."

He glared at her, then continued pacing.

"Good sex is *not* love," he informed her. "I could fuck dozens of girls and they could all probably blow my mind. That wouldn't mean I would love them."

"Who said anything about sex?" she asked.

"That's what it is," he stressed. "My muscles, my skin, they're remembering her. Not my brain, but my *body*. The way she moves and tastes, those sounds she makes, I recognized them all."

Another silence.

"Recogniz*ed*, huh? You're using the wrong tense if you're trying to hide something," she told him. He refused to blush.

"I'm not hiding anything."

"When did it happen?"

He finally stopped walking and stared out a window.

"About a week ago," he said softly.

"Does Kitty know?" she asked, with no judgement in her voice.

"No, I haven't seen her yet. She's upstate, visiting a sick aunt. I'll tell her," he promised.

"Are you going to see Delaney again?" she broached the subject in a delicate voice.

"I haven't seen her since then. I texted her once, and she messaged right back, but …" he let his voice trail off.

"But … you don't know what you want, so you don't want to string her along," Sloany filled in for him. He glanced over his shoulder and nodded.

"Yeah. Am I going to hell?" he asked. She started laughing again.

"Are you joking? Jon, I found out my ex-husband was going to sex clubs behind my back. You're caught between two women, and you've been very clear to both of them about not making any promises. You're not an angel, but you're doing pretty okay," she assured him.

"You were married, Sloany!? I feel like my whole life has been a lie. I can't ever be with you now," he gasped, pressing his hand to his chest as he turned to face her.

"Damn, I'm *sooooo* bummed," she groaned, the sarcasm so thick he could cut it with a knife.

"I didn't plan it, just so you know. I never put the moves on her," he started up again on the subject. "I was always respectful. Polite. You saw me. I went to her restaurant just to … talk to her, figure out what had happened. Why she stopped speaking to me."

"And did she ever say what happened?"

"Something about Kitty talking to her, but she wouldn't say what. Anyway, she said something, I can't even remember what. I was just so angry, you know? Angry that here's this person my body clearly remembers, but I can't, but she can, and god, *I was so fucking angry*. She'd been walking with this guy from her work, he started touching her, and I … I lost my shit. Like a wave of rage and jealousy, I wanted to tear him apart. After I scared him off, she and I started screaming at each other. I've never fought with anybody like that before," he told her.

"Doesn't sound like a good start. How did you end up in bed?" she asked. Good ol' Sloany, not shy about anything.

"It was crazy. She was yelling, I was yelling, and it was like, *snap!*

I kissed her like I was taking a breath. It all felt so … natural. There wasn't one awkward moment. Like, usually with a first time with somebody, I'd assume it would be awkward. Figuring shit out, learning what each other likes, blah blah. Not this chick. I knew every spot to hit, every part to touch, what to say, how to move," he said. She held up her hand.

"I don't need the graphic details, thanks. I'll buy the porno when it comes out."

"Sorry," he laughed. "I'm just trying to say, I didn't do it on purpose. I wasn't like 'let's cheat on Kitty, now!' or anything. It literally just … happened. I just breathed her in."

"I'm shocked to be saying this, but you, Jon, are a romantic," she informed him.

"Me!?"

"Yeah. I think she pulls it out of you."

"Well, I wish she'd stop."

"Really?"

I don't want her to ever stop.

He remained silent and she got the hint.

"Sounds like this is a situation only you can get yourself out of," she sighed. "So let's talk about something else. How's the book going?"

He was still reeling from the phone call he'd had the other day. He'd sent the rough draft to the writer for the Times at the beginning of the week, and the guy had taken it around to a couple of friends in publishing. Everyone said it was good. Of course it needed a good editor, but that would be no problem. Bids were already coming in from publishing houses and the journalist had arranged for Jon to meet with an entertainment lawyer who specialized in literary law.

"It's going to get published," he said. She gasped.

"No! Are you serious!? *No!*" she gushed. He smiled and nodded.

"Yeah. A couple publishing places asked for it. I narrowed it down to two offers that I thought were pretty okay, and I'm gonna go over them with this lawyer," he told her.

The most shocking thing of all happened, then. Mrs. Sloan's eyes filled with tears.

"Jon, I am so incredibly happy for you," she breathed. "It could not have happened to a better person."

"Sloany, I'm a homeless drug addict who just cheated on his girl-friend with a woman he technically doesn't know."

She snapped her hand out and punched him in the stomach.

"And an asshole, don't forget that."

Two days later, Jon all but skipped down the street.

He couldn't believe it. He'd officially been signed to a Big 5 pub-lisher, and he had a very impressive advance coming to him. Best of all, he wouldn't need Sloany to take care of it for him—Delaney had found his wallet amongst her stuff. He was officially Jayson Fairbanks again, resident of New York state.

Though he still went by Jon.

He was at a loss for what to do with himself. He wanted to yell and skip and jump. He was a productive, contributing member of so-ciety! He had to celebrate. But where? How?

Kitty was coming back that day, she'd be getting home in the af-ternoon. They were having dinner together later in evening. Just the thought of the conversation they were going to have dampened his spirits a little.

He walked through Times Square, cheering up a little, smiling at the bustling plaza and all the busy tourists. He buried his hands in his coat pockets and whistled a tune as he strode along. Sloany was busy, he knew, and Gary Tupper and the guys at the Benson House were too far away—he didn't want to schlep out to Harlem so late in the afternoon, knowing he'd have to be back in time to meet Kitty.

He was just happy to be alive, so he walked aimlessly for a while. Or so he thought. When he realized he was a couple blocks over from Penn Station, he knew exactly where his feet had been carrying him to.

Delaney.

She'd given him her address, "just in case" he ever needed her. It was written down on a piece of paper in his hotel room, he hadn't even realized he'd memorized it. He also knew she wasn't supposed to be at work that day. He argued with himself for a moment. He didn't want to give her—or him—any false hope. He didn't want to hurt Kitty anymore than he already had, either.

But I also have to tell someone this news.

Next thing he knew, he was slipping through the security door of Delaney's building as another tenant left. He hurried up the steps and knocked on the door to her apartment.

"*I'm getting it!*" a voice screeched as the door fell open. Then an angry looking girl with long brown hair was staring up at him. "Can I help you!?"

"Uh, does Delaney … Carter live here?" he asked, glancing over her head.

"Who?" she asked, scrunching up her noise.

"*Del!*" barked a voice from inside. "Jesus, let him in!"

The door fell all the way open he and stepped into the apartment. There was a large, comfortable looking sofa facing a ridiculously huge television. A couple sat together on the couch, aggressively making out, completely oblivious to the guest in their home.

The girl who'd opened the door for him walked into the kitchen, slamming around pots and pans. She occasionally glared back into the living room at a young man who was sitting in a reclining chair next to the sofa. He was putting a jigsaw puzzle together and he glanced up at Jon.

"Her door is right there," he commented, pointing across the room.

Jon smiled his thanks and walked over and tapped on the wood.

"Please," her muffled voice came from inside, and he listened as she shuffled around the room. "I told you, I don't want to be bothered. I don't—" Her jaw dropped when she opened the door and saw him standing there. "Jon! What are you doing here?"

"I wanted to tell you something. Are you okay?" he asked, suddenly concerned. Her nose was red, and her lips and eyes were puffy. "Are you sick?"

She blinked up at him for a second, then opened her door wide and gestured for him to come into the room. The space was very neat and tidy, except for a couple balled up tissues around the head of the bed.

"Uh, yeah. I think it was from being in the rain. Stupid cold," she said, hurrying around him and grabbing the tissues, throwing them all in a tiny trash can.

"I'm sorry. I feel like it's my fault," he said. She waved her hand at him, then pulled out her desk chair.

"What? That's stupid. I was walking in the rain for a while before you showed up. Please, sit down. What's up?" she asked, leaving him the chair and sitting cross-legged on her bed.

Jon looked at the chair and desk. The space was very orderly, with a neat stack of papers on one end. Behind it, there was a subway map of New York City taped to the wall. There were dozens of pins in it, and a piece of notebook paper was also taped up. He leaned closer to it and saw the names of hospitals, most with check marks next to them.

"You really did look everywhere," he breathed, his gaze wandering over the dozens of pins.

I wasn't alone. She was always there. Always looking for me. Caring about me. **I was never alone.**

"I did," she sighed, then he heard her pat the desk chair. "C'mon, sit down, take a load off."

Jay turned and glanced between her and the chair, then sat down on the edge of the bed.

"I have some big news, and I … I wanted to share it with someone. I was walking around and realized I'd come here. I hope you don't mind," he said.

"Mind? Of course not. I told you, anytime. What's the news?" she asked.

"That book I wrote? About the accident and my amnesia? It's getting published," he said.

She let out a scream, scaring him, then she lunged forward and hugged him. They almost fell off the bed, but he managed to keep them upright.

"I knew it!" she laughed in his ear. "I knew you could it! I am *so happy* for you, Jon!"

"Maybe wait till you read it," he chuckled after she'd pulled away. "You're in it, you know."

"I don't care what you wrote about me," she waved him away. "You're doing what you always dreamed of doing. *That's* all I care about."

"You are an amazing woman, Delaney," he said with a smile. She grinned back at him.

"Damn straight I am. What did Kitty say?"

He paused for a moment, then nervously yanked at his shirt collar.

"I, uh, haven't told her. Yet. She's been out of town. I'll see her tonight, though," he said, feeling awkward as fuck.

"Well, I'm sure she'll be even twice as happy as I am," Delaney said.

Sometimes, just sometimes, he wished she wasn't so pragmatic.

"Yeah, maybe. Look, I didn't mean to barge in, I don't want to bother you while you're sick. I just wanted to tell you the news, and, uh … see how you were," he stammered. Her grin dimmed into a smile, but it was still just as beautiful.

"Same ol' me," she told him. He frowned.

"I didn't … do I need to apologize for anything?" he asked, suddenly nervous. She blushed high on her cheeks, but didn't look away from him. Didn't lose her smile.

"I hope not. Have you done something *bad?*" she teased, finally getting a smile out of him, as well. He rose to his feet.

"Thank you, Delaney."

"For what?" she asked, standing up as well.

"For being a great friend. An *amazing* friend," he corrected himself. Her smile faltered for a moment, but then she cleared her throat and it was back.

"I do try," she said, then her eyes wandered down to his chest. "Look at you! In a *suit!* I could never, ever have imagined you in a suit."

"You like it?" he asked, holding his overcoat open wide. "I wanted to look professional, I met with a bunch of people today for the book deal."

"I love it," she assured him, reaching out and smoothing her hand down his tie. "You look *incredible.*"

"I feel incredible. Look, things are gonna be crazy this next week, but … can I call you?" he asked.

"You'd better. I gotta get in my time with you now, before you're all big and famous," she laughed. He chuckled as well, then leaned down and hugged her. She wrapped her arms around him and squeezed him back.

It was purely platonic for a moment. Just two friends, hugging each other. When he pulled away, though, something stopped him. He had his cheek pressed to her temple, his hands on her hips, and he froze. She had her palms flat on his back and her nose against his collar bone, and she froze, as well.

That ol' sledgehammer, it got him every time. He felt like he couldn't breathe as snap shots began flipping through his brain.

Delaney in the gold sweater and black panties, from the photos she'd given him. But this was real life. She was biting her lip, then whispering his name. Crawling over and twisting around on him, begging him to touch her. He knew he'd eventually ripped those black panties off her and had used them to tie her wrists to a sink pipe. Then he'd done anything he'd wanted to her.

He caught his breath again and stepped back. She was staring up at him, her eyes full of concern.

"Are you okay?" she asked, smoothing her fingertips across his forehead. It was too intense, too soon. He jerked back, stumbling into her door.

"Yeah, yeah, fine," he murmured, fumbling with the doorknob. "I just … remembered something I forgot. I gotta go. I'll call you, okay?"

"Okay. Take care, Jon," she said in a soft voice. He gave her a tight smile, then all but leapt out the door.

He jogged a couple blocks away before stopping and resting. He leaned back against a wall and stared up at the sky.

What the fuck had that been? A memory. It couldn't be. He never remembered anything, except smoking, which he didn't even do anymore. Why would he now suddenly remember something? And so randomly?

If he was going to remember something like having sex with Delaney, wouldn't he have remembered when he'd been actively fucking her? Why on earth would something as simple as a smile and a hug trigger it?

It was a fantasy. It was those pictures. There were several of them from that evening, her in the gold top, with those red lips. They'd stuck in his mind, for obvious reasons, and now his brain had turned them into a flip book. It borrowed actual memories from their night together earlier in the week and spliced in the photos. That was it. No big deal.

Yeah, no big deal at all. This raging hard on means absolutely nothing.

CHAPTER
seventeen

"You ou seem distracted."

Jon snapped to attention and looked at Kitty.

"Hmmm? Oh, sorry. It's just … it was a big day to day," he gave her an excuse, and she smiled at him.

"It was. I'm so proud of you. I wonder if they'll send you on a book tour? I'll have to buy a new wardrobe," she sighed dreamily, and she snuggled closer to him.

She'd come over earlier and he'd told her about his book deal. After much squealing and excitement and talking over him, she'd ordered up some champagne to celebrate. They were now sitting on the sofa in his room. Correction, his hotel suite. He would be leaving it soon, he was sure. The advance had been plenty big enough to get him his own apartment, he just had to decide where. Back in Harlem? Stay in Midtown? Check out the Flower District?

Maybe Brooklyn …

"Why would you need a new wardrobe?" he asked, staring out

the window and playing with a strand of her hair.

"If I'm gonna be traveling with you everywhere and going on television, I have to look good, silly," she laughed at him. He frowned and looked down at her again.

There had been no mention of a book tour, and she was already planning on going on camera with him? Something about that really rubbed him the wrong way. This was his moment. His accomplishment. She had helped, and he was thankful, but why was she making it about her?

Why does she always do that?

"Kitty," he sighed, realizing the moment he'd been dreading all night had finally come about. He slowly pulled away from her so they could face each other. "I think we should talk."

"Oh god," she whispered, the color draining out of her face. "That's the worst thing a person could say. What? Oh god, this is it, isn't it?"

"If you'd let me speak, I could tell you," he said, reaching out and holding her hands. "This book—I don't want it to change me. I'll always just be Jon, the guy with a crazy story. If the book flops, if the book's a hit. Just Jon. There hasn't been any talk about a book tour, and even if there was, I'm not sure I'd want to go. I don't know if I'm ready to leave New York."

"Ready to leave? Jon, we've talked about leaving New York lots of times. We talked about going to the Bahamas for my birthday in August," she pointed out. "So what's really going on? What's changed? Why don't you want to leave?"

He couldn't even answer that question for himself.

"I don't know, I'm just not sure I do," he said. She frowned and let go of his hands.

"It's because of *her*, isn't it?" she demanded. He sighed and rubbed his fingers over his eyelids.

"No, but maybe we should talk about her," he said.

"What? Was she here? Did you see her while I was gone? You

did, didn't you," she accused him.

You have no idea.

"Yes, I saw her. She was here," he was honest. Kitty let out a muffled shriek and jumped to her feet.

"I knew it!" she cried. "I just knew it! I knew she couldn't stay away. You should've seen her face when I talked to her. She's never stopped loving you, she wants you all to herself."

"Wait, wait, wait," he said, holding up his hand. "She mentioned you'd talked to her."

"Oh, yeah, I did. Fat good it did me! She just waited till I was gone to get her hooks into you. What did she do? Just show up here in a raincoat and panties or something!?" she asked, her eyes brimming with tears.

"What? No, I brought her back here. I couldn't figure out why she'd stopped talking to me, so I went and found her. Kitty, what did you say to her?" he asked, slowly climbing to his feet.

"I love you, Jon," she cried. "And it's not fair! I was the one who nursed you back to health!"

"What are you talking about? I was perfectly healthy when we met, Kitty. What the fuck did you say to Delaney?" he demanded. She sniffled and wiped at her eyes.

"I told her what she needed to hear," she said simply.

"And what, exactly, was that?"

"That we're in love," she proclaimed. "And that she was coming between us. It's the truth, isn't it?"

He gaped at her.

"You said that to her!?" he yelled.

"Yes. I told her how all the stress of being around her was killing you. It was, Jon. I could see it because I care about you!" she yelled back.

"You sound fucking crazy right now! How could you do that to me? What if she'd gone away for good?" he shouted.

"Then we could continue on being happy together forever!"

she shrieked.

"*I could never be happy with you!*"

His words shattered something. As it broke and fell around them, they stood in silence. Staring at each other.

Me and my mouth. I have to learn to control it.

"Do you mean that?" she whispered. He groaned and dropped his head.

"No. Yes. I don't know? Kitty," he sighed her name. "I … care about you. So fucking much. You're one of the best things to ever happen in my life. But things are confusing right now. I don't know what's going on, or what I want."

"Did you sleep with her?" she asked, her voice high pitched. He took a deep breath.

"Yes."

"Are you leaving me for her?"

"*No,*" he stressed. "I've only seen her once since it happened. Just today, and only to talk about the book for two minutes. That's it, I swear."

"It doesn't have to end us, Jon. We can work through it," she insisted, and his heart sank.

"I just don't have it in me right now. Not for *anyone,*" he told her. "I told her the same thing, and she understands."

"Oh, I'm sure she *understands.* Understands how to steal someone's boyfriend."

"She didn't steal anything, it was all me, okay? I went and found her. I wouldn't leave her alone. I kissed her. I brought her back here. *Me.* She told me to tell you she's sorry, but I didn't think you'd believe her," he laid it all out. Kitty started crying in earnest.

"I love you," she sobbed.

"If that were true," he spoke softly. "Then how could you have done that? How could you scare her away? Like it or not, she's my only memory, and you tried to destroy that. You know what getting my memories back means to me. How could you try to ruin that?

That's not love."

"You don't know what love is!" she screamed.

"No, probably not. I wanted to learn about it with you. I'm sorry I ruined it," he apologized. She gasped and hurried over to him.

"No, I'm sorry. You didn't ruin anything, not yet. We can work on us," she assured him.

"I think I need to work on myself, first. I should've done that from the start."

"Please, don't leave me! What will my family say?"

"Probably that they wouldn't want their daughter in a relationship with a guy who doesn't love her and cheats on her," he guessed glibly.

She slapped him, and even he couldn't deny he kind of deserved it.

"Screw you, Jon. My family is gonna be pissed. My mother will be so embarrassed, and my father! After all the time he put into you, this is how you treat him?" she snapped.

"Treat him?"

"He's a very powerful man. You don't want to be on his bad side, so just think about that."

"I'm sorry, is that a threat, Kitty?" he asked, looking at her with new eyes. She sniffled and leaned over the sofa, grabbing her purse.

"No, it's a fact. Look, we're both angry right now and being stupid. I'll go home and we'll cool off, then we can discuss this," she informed him.

"I think it's been discussed," he replied. She flicked her hair over shoulder and stomped to the door.

"This isn't over, Jon!" she called out as she stepped into the hallway. "I can fight for you just as much as she can!"

Then the door slammed shut and he was alone, his hands on his hips and his mind swirling.

Fight for me? She let me go and wished me well.

CHAPTER
eighteen

Delaney sat out on her fire escape and took a deep breath. The air was crisp, still with just a hint of winter in it.

What was I doing this time, last year? Beginning of May—I was in beauty school. Jayson had kissed me for the first time just a couple weeks ago, and things were getting serious between us.

She frowned and looked down at the street.

Their fight from the other night kept rattling through her brain. Did he really feel that way? That they had been *toxic* for each other? Sure, it would look that way to an outsider. Even she looked at it with different eyes. She was older, she'd had a couple years scared off her life, and she was sober. Yes, she could admit there had been unhealthy aspects to their relationship.

But they'd both been sober when they'd met. They'd spent plenty of time together sober, too. It wasn't like they'd been stoned *all* the time. Just towards the end, when things had gotten really rough. It wasn't okay, but that it invalidate their entire relationship.

She knew without a shadow of a doubt she had loved Jayson Fairbanks, just like she knew she was completely in love with Jon Doherty. Drugs or no drugs, memory or not, she loved him. Inside and out.

"I'm glad I forgot us."

When he'd said those words, her heart had truly broken. For the first time ever. She'd never given up hope, not once. Not when he'd fallen, not when she hadn't been able to find him, and not when she'd found him again in a different person.

But those words.

He'd apologized for them, later in the night. Told her he hadn't meant them, said he'd just been trying to hurt her. Explained how he wished he could remember them, and that he *wanted* to remember. He knew not remembering caused her a lot of pain, and that killed him.

He wants to remember for me … but not for him.

"I'm glad I forgot us."

Sometimes, just sometimes, Delaney wished she could forget, too.

"What's doing?"

Eric, her jigsaw puzzle enthusiast roommate, crawled through the window and sat on the escape next to her. She smiled at him and wrapped her arms around herself.

"Nothing, just sitting. Thinking," she replied.

"So the other day, was that the guy?" he asked, taking out the supplies to roll his own cigarette. She nodded.

"Yup, that was the guy."

Everyone knew about her ex-boyfriend, the amnesiac.

"Seemed nice enough, but too tall," he teased. Eric was only five-foot-five.

"He is tall," she agreed.

"You guys gonna get back together?"

"No."

"Why not?"

"He has a girlfriend."

"For reals?"

"Well, he used to. I think he broke up with her," Del said. "Or he was going to, at least."

"Obviously he's doing that for you, so what's stopping you from getting him back?" he asked, sprinkling tobacco onto a piece of paper.

"He doesn't want me back," she sighed.

"Didn't look that way to me."

"Excuse me?"

"Just the way he looked at you when he was here. I think deep down, he's still in love with you," Eric told her. She smiled.

"It's a nice thought, but no. He doesn't know what he wants, and you know what? That's okay. Maybe he never will, and that's okay, too. Because he's not dead. I get to walk around in a world with him in it and breathe the same air he does, and that's good enough for me."

"Horseshit."

She snapped her head to the side to stare at him.

"What did you just say to me!?" she exclaimed.

"I said, you're full of horseshit," he replied, slowly rolling the cigarette up. "No one *actually* feels that way. You want him, and he's too fucked up right now to realize he wants you, too. Pound it into his brain, man."

"That's not how it works. Look, he made his choice, and I respect it. He wants to figure himself out, find out what he wants in life. If it's me, I'll be over the moon, but if it's not, well … I have to protect my heart, too," she pointed out.

"How? By shutting him out?"

"Shutting him out? Eric, I had sex with for almost thirteen straight hours. I put myself as out there as I know how," she laughed.

"Thirteen hours, huh? I'm sleeping with the wrong roommate," he sighed, making her laugh harder.

"I admit it—I don't like it. I hate it. I want to scream, and yeah, I want to pound his head against a wall. But that won't change anything, except make him more confused and make him want to pull even further away. It's cliché, but it's the truth—I'd rather have him as a friend than nothing at all," she said. He snorted.

"I wish my friends fucked me for thirteen hours straight."

He lit up the freshly rolled cig and took a deep puff. She closed her eyes and inhaled the scent. Delaney had never smoked, but Jayson had. Not a lot, just occasionally or socially. She'd always tried to break him of the habit, but it had been impossible. Now the smell, as awful as it was, made her feel good. It reminded her of a time in her life when she'd been blissfully happy.

We had nothing. Nothing at all, barely two pennies to rub together, but we were happy. **That's** *true love.*

"Well," Eric sighed, flicking ashes to the street below. "I still say horseshit. Nobility is for pussies. Tell him exactly how you feel and how you'll die if he doesn't take you back."

"Even I have more pride than that," she snorted. "Besides … it wouldn't be fair. He's had it hard enough. I'm not going to be another problem for him to deal with. I couldn't stand it."

"Horseshit."

As stimulating as the conversation was, Delaney excused herself and headed back inside. Smiled at Eric's girlfriend, who was perpetually angry at him. Ignored the other couple who seemed to be permanently attached at the mouth.

She sat in her room and looked at her small little existence. So controlled, so empty. Once upon a time, her room would've been filled with stuff. Clothing everywhere, and the desk completely covered in makeup. Now, she didn't even have a mirror in her room, let alone any desire to paint her face.

No, the desk was piled with stacks of papers, and a map was on the wall behind it. On it were pins with little red heads—one stuck into every hospital she'd gone to looking for Jay. She stood up and put her hands on the desk, looking at the map.

Lenox Hill Hospital. She hadn't gotten that far north yet. She'd wasted so much time in Brooklyn. Though at least back then, she hadn't had a job to get in the way. She'd trained in everyday from Connecticut, early in the morning, and stayed till the last train was heading back. When she'd decided to take her search into the city, she'd made the decision to just move there, which meant getting a job. Eight hours a day she couldn't spend looking for him.

She lowered her gaze to the papers on the desk. They were fliers, all with Jay's picture front and center, and his description below it, along with her contact information. She would show them to customers at the restaurant, then walk around Times Square after work, handing them to anyone who would take them.

She snorted and slammed her hand into the stack, sending the pieces of paper flying across her room. A lot of good they had done her—she'd been looking for a person who hadn't existed anymore. Even if someone had seen him, and then saw her flier with his picture, it wouldn't have helped. He looked like two totally different people. Answered to a totally different name. Of course she hadn't been able to find him! Asking all those fucking doctors *"have you seen a man named Jayson Fairbanks?"* when *of course* they hadn't—Jayson Fairbanks had never been to *any* hospital in New York, and she hadn't known to ask for John Doe.

For Jon Doherty.

She sank to her knees and pressed her forehead against the desk. Panic attacks were a thing in her life now. Xanax would help, her doctor had told her, but she refused to take anything. So she just had to live through it as best as she could.

Day after day after day.

*I love him. I love him so much. It's like he's dying all over again. Like **I'm** dying. God, please help me. Help me get through this. Make him remember me, or make him go away, because I don't know how much more of this I can take.*

CHAPTER
nineteen

Jon was told, very politely, that his stay at the hotel had come to an end.

Kitty must have told her dad about the conversations she'd been having with Jon. The Beaumonts were stopping payment for his hotel room.

It didn't matter much. He could afford to pay it himself now, and in fact planned on paying Mr. Beaumont back. But Jon didn't want to stay there anymore. It was a room filled with memories of people he didn't really know. Kitty, Delaney. *Himself.*

Once again, he longed for the halfway house. It had been shitty and there hadn't been any real privacy, but every memory there was one he'd carved out for himself. *By* himself. Just Jon. It wasn't possible to go back, though. There were other people who really needed the help Benson House and Gary Tupper provided. Jon didn't get to have the room just because he was feeling depressed.

Sloany once again solved the problem by inviting him to stay at her place. She said since his case was all but closed, there wasn't really a conflict of interest. It wouldn't be considered unprofessional. He'd grown on her a lot during their months together. She liked being around him, so she didn't mind sharing her personal space.

Plus, he wouldn't be staying very long.

"This is *exactly* how I pictured your home," he said the moment he walked in the front door.

"So you've been picturing where I live, huh? Jeez, you must be hard up."

She bumped his shoulder as she moved past him, giving him a general tour of the house. It was a small Craftsman style home, just shy of being in the Upper East Side proper. Apparently, her husband had been very wealthy. She'd done very well in the divorce, scoring an impressive alimony and her quaint little home.

There was a living room to his left, den to the right, kitchen at the back. Up a set of perfectly creaky stairs, she showed him to a guest room. It had all been done in gauzy whites, and the duvet cover had little rosettes stitched onto it. He raised his eyebrows at her.

"Shut up, Mr. Sloan had a niece who came over all the time. Besides, pink suits your coloring. And your crybaby attitude."

He slammed the door in her face and listened as she cackled her way downstairs.

He didn't care about the colors in the bedroom. It was warm, and it belonged to a good friend. A friend he remembered and trusted and knew, through and through. That was all that mattered.

He stared at his suitcase for a while. Sloany had gotten it for him. It was black, on the smaller side, and had wheels that rolled in any direction. Between it and a messenger bag, he was able to carry all his worldly possessions around with him. Which was handy, because he wouldn't be in New York for much longer.

There was *a lot* of interest in his book, even though it wasn't even published yet. After Delaney had found him, his story had made national news. Everyone wanted to meet Jon/Jay. His lawyer, now acting as his manager, had offers for Jon to appear on eight different talk shows, and more were coming in every day.

All of them, so far, were in L.A. His publisher wanted to fly him out there and get him settled in, then arrange a proper press conference. Afterwards, he would do the rounds on talk shows, promoting the book and talking about what had happened.

They'd all wanted Kitty to come on the show, but he'd said no. And of course, Delaney was necessary, they'd said—a woman bumping into her long lost love and discovering he had amnesia? It was the stuff daytime Emmy's were made of! Her story was almost wanted more than his own. The thought had made him ill, so he was glad when she said a hard no to the offer. She had crippling stage fright, she said, and absolutely no interest in being famous.

He'd wanted Sloany to go, but she didn't want to leave her job. During a late night heart to to heart, she'd told him if he really wanted her to go, she would ask for a leave of absence and she would go. But he couldn't do that to her. He felt like he'd derailed enough peoples lives. So he just said he'd call her after he got there, and she made him promise that he really would.

She also made him promise to talk to Delaney again before he left, and made him promise not to fall for Kitty's antics.

Jon glanced down at his cell phone when it started vibrating in his hand. *Kitty.* He wasn't ignoring her—he wouldn't do that to her after everything she'd done for him. But he wasn't going to get back together with her. Not a chance in hell. That part of his life was just as over as everything before the accident. They'd spoken on the phone several times, at length. Sometimes it was good. Most of the time it was bad and ended with them shouting at each other.

Please, let this be a good time.

"Hello?" he answered.

"How are you?" she asked in a soft voice. She sounded like she'd been crying.

"I'm okay. How're you?" he asked, laying back flat on the mattress.

"Not so good. I'm sorry, Jon."

"For what?"

"Dad told me he pulled the plug on your hotel room."

"It's okay," he assured her. "I'm a grown man, I shouldn't be living off your dad. I've already arranged to have him paid back for all the money he spent on me."

"You don't have to do that," she insisted.

"I do. I really do, Kitty," he sighed.

"And ..." her voice faltered. He was worried for moment she'd start crying again. Then she took a deep breath. "I'm sorry for how things ended between us."

"It's oka-"

"*Stop* saying that!" she snapped, then took more deep breaths. "Sorry. It's just ... it's *not* okay. I was horrible. I really, really was, and I'm so ashamed of myself. I just cared about you *so much*. I felt like ... I don't know ..."

"I cared about you, too. I still do. I always will," he promised, and it was the absolute truth.

"I really did think I was in love with you," she said, and he was glad to hear it.

"But you weren't," he finished. She let out a deep sigh.

"I don't know. It sure felt like love. I just ... I wanted to be by your side and watch you grow and blossom and turn into this amazing person that I just know you're going to be," she explained.

"Kitty, that's great, and you did help me grow and all that jazz. But you should want to be with someone because you *want to be with them*, not because of what you think you can do for them, or what you think you can turn them into. You're so amazing, yet you just throw yourself into everyone and everything around you. Maybe relax. Let someone take care of *you* for a while," he suggested. There was a long silence.

"And you couldn't be that person?" she whispered.

"No. I can barely take care of myself."

"I'm going to miss you, Jon. So much."

"I don't know why, because you're never getting rid of me," he teased, and his heart swelled when she finally laughed.

"Can we have dinner? Before you go?" she asked.

"I don't know if that's such a good idea," he said, instantly on guard.

"Just as friends. You can invite Mrs. Sloan," she offered.

"Kitty …" he breathed out her name.

"You can even invite Delaney," she suggested, her voice soft and sad. He closed his eyes and tried to ignore the hurt in his chest.

"Okay," he said. "I'll come to dinner. Just the two of us."

"Really?"

"Really."

"I'd like that, Jon," she sighed. "I'd really like that."

Jon was nervous about the dinner. Would she throw herself at him? Threaten him again? Make a scene? Any or all of the above? He resisted the urge to chew on his fingernails, then caved and nibbled at his thumb. Thankfully, she walked into the restaurant before he could do any real damage.

"It's good to see you," she gushed, practically running up to him and enveloping him in a big hug. He hesitated for only a second, then hugged her back. Squeezed her. Crushed her to him. They'd seen each other almost every day for over four months, and then had gone the last two weeks without seeing each other at all.

I missed her.

"You, too. You look great," he complimented her when he pulled back, and he meant it. She was wearing her hair down and the same clothing she'd probably worn to her volunteer job. She hadn't dressed up for him, which made him feel good. Like she wasn't trying to pull anything.

"Thanks. You, too. Your hair is getting long," she laughed, running her fingers quickly through his thick locks. He didn't want to grow it out, but he'd been letting the top get a little wild and unruly.

They both sat down and ordered drinks. Made brainless chit chat about her work, Mrs. Sloan, everything but the elephant in the room.

"So ..." she cleared her throat. "How's Delaney? Are you two ..."

"No," he answered quickly. "I haven't seen her since you and I broke up."

"Oh, wow," she seemed genuinely surprised. "Not once?"

"No."

"But you talk, of course," she said, and he slowly nodded.

"Yeah, we text each other about once a day," he said.

"That's good. But why ... I'm sorry if this is personal," she cut herself off. He shook his head.

"No, it's okay, I don't mind telling you. You already know everything else about me," he managed to laugh. "I just decided ... everything is complicated right now. I was with you, and what she and I did wasn't right. And apparently, that was kind of normal for the relationship we used to have, doing things that aren't right. We're both in such good places right now. I also don't want to get into something when I don't know I can offer her my best, and she really deserves the best in life."

Kitty let out a deep breath and stared at him with so much love, he almost felt guilty.

"You really are a good person, Jon," she whispered. Then she cleared her throat again. "And you shouldn't ... shouldn't sell yourself so short. You have a lot to offer, and you clearly care about her. I think you maybe even still love her."

"I do care about her," he agreed, becoming uncomfortable with the conversation. "But how could I possibly love someone I barely know?"

She thought for a second, toying with her napkin. Then she started smiling.

"Well, it's just like you said, isn't it?"

"What?"

"It's all in the muscle memory."

Their food was served and they turned back to more mundane topics. She was thinking of going back to school and moving away from her parents. He told her it was a good idea. He told her about moving to L.A., and though it clearly made her sad to hear he was going so far away, she was genuinely happy for him.

"And it won't be forever. New York is home," he told her, leaning back so a waiter could clear the table.

"Yeah, but you'll be so different when you come back," she sighed. "So much more … *you.*"

"God, I hope so," he laughed. "I have to ask, Kitty—where'd this turn about come from? What changed your mind?"

She waved her hand at him and he smiled as she started blushing.

"I just had a long talk with myself, and Geraldine."

"Who?"

"Geraldine—the lady who worked in the kitchen with us, when you first started volunteering?"

"The grump?" he was shocked. He'd forgotten all about her.

"Yeah. She caught me crying in the office and asked what was wrong, so I pretty much raked you over the coals. Big mistake. She's half in love with you herself," she snickered.

"*Me!?*"

"Yeah. She always liked you. And she said I was being stupid, and how I would fall in love with a baby bird that fell in my lap, and how it wasn't right putting so much pressure on someone in your position. Then she told me I was going to hell for what I'd done to Delaney, and that really kind of scared me. I thought about it for a while and ... well ... I realized how selfish I was being, and how I wasn't one step closer to getting you back. I was just pushing you away. I guess I'd rather have you as a friend, than not in my life at all. I didn't want to lose you," she finished.

Jon stared at her for a long second, then abruptly stood up. As he came around the table, she asked what was wrong, but he ignored her. Just grabbed her by the arms and yanked her up into a hug.

"You know what, Kitty?" he whispered as he held her tightly. "I do love you, and I wish nothing but good things for you, and nothing could ever make you lose me."

She hugged him back, her face pressed against his neck. He could feel her tears.

"I love you, too," she said in a shaky voice. "I'm sorry we couldn't be *in* love, though."

"I'm not. Not at all, because this way, we get to hold onto each other forever."

"That's true. You have such a beautiful way of looking at things."

"Thank you, Kitty. So much."

"You're welcome, Jon."

CHAPTER
twenty

Delaney hadn't been interested in meeting Kitty Beaumont again. Not one little bit. But then she remembered Jon's happiness was her priority in life—not being a massive bitch. So when the other woman called and invited her to lunch, Del gritted her teeth and said yes.

They met at a fancy place near Central Park. She felt uncomfortable in her jeans and sneakers. Of course, Kitty was in slacks and cashmere, fitting right in. She still wore the little gold locket around her neck. Still looked perfect.

I hate her. No, I don't. It's not her fault. But still. **I hate her**.

"How are you?" Delaney asked politely.

"Not so good," Kitty sighed, tucking a strand of perfect blonde hair behind her ear.

Oh god. This is it. She's going to kill me. Jay told her everything that happened, and now she's come to finally kill me.

"I'm sorry to hear that," Del replied, glancing around.

"I wanted to tell you something," the blonde seemed to be struggling with her words. Every second was making Delaney feel like she wanted to throw up, so she finally let out a deep breath.

"We're not together," she blurted out, startling Kitty. "Not at all. I haven't seen him in like two weeks. I never wanted to come between you, I promise. I just wanted you two to be happy together, and I—"

"I'm here to apologize, Delaney," she interrupted her. Del sat back in her seat, stunned.

"What?"

"I did something really bad," Kitty said. "And you didn't deserve it, and Jon *really* didn't deserve it, and I just feel awful."

Delaney was really confused now and her imagination started working overtime.

"What? Did something happen? Is Jon okay?" she asked, leaning forward in her seat.

"He's fine, he's fine. I told you some things that weren't true. Last time we met," Kitty said.

"Oh. Like what?"

"You're just … the way he looks at you. Like he's finding himself in your eyes. I couldn't stand it! You guys hadn't slept together yet, but I knew it was gonna happen. I just wanted to stop it," she babbled.

"What did you lie about, Kitty?" Delaney pressed.

"Almost everything I told you that night," she said. "I mean, yes, he was stressed, and yes, it hurt him to see you hurting, but he never wanted to stop seeing you. He *wants* to remember you. I think he does, in some ways. He doesn't know this, but after you found him, he used to say your name in his sleep. He started dreaming about you all the time."

"You lied …" Delaney breathed. Kitty blushed, but kept talking.

"I was so scared of losing him. You never made him feel like you were trying to make him live in the past. And yeah, my family took him in and he spent a lot of time with them, but … it wasn't like I said. We were never … we were never …" she started to stammer, and her brown eyes shimmered with tears.

"You were never what?" Delaney asked.

"We were never in love," Kitty whispered, looking down at her plate. "I thought he was going to leave me, so said I loved him, but he never said it back. He was never in love with me, ever. And I don't think … I don't think I was ever really in love with him."

Delaney fell back in her chair. Of course she'd known Jon had ended things with Kitty. He'd told her right after it had happened. Delaney had felt *so guilty*. Here she was, making promises to keep him happy, and then she'd gone and broken up his relationship. He'd told her repeatedly that she didn't really have anything to do with it, that even if she'd never found him, he and Kitty wouldn't have lasted. Still, it was hard on her.

She'd kept her distance from him ever since then. If he wanted her, he knew where to find her, and he certainly wasn't coming around. He called a couple times, and texted her quite a bit. Sometimes she thought he sounded lonely, and it hurt her soul to think he might be. But she never invited him over. Never offered to go see him. He seemed to be playing the same game, because he never asked her, either. She'd sort of assumed it was because of the way things had ended with Kitty.

All a lie. I've felt guilty for so long …

"So … you just wanted to get me out of the picture?" Delaney checked. Kitty nodded.

"Mmm hmmm. I thought maybe without you there, he would start to forget you again."

"And did he?"

"No," Kitty smiled sadly. "If anything, it just made things worse. He was obsessed with finding out where you'd gone. I … I told him you'd probably left because seeing us together was too hard on you."

"I'm sorry, Kitty," Delaney blurted out. The blonde head jerked up and confused brown eyes met Delaney's blue ones.

"What? Why? You didn't do anything. *I'm* apologizing," she

pointed out.

"I know, and I accept your apology. But I caused a lot of pain for you, and when you hurt, I know Jon must be hurting, and I hate that. I'm really sorry. Sometimes I wonder ... maybe he would've been better off if I'd never recognized him," Delaney voiced her fears.

"Oh no. Don't ever say that. I was angry for a while, but now I really am glad you found each other. So many great things happened because of it. He wrote his book, he's going to L.A., he's got his family, he—"

"He's going to L.A.?"

Another awkward silence descended on the table.

"He didn't tell you?" Kitty asked slowly.

"No. He messaged me earlier today. I told him how you and I were meeting. He just said he was glad, and how he hoped we could be friends, but nothing about L.A.," Del replied.

"Oh, well, maybe he meant to surprise you, or something. I'm sorry if I ruined it," Kitty babbled. Delaney took a deep breath.

"I'm sure you didn't, he'll tell me when he's ready."

"So ... I'm sorry," Kitty repeated herself. Delaney managed to smile again.

"Me, too."

"Friends?"

"Maybe. Someday."

"Maybe," Kitty nodded. "My family is throwing a going away party for Jon. Of course, you have to be there."

"Oh, I don't know," Delaney started feeling nervous again. "I think it would be kind of strange. Two ex-girlfriends in one room."

"It would be strange if you *weren't* there. You're the most important person in his life."

Kitty said it simply and genuinely, as if she were announcing a fact. Like it was one in the afternoon, the sun was shining, and Delaney Carter was the most important thing in Jon Doherty's life.

"Thank you. I'll think about it," Del whispered. Kitty nodded and opened up her menu.

"Besides, technically there'll only be one ex-girlfriend in that room," she pointed out while she perused the lunch options.

"Excuse me?"

"He broke up with me. He never broke up with you."

CHAPTER
twenty-one

Jon had only been to Delaney's apartment once, and she was glad—New York was full of memories of them. They hadn't spent much time together in the city, but everywhere made her think of Jon. And being in Brooklyn made her want to kill herself. It was *filled* with Jayson.

Her bedroom was her safe space. He'd only been in there for a couple minutes, so it wasn't stained with his presence yet. She could go there to escape and just be Delaney for a while. Not Delaney-and-Jayson. Not Delaney-helping-Jon. Just her.

Do I even know who "her" is anymore?

So when Jon called and asked to come over, she wanted to say no. Wanted to suggest they meet somewhere, anywhere, else. Before she could, though, he said please. Said he had things to say to her. He was already on his way—was that alright?

She'd closed her eyes and images of their one night together played in her mind. His smile and his touch and his soul. She wiped her tears away and told him yes, he could come over.

She was glad he wasn't in a suit again. He'd been dressed up the night he'd followed her, and the last time he'd come he'd been in a suit. It was nice seeing him in jeans and t-shirt. The hair was going to take her a long time to get used to, but he looked good.

Better than good. He looks the best. The best thing that ever happened to me.

"How are you?" he asked as she lead him into her bedroom. She turned around, a little overwhelmed by how big he was in her room. How much space he took up.

"I'm good. Tired—things have been picking up at the restaurant," she sighed, sitting down by her desk. He nodded and lowered himself to sit on her bed.

"I can't imagine being a waiter … wait, was I ever a waiter?" he asked. She smiled at him.

"Yes, but it was before we ever met," she told him. He nodded and rubbed his hands together.

"I'm sorry I haven't been able to see you lately," he said, looking around her room. She was pretty sure he hadn't looked at her once since she'd let him into the apartment. "Things have been crazy busy. So many people are interested in my story, in that book. It's kind of gotten away from me. They, uh, they want to fly me out to L.A. next week. I'll be out there for a while."

"That's really great, Jon," she told him. He still looked uncomfortable, and she felt uncomfortable, so she didn't know what to do. She leaned forward and rubbed his knee. "It's scary and crazy and probably a little too much, but really, it's great."

"When you say it, I almost believe it," he chuckled, and his hand slid over the top of hers. They held still for a second, then both pulled way at the same time. "So. Lunch with Kitty, huh? How'd that go?" Delaney laughed and he finally looked at her.

"Interesting," she admitted. "She told me a lot of stuff I didn't know. She's the reason I disappeared for those couple weeks."

"Yeah, I know. She told me when we broke up."

"But I'm not mad. I kind of understand, you know? I can imagine how she must have felt," she said softly. He nodded.

"I'm not surprised. I bet you were always understanding."

"I wouldn't say that. You haven't seen my temper yet."

"I don't know, I seem to remember someone slapping me and telling me to suck it, then giving me the finger."

"Which time?" she laughed again, but he just looked confused.

"Huh?"

"Never mind," she sighed. "I don't know if Kitty and I will ever be best friends, but at least we understand each other now. She's nice. I can see why you fell for her."

"Thanks, she is nice," he mumbled, looking down at his hands.

"So what've you been up to? You look good," she told him. He smiled.

"Thanks. I moved out of the hotel, I'm staying with Sloany now. Er, I mean, Mrs. Sloan," he answered.

"Oh good, I really like her."

"She likes you, too."

"She also has excellent taste."

They both laughed.

"I think it's my turn to apologize," he said when they'd fallen silent. She went very still.

"For what?" she asked, pulling her legs up so she could wrap her arms around her knees.

"For not making time for you," he said. "For not being the guy I used to be. For not remembering. For not knowing what I want. For not knowing what I should do at any given time."

It was a lot for him to all lay out at once, Delaney's head was spinning. She swallowed thickly, then nodded and rested her chin on top of her knees.

"It's okay," she said softly.

"God," he groaned, raking his hands through his hair. Apparently now that he'd started to speak, he was finding it hard to stop. "I just wish things were different. I want all these good things for everyone. Sloany, you, Kitty, and I don't think I can do it for you guys. I can barely figure out my own way around—how can I be with anyone?"

"Really, it's okay, Jon," she insisted. "No one expects anything from you. We just want you to be happy. That's it. That's all."

"But it's *not*. Sloany wants me to be successful. Kitty wants me to be in love. And you … you just … you want …" he stammered.

"I just want you to be happy," she promised.

"That's almost worse!" he snapped. "Why don't you ever get mad? Don't you hate me, or Kitty, just a little?"

"No. Not a little. Not even at all."

"You thought I'd left you, or died, and then I went and found a new life without you. Doesn't that make you angry?" he asked. She shook her head.

"No, I'm glad you're alive, and I knew no matter what, we'd find each other again. That's just the kind of people we are. We find each other," she told him. He shook his head.

"I don't know if I believe that," he was breathing hard. "I'm not … I can't remember our relationship, and I believe everything you said, how we were in love and we were happy. But Delaney—we were *homeless*. We did drugs all the time. And then later, the first time we were alone together, we cheated on my girlfriend. We weren't—*aren't*—healthy. And on top of that, I'm afraid … afraid you won't love this guy as much as you loved the other guy. I don't want to ruin your memories of him."

Delaney was breathing fast, too. She couldn't be listening to this. Didn't know how to tell him he was *already* ruining those memories.

"I understand," she whispered, wiping at her eyes. "And like I said, I'm not asking for anything, and I'm certainly not going to try to convince you of anything. But Jon … *Jayson*, it wasn't all bad. I swear to you. On drugs or off, I've never been that happy in my life. Just being near each other, it was like sunshine every day. For both of us. So please, whatever happens between us from this point on, *please* don't ever say it was bad. Okay? I can handle most things, but that's just too much."

Jon groaned and stood up, then started pacing.

"I'm sorry. I just fuck everything up for us, don't I?" he said, his hands in his hair.

"You don't," she told him, standing up as well.

"Delaney," he said, turning towards her. "God, I have tried *so hard* to remember. And it's like your always there, at the edge of my vision, just out of sight. I can feel you and taste you and smell you, but you're not there. I even dream about you, but I *can't remember.*"

"Why are you telling me this?" she whispered, ignoring the tears running down her face.

"Because I can't ... Delaney, I just can't. *I don't know you.* I don't know if I'm any good for you, or worthy of you. I don't even know what I want, so how can you possibly expect me to give you what you need? I wish I could. Everyday, I hope I'll remember. That I'll wake up and you'll be next to me and it'll be like it was. But it can't. It just can't. That time in our life is over, now. Gone. *Forgotten,*" he finally finished.

She was crying too hard to respond. Of course she'd already told herself all the same things, but it was different hearing it from him. Hearing it from the only mouth she ever wanted to kiss.

When his arms went around her, she wanted to push him away. Wanted to shove him onto another set of train tracks. But instead, she clung to him and cried into his chest. Her heart was breaking for a man who didn't exist anymore. For a love that should have lasted forever.

"I'm sorry," he was whispering into her ear. "I'm so sorry, Delaney."

"I miss you," she sobbed. "I miss you so much."

"I know. I bet he would miss you, too."

She cried even harder.

"Why did this happen to us?" she said between gasps for air. "What did we do to deserve this? *We were happy.*"

"I'm sorry. Please, don't cry anymore. It kills me. Please," he begged through clenched teeth. He gripped her arms and gently pushed her away so he could look her in the face.

"There's nothing now," she was crying so hard she was shaking. "Nothing for me."

"Don't say that," he moaned, leaning down and pressing his forehead to hers. "I'm not him, but I'm still here."

"I can't … I can't … I can't …" she couldn't even breathe, let alone talk.

"Shhh. Don't cry. Please, babe, don't cry," he whispered. *Babe.*

She gasped and looked up at him. He stared down at her for a second with those steely green eyes of his. So familiar, yet so distant. She stared right back, blinking away tears.

Then he was kissing her. Tenderly, almost nervously. She held still, freezing her heart. Refusing to let this stranger in again. He sighed and his arms went back around her, holding her close as he kissed her again.

"Please, please, please," he whispered against her lips.

The first time Delaney had ever met Jayson, she hadn't been able to resist him. Not even when he was a complete jerk to her—her tough guy act had been just that, a total act. Now all this time later, even with all the distance between them, she still couldn't resist him.

She cried and she kissed him back, smoothing her hands over his shoulders. He shuddered and his mouth opened, his tongue lightly sliding across her bottom lip.

"Jon, please …" she breathed. Begged him.

He didn't pay any attention to her words. He seemed to be tuned into her heart only. He forced her backwards till they were up against a wall, then his tongue was back in her mouth. She moaned when she felt his hands on her wrists, then he was pinning her arms to the wall above her head.

"I remember this," he sighed.

"I know you do," she replied, arching away from the wall so she could press against him.

This was a bad, bad idea, she knew. It was only going to cause her more pain. The night they'd shared together had been amazing. Like a dream. Like going back in time. But it had taken her *days* to get over it. To rebuild her walls and her strength. To remind herself that he no longer belonged to her. He was free, and she had to let him go.

He let go of her wrists and ran his hands heavily over her body, pressing down against her breasts and hips. She combed her fingers through his hair, wanting to remember every follicle. They kissed again, pushing against each other. Trying to push *through* each other.

Trying to remember something that doesn't exist anymore.

"I loved you once," he said as he kissed along her jaw. "I know I did."

"You did," she agreed, wrapping her arms around him and holding him close. Never wanting to let him go.

"Maybe I could learn to love you again," he whispered. Her heart swelled and fluttered for a moment, then fell back down. She smiled and buried her face in his neck.

"No," she whispered back. "Those times are over. Gone. *Forgotten.*"

He stopped kissing her. His arms went around her waist and his palms went flat against her back, crushing her to him. Making it hard for her to breathe. She squeezed just as hard, wanting to become one with him forever.

For the last time ever.

"But I did love you," he said in her ear. She sniffled.

"And now you need to love yourself. Go to L.A., go see the world. Find out who Jon Doherty is. Maybe he'll think of me sometimes," she said.

"He thinks of you *all* the time."

"I can't ask you stay," she whispered. "You were right. We don't know each other. Go, and be happy. Do all the things you were meant to do, and if you ever find yourself in New York again, maybe look me up."

"Wherever I go, I promise you, Jayson and Delaney will be with me," he assured her. She smiled and gently pushed him back.

"Good. I'm glad. I hate to think you might be lonely."

They awkwardly fell apart. The moment was over. Dead. Lost, along with Jon's memory. It never could have lasted. Just a bright flash of recognition, gone as quickly as it came. Two strangers faced one another, missing each other already.

She held his hand as she walked him to the door, selfishly reveling in the feeling. When he was in the hallway, she squeezed his fingers and started letting him go.

"You're coming to the party?" he asked, clinging to her fingers.

"I don't know, Jon. Kitty invited me, but I just don't know," she replied, leaning against her door frame.

"I get it. I totally do. But honestly, it would mean a lot to me if you were there," he told her. She smiled at him.

"I think it will just make things harder," she said. He nodded.

"Maybe. But I'd rather something difficult, than nothing at all."

"That's so you," she breathed, and his brows drew together in confusion.

"What?"

"Nothing," she shook her head, then finally jerked free from his grip. "I'll try. I won't promise you, but I'll try."

"That's all I can ask. I leave soon, I don't know when I'd get to see you again," he warned her. She nodded.

"I know. And Jon?" she asked as he started taking a step away.

"Yeah?" he responded, holding still.

She chewed on her bottom lip for a moment, then stood on her tiptoes and kissed him quickly.

"You were the best time of my whole life. Thank you for that," she said. He looked stunned for a second, then he smiled down at her.

"Thanks. I think … I think I felt the same way about you," he replied, and she smiled back.

"I think you did, too."

CHAPTER
twenty-two

Delaney didn't go to the party.

Jon spent most of the night looking for her, his head always turning back to look at the doors. But she never appeared. Halfway through the event, he got a text message.

I'm sorry. It would be too hard for both of us, and I never want to make things hard for you. Just know that I believe in you, and I love you, and I hope wherever you end up, you're happy.

She was right, of course. It had been hard enough in her apartment. His brain had been at war with his body, creating a cacophony of confusion. If she'd shown up at the party, it just would've been worse. She would've cried again, and that would be *the* worst. He didn't like to make women cry in general, but when it was Delaney, it broke his heart. Made him feel sick to his stomach. Made him want to pick her up and carry her back to a time and place where they'd known each other.

I'm so broken, though. Lost in this fog. I can't drag her in here with me. She said it—I need to find myself.

Kitty did a good job distracting him, and not just by helping him mingle. He believed everything she'd said during their dinner, but old habits die hard. She hung on his arm, smoothed her hand down his tie. Fawned over him, fussed.

I feel like I'm on a date with my mother.

"Kitty, stop," he grumbled, shoving her hands away. She'd been trying to fix the knot in his tie.

"I'm sorry! I just want you to look your best. There's photographers," she reminded him.

"I don't care."

"Well, I do—I'm in these pictures, too. Do you want us to look ridiculous?"

I want us to not be in photos together.

"I'm too tired to deal with this," he complained, glancing around the room. "Would it be awful if I went home early?"

"Yes! Jon, my parents spent a fortune on tonight! Please, just stick it out for another hour, then I'll take you home myself," she promised him.

Then she paraded him around for another hour, introducing him to people he didn't care about and he wouldn't remember.

"Kitty," he started asking after another random couple walked away. "Do you ever think about what ifs?"

"Oh lord, all the time. What if I'd missed that sale? What if I'd gone to vet school? What if I hadn't started working at the community center?" she prattled off, ending with a smile.

"What if I hadn't fallen on those tracks? What do you think would've happened?" he was curious. She thought for a second.

"I probably would have left the community center after Christmas," she said. "I'd been thinking about going back to school again even before you showed up."

"So there's another thing I ruined," he muttered.

"Excuse me?"

"Nothing. And what about me? Where do you think I'd be?" he asked. She smiled sadly.

"I don't know, somewhere in Brooklyn with Delaney."

"You think?"

"I know so. Probably doing awful," she added. "But probably really happy."

"We never would have met. Ever. Del said we almost never came to the city, and never ever up to Harlem. I wouldn't exist to you," he pointed out.

"And you wouldn't exist to me. Isn't that sad?"

He nodded out of reflex, but his brain was still working. It would have been sad—despite all her faults, he really did like Kitty. They had good conversations, and sometimes he even kinda liked the way she mothered him.

But being in Brooklyn with Delaney—would that have been so bad? He couldn't remember it, but sometimes when he kissed her, he felt like he almost could. Like the feelings were all still there. Laughing with her and laying with her. Just being.

"Yeah," he finally responded. "It would be sad."

Shortly after, they snuck out. Caught a taxi out front and gave the directions to Sloany's house. Kitty scooted over on the seat, pressing up against his side and laying her head on his shoulder.

"I'm going to miss you, Jon," she sighed. He nodded.

"I'll miss you, too."

"Oh, maybe. For a little while. Then life will move on. There'll be so much to do and see, so many people to meet. Think of me once in a while?"

"I will."

The taxi was rolling to a stop when her hand slid onto his face. Pulled him around so he was facing her. Then she was pressing her soft lips to his, kissing him. Her fingers moved into his hair, curling around the dark strands.

He let it happen, didn't push her away. Let his lips stay soft and loose. But he didn't touch her, and he didn't kiss her back. When she finally pulled away, it was with a sigh.

"A girl's gotta try," she laughed softly, then she swiped her thumb over his bottom lip, wiping away her gloss.

"An excellent attitude," he chuckled, opening the door and climbing to his feet. "Now start applying it to someone else."

As soon as he shut the door, she rolled down the window and leaned out of it.

"I'll be here at nine in the morning," she assured him. His plane left at one, Sloany was driving him to the airport around ten. Nowhere in those plans had it been mentioned that Kitty would be coming along.

"Oh, no, please don't," he said. "Let's just have tonight, okay? I don't want to make it harder than it's already been."

"Please, I can't let you go without saying goodbye," she replied.

"But we can say it—"

"You're not getting away from me that easy, Jon Doherty. Just one more breakfast together. One more car ride. Deal with it, then you'll be rid of me. See you at nine," she called out, then the cab started to roll away.

He cursed, then stomped up to the house. He took a couple deep breaths before going inside. It was after one in the morning, Sloany was asleep. He tiptoed upstairs, then crept around while he got undressed, carefully packing his suit into his luggage.

Only wearing his boxer briefs, he laid down on top of the girly duvet and stared at the ceiling. He was scared, he could admit it. As far as Jon's memory went, he'd never traveled. Never been on a plane. Had he ever even lived alone before? He'd never thought to ask Delaney.

Delaney.

He didn't stop to question what he was doing, just picked up his phone and texted her.

Have I ever lived alone?

It was so late, closer to two now. He didn't necessarily expect her to answer, but he also wasn't surprised when his phone vibrated with a response.

I don't think so. Maybe in college? You moved to Brooklyn with a bunch of friends when you were young, like twenty. You were still living with some of them when we met.

So I went straight from my parents' house to college to room-mates to living with you.

Don't be scared, you'll do great in L.A.

Sometimes, he swore she was psychic.

I suppose it's better than being homeless.

Hey, don't knock it till you've tried it.

Come to the airport tomorrow.

He held his breath, waiting for her response.

No.

Why?

Because—this is something you need to do for yourself.

I'll be doing it all by myself—I just want to say goodbye to you.

We already said goodbye.

Please?

Can I tell you something about Jayson Fairbanks?

Okay.

There was a long pause. The little dots blinked continuously on the messenger app, telling him she was still there. She must have been writing a novel. After a minute or so, it finally came through.

Jay was fucked up. He did way too many drugs and he didn't take anything nearly seriously enough. He forgot appointments, couldn't hold a job to save his life, and made me so mad sometimes, I fantasized about killing him. But he was also fearless. He didn't care one little bit about what anyone else thought of him. He would give you the shirt off his back and ask for nothing in return. He marched to his own drum, and he made the people around him want to march to it, too. He moved to Brooklyn with no money, no job, nothing. He'd never even been there before, didn't know anyone there, yet he didn't hesitate. He just went, because everything is an adventure if you look at it from the right angle. So just go, Jon, and have your own adventure.

He read her text over and over again. Late into the night, long after she must have fallen asleep. He read until the screen on his phone dimmed and eventually died on him. Then he stared back at the ceiling again.

I was fearless once, she said. Maybe I can be fearless again.

CHAPTER
twenty-three

"**N**ice ass."

Jon turned around and glared at Sloany. She was leaning against his doorway, grinning at him. He was standing in his room in a t-shirt and underwear, rooting through his suitcase.

"Shut up. I lost something," he grumbled, going back to searching through everything in the luggage.

"What is it? Gold? Slow down, you're gonna rip something," she warned him.

"My mood ring."

"Your what?"

"*Mood. Ring,*" he growled, picking up the entire suitcase and slamming it back down. "It's one of the only things I had on me when they admitted me into the hospital. I can't fucking find it!"

"Jesus, Jon, calm down. We'll swing by a store and grab you another," she said.

"I want *that* one."

She moved into the room and he felt her hands against his back.

"You packed everything from the hotel, yes?" she asked, and he nodded. "Then it's in there. Just chill out. Come downstairs and have breakfast, relax. When you get to L.A., you can unpack thoroughly and methodically. The way you're doing it, you'll probably fling it out a window or something and not even know it."

Of course she was right, but it didn't make him feel any better. He wanted the ring with him. Wanted to feel it in his palm, just to know it was there. That it existed. A tangible memory he could hold and take with him, wherever he went.

He put on some pants and went downstairs with her. She'd put out a whole spread for him—eggs, bacon, pancakes, sausage, hashbrowns. His stomach felt like a lead weight, but he put a little bit of everything onto a plate and sat down. He could get through one meal.

"*Helloooo!*" Kitty's voice suddenly called out from the entryway. *Maybe I can't.*

"In here," Mrs. Sloan called back before blowing on her hot coffee.

Kitty traipsed in, smiling big at everyone, her arms full of bags.

"I come bearing gifts."

It actually cheered him up a little, sitting around a table with two people he cared very much about, just laughing and talking. Kitty had gotten California themed gifts for everyone. Sloany got a coffee mug shaped like a woman in a bikini. Every time she took a drink out of it, Jon cracked up. There were also sea salt scented candles and funny beach towels. Even a "Men of California" calendar, which Mrs. Sloan promised to hang up in her office at work.

For Jon, there were board shorts and tank tops. A pair of nice flip flops, and a really expensive pair of sunglasses. A pen with a girl in a bikini on it, but when he flipped it upside down, the bikini disappeared. He also got a bikini girl mug, but it wouldn't fit in his luggage. Sloany offered to keep it safe for him.

"My entire life fits in these bags," he sighed, staring at the small suitcase and his messenger bag. Kitty coiled herself around one of his arms and hugged it tightly.

"It's kinda handy. Whenever I travel, I can barely fit a weeks worth of clothing into two bags and two carry ons."

"Yeah, but this is *literally* my life," he pointed out.

"Exactly. Everything you care about is right there. You can always take it all with you wherever you go."

Please, god, let that mood ring be in my bag.

They all piled into the silver Corolla. Who would've thought he'd feel nostalgic about a shitty car? As they drove and Kitty chattered away from the backseat, he rolled down the window and smoothed his hand over the door.

"You'll call as soon as you land, right?" Kitty asked almost an hour later.

"Jesus, let the man breathe!" Sloany laughed, taking the exit for the airport. "He's not your kid going off to summer camp."

"I know that, I just worry."

"Well, worry about something other than a grown man living his life." There was silence for a moment, then Sloany cleared her throat. "Call as soon as you get to the hotel, instead."

They all laughed together.

He was glad when Mrs. Sloan didn't take the exit for airport parking. Instead, she drove right to departures, which meant they wouldn't be able to go inside with him. He was pretty sure if they had parked, Kitty would try to get all the way to the gate with him. Possibly on the plane. As it was, he was treated to an emotional goodbye at the curb.

"I told myself I wouldn't cry," she sniffled. He chuckled and rubbed her back.

"You are a wonderful cliché, Kitty," he sighed.

"I try. Take care of yourself? Eat right, please. And go to the dentist—you missed your last appointment. And remember—"

"Kitty," he started laughing again. "I'm not your charity case to worry about anymore, remember?"

"No," she pulled away from him. "You're my friend, so I'll *always* worry about you."

They kissed quickly, then he turned to Sloany.

"I am not kissing you," she warned him.

He felt like that was a challenge, so he pulled her into a deep dip before kissing her hard. She squirmed the whole time, pushing at his shoulders.

"Was that really as bad as you thought it would be?" he asked when he stood her upright. She glared at him and straightened out her pantsuit.

"*Worse*," she grumbled, but then she hugged him tightly. "I'm gonna miss you, kiddo. She's right—take care of yourself."

"I will," he whispered back, burying his face in her blonde hair. "You've been the best friend a guy could ask for. I think I'm going to miss you the most."

"Somehow, I honestly doubt that."

Neither of them said her name, but they were both thinking about Delaney.

A couple more hugs, a firm goodbye to Kitty when she tried to come inside, and Jon was free. He didn't look back as he wheeled his stuff up to the ticket counter.

He was happy to learn his suitcase was small enough to count as a carry on, so he opted to keep it with him. He didn't want it out of his sight until he found his ring.

He went through security. It was all strange and confusing, but oddly familiar at the same time. He took off his belt and shoes, watched as his belongings went through the x-ray. Then he got dressed again and went off in search of his flight.

"*Flight 267 to Los Angeles ... United Airlines ... has been moved to ... Gate 34.*"

As he listened to the announcement come over the P.A. system, he glanced at his ticket. It was his flight, so he started heading off towards Gate 34.

What a crazy life.

Six months ago, he was in the hospital. Four months ago, he was trying to convince himself he could fall in love with Kitty. Two months ago, he was given a glimpse into his past and he'd started writing a book about it. Now he was on his way to Los Angeles, to start a whole new crazy life.

And a year ago, you were falling in love with Delaney.

He stopped walking, staring straight ahead as people flowed around him. The airport was crowded, but he didn't see anybody. Just started to mildly hyperventilate as his vision went black at the edges and he was transported through time.

"You know you could do better than me. You're gorgeous, you're funny, you're so goddamn caring ..."

"Thanks, but I think I did pretty good with you ..."

"Still not anywhere near good enough for you, babe, and also not strong enough to let that stop me. I fucking love you, Delaney. You are the first thing I think about in the morning and the last thing I think about before I go to bed. I want to be inside you forever. Want to lay with you and love you and make you laugh until we're old and gray. Delaney Carter, will you marry me? I know this ring isn't much, and I can't even promise you that someday I'll do better. But it's for you, and only you."

"It's a mood ring. Blue means love."

"It does?"

"It does. Oh my god, Jay. Yes. To everything. To always. To you and me, forever."

"Forever and ever and ever."

It was mostly audio, no video. He could hear Delaney's voice, feel her in his arms, but he couldn't quite see her face. Still, he knew it was a memory. That's how he'd proposed to her. That's how he'd felt about her.

God, how he felt ... he could feel it coursing though his veins, pumping through his heart. Jesus, how could somebody love some-one so much? He hadn't known it was possible. He felt faint. It was taking him over, overwhelming him. *He'd loved her.* So much. More than was sensible or smart. More than anything else on the planet. *So fucking much.*

He dropped to his knees and knocked over his suitcase. A wom-an let out a startled shout, tripping over the handle, then called him a few choice words. He ignored her and opened the luggage, then started rifling through everything. Fuck what Sloany said, he had to find that ring *now*.

He threw his clothing everywhere, not caring about anything or the scene he was causing. He turned pants pockets inside out and ripped pockets off shirts. Tipped over shoes and went through toiletries.

Finally, he came to an old jacket. One he hadn't worn since his trip home from the hospital. He had his hand in one pocket and was squeezing the other when he felt it. Like a small hard ball in his hand. He struggled to yank it free of the material, then chucked the jacket under a row of seats.

He stood back up and stared at the ring. It was cheap, of the car-nival or fair variety, with an adjustable band. The stone was opaque black, he'd never seen it turn any color.

I know this ring. I know that woman. I know what love is.

His hands were shaking when he slipped the ring on. He willed the memories to come forward. Went over the proposal memory again, then prayed something would follow it. Closed his eyes and begged every god he could think of.

And yet … nothing. Just swirling blackness and fog. Their voices fading in, then their voices fading out. Just like the memory of her in the gold top. Barely a moment in time, surrounded in black on all sides.

Why!? How can you show me something, and not everything? With no explanation? What does this mean?

He opened his eyes and stared at the ceiling. Then glanced around at the people looking at him. Looked down at his belongings strewn everywhere. Then he zeroed in on his hand.

I don't ever want to lose this feeling. I don't ever want to forget her.

The mood ring was practically glowing on his finger, swirling into an intense, deep blue. He couldn't rip his eyes away from it, watching as the color grew bolder. More intense. Almost blinding.

"... blue means love ..."

Jon was back at security before he even realized he'd started running. His luggage and all his clothing were still in a pile on the floor back by Gate 34. It didn't matter. He wouldn't be catching his flight.

He got yelled at by TSA, but kept running. He sprinted past the ticket desks, then hurtled himself down the escalator to the arrivals level. Almost got stuck in a crush of tourists by the doors, then practically knocked down a little old lady in order to steal her taxi.

"Times Square," he was gasping for air.

"Traffic's shit down there right now," the cabbie commented. "Fair warnin'."

"Get me downtown as fast as possible, and I will pay you five hundred dollars."

When he held up the bills to prove it, the driver hit the gas so hard, Jon was flung back into his seat. They practically flew out of the airport and he scrambled to put on his seat belt.

"Also alive," he called out. "As fast as possible, and *alive.*"

"So what's the big rush?" the guy asked, flicking the butt of a cigar out his window. Jon took a deep breath and watched other cars as they zoomed by.

"I have to tell a girl I love her. Again," he replied.

"*Again?* What happened, you break up with her?"

Jon smiled to himself.

"No. No, I never really did."

CHAPTER
twenty-four

Jon all but leapt out of the cab, throwing hundred dollar bills into the front seat before sprinting through the crowds. The cab driver hadn't been lying—Times Square was insanity. Cars everywhere, and good lord, so many people. He busted up more than a few photo ops, not bothering to apologize as he sprinted across the square.

"Delaney," he was panting when he ran up to the podium at the front of her restaurant. "I need to speak to Delaney Carter. She's a waitress here."

"Oh, she's not here," the hostess said, looking a little startled.

"What!?"

"Yeah, uh …" she looked down at a notebook in front of her. "She switched shifts with someone. She should be here in like … gosh, any minute now."

Jon glanced at a large clock. It was almost one. He swore and turned around, slamming through the door.

He stood on the corner for a moment, his hands in his hair,

wondering what he should do. Of course, he could wait for her to show up, that was the logical next step. But he was scared if he stopped moving, if he slowed down, the feeling would go away. Would slide back into the fog, and the way he was feeling would disappear forever.

I can't let that happen. I remember us. I can't let her go.

He took off running up the street, grateful for all those early morning runs with Gary Tupper.

He knew Delaney usually walked to work, but not necessarily always. If she was running late, she might catch a taxi or an Uber or something. And even if she was walking, there was no guarantee he'd see her. The streets were filled with people out enjoying the sunshine, and the road was wide—if she was on the opposite side, he'd miss her entirely.

As his feet pounded the pavement, images and photographs went around in his mind. Him and Kitty at Christmas, feeling so unfulfilled. Delaney in the bathroom at his hotel, his arm around her. Kitty reminding him it was all in his muscle memory. Delaney crying in the rain, wanting to be with him. Kitty crying in the hotel room, having to let him go. Delaney smiling at him outside of Crash's house. Laying with him in his hotel room. Screaming on a rollercoaster. Sitting in her small bedroom. Just loving him.

*Keep running. Look for her. Remember her. **Find her.***

Her apartment was only about a twenty minute walk to Times Square, maybe less. He made it in under ten minutes. He careened around the corner onto her street and sprinted towards the security door, his hand outstretched to press the buzzer for her apartment. Just as he was about to reach it, though, the door was pushed open and he slammed into someone.

"*What the shit!*"

They ricocheted off each other, but Jon's adrenaline was pumping too hard to let him go down. He grabbed the handle of the door for balance, then lurched forward and wrapped his arm around her waist, catching her before she could hit the ground.

"I've got you," he breathed.

Delaney looked up at him, her eyes as wide as he'd ever seen them.

The most beautiful eyes I've ever looked at, and I really do know that for a fact.

"Jon!" she gasped, bracing her hands against his chest. He stood upright, pulling her with him.

"Delaney," he managed to pant out, his chest heaving against hers.

"What are you doing here? Shouldn't you be on a plane ..." she glanced at her watch. "Like right now?"

"No," he said, refusing to let her go when she went to step back. "No, I don't need to be anywhere else."

"What's going on? Are you okay?" she asked, reaching up to brush his messy hair away from his forehead.

I always loved it when she did that.

"Better than I've ever been. I need to talk to you," he said quickly.

"Okay, but it'll have to wait. I was on my way to work," she said, gesturing outside.

"No, this can't wait."

"Jon, I have to go to work. I missed so many days last month."

"I don't care."

"Well, I do. My paycheck was non-existent."

"*I don't care.*"

"Jon," she said, and he felt her palm against his cheek. "I'll come back."

No, you won't. You might be gone forever by then.

Someone else came down the stairs behind them and made a fuss, trying to squeeze out the door around them. Delaney tried to pull free, to move onto the sidewalk, and he panicked. He wouldn't let her go. Not ever again.

So he picked her up and threw her tiny frame over his shoulder. She shrieked as he bolted up the stairs, taking them two at a time.

"What are you doing? Put me down! *Jon!*" she was yelling, struggling against his hold. In response, he wrapped his arm around her hips even tighter.

"Just stay," he was panting as he moved. "Just stay with me a little longer."

Fucking walk up. It took forever. He was sweating and gasping for air by the time he got to her floor, but he still wouldn't let her down. He fumbled around with one hand, digging through her jacket pocket. He finally found a set of keys and pulled them out. One had a bright yellow sticker with *HOME* written in marker on it. He shoved it into the lock and twisted it, then kicked the door open.

An entire room of people jumped and gasped at the unusual entrance. He marched across the place, leaving the door wide open behind him. He ignored the couple fighting in the kitchen, as well as the couple dry humping on the couch, as they all turned towards him. Delaney bleated out excuses, assuring everyone it was okay, and to go back to what they'd been doing.

Once in her room, he dropped her to her feet so abruptly, she teetered over and fell on her bed. She gaped at him as he started rifling through her desk drawers.

"What the fuck do you think you're doing!?" she demanded, scrambling around to get on her feet.

"Where is it," he breathed, shuffling papers and pens around, glancing briefly at a flier with his face on it.

"Jon! Did you have a mental breakdown? Should I call Mrs. Sloan?" she threatened, moving to stand behind him.

He slammed the desk drawer shut and whirled around, but didn't look at her. His gaze bounced all over the small, tidy bedroom. All the surfaces were bare, no trinkets or jewelry anywhere he could see. While she continued ranting at him, he closed his eyes.

Where is it, where is it, where would she put it …

The fog shifted and moved. Never lifted completely. But it was there. In his blood. In his muscles.

He opened his eyes and went straight for her dresser. Dropped down into a squat and yanked open the bottom drawer. A treasure trove of satin and lace and cotton looked back at him.

"A breakdown *and* you've turned into a pervert, great," she grumbled. "Wait! What are you doing? *Stop it!*"

He listened to her scrambling around behind him, picking up all the underwear he was tossing over his shoulder. Bras flew past her, as well, making her yell at him more. He ignored her until he found what he was looking for tucked into the back of the drawer. A white cotton pair of panties with red hearts all over them. He unrolled them and caught an object as it fell away from the fabric. Then he stood up.

"I knew it," he whispered, turning around to face her.

"Are you *insane?* You're freaking me out! Why are you doing this, Jon? It's already hard enough, you know that, and this will just make it worse! Just go and get ..." her voice trailed off when she saw what was in his hand.

"I gave this to you," he said, holding up her mood ring. When he finally looked at her, he almost laughed. She was paler than ever before and she was clutching an armful of underwear to her chest.

"Yes, you did. I told you that," she replied, her voice shaking. He walked up close to her and with his free hand, he pulled her arms apart, making her drop the panties and bras.

"What you didn't tell me was how you cried," he said, grabbing her left hand. "That it was windy out and you got scared on the rides, but you loved it. How all you wanted was that ridiculous cotton candy, and then I made you drop it. You never said how you didn't even hesitate before you said yes, and that you already knew what all the colors meant."

"How do you know that?" she whispered, her hand trembling as he slipped the mood ring back on her finger.

"You told me blue means love," he said simply, smiling down at her.

"*How can you know that?*" she cried, staring up at him as two big tears rolled down her cheeks.

"Because, it's not only about the memory, Delaney. Sometimes it's more about how you *feel*," he told her. She took a deep breath.

"And how do you feel?"

"Like I've never been more in love in my whole life. With this day, with these rings, and with you."

She broke down. Her knees went weak and as she sobbed, she started crumbling to the ground. He wouldn't let go, though. Never, ever, again. He sunk down with her, standing on his knees and clasping her hand tightly in his.

"You can't mean this," she sobbed. "You don't remember me. I can't live through this."

"I mean it," he assured her, working his free hand into the back of her hair. "And I remember enough."

"You're killing me," she gasped for air.

"Then I'll die with you," he whispered, pulling her close.

She was still crying when he kissed her. Still sobbing when he took her face in both his hands and gently urged her up onto her knees. Her whole body was shaking as he held her tightly.

"How did this happen?" she breathed. "Is this real?"

"It's like you said," he replied. "Forever means forever. I may never remember everything, but god, I will *never* forget you, Delaney. Ever."

"Never, ever," she repeated, her lips trembling beneath his own.

"My brain couldn't remember," he said. "And my heart wasn't sure. But my soul ... how could I ever forget it belongs to you?"

She was kissing him back, finally. Just like before. Just like always. She was crying and she was happy and she was in love, and he knew all that because he remembered her. He could read her face better than his own. Amnesia and injuries and other people and distances between them and all the fog in the world couldn't keep them apart. Couldn't make them forget each other.

Because when true love finds its counterpart, it always recognizes it.

It's all in the muscle memory ...

EPILOGUE

"Picture!" Delaney called out. "Picture, picture, picture!"

Jon groaned as he heard her scampering across the floor. He was carrying a heavy box full of books in his arms and managed to put it down just before she launched herself at him.

"What is it with you and pictures? Were you a photographer?" he asked, stumbling around, trying to keep them upright.

"No, never. I did makeup," she reminded him, then she wrapped her leg around his and tripped him, sending them both down onto a futon mattress on the floor.

It should have been strange, not remembering basic details about the love of his life. But it never was. He asked questions, and she always answered. Sometimes, it came back to him. Most of the time, it didn't. And it never, ever, mattered.

She was holding a bulky, funky looking camera in her hands. He almost thought it was a toy, but he went along with it. Laid down flat on his back on the mattress. She scooted up close to him, tilting her neck to the side so her head was at an angle, almost against his shoulder.

"Say cheese," she ordered. He grinned broadly and she took the picture. There was a flash, a whirring noise, and then a tiny picture began to print from the side of the camera.

She took pictures of him constantly. Of them together. She never said why, but he knew it was because deep down, she was afraid. Scared he might forget all over again, so she wanted all the proof possible to remind him of who he was, and how in love they were.

I could never, ever forget.

His publishing house hadn't been happy about him missing his flight, and even more upset when he'd canceled all his appearances in L.A. There had been lots of ugly phone calls, and finally he'd gotten Mrs. Sloan and a doctor to write letters on his behalf, saying the strain of traveling was just too much for a man with his medical condition.

Besides, Good Morning America wanted him on their show just as much as anyone else, and they were right in Midtown.

He stayed in New York, stayed with Mrs. Sloan while his book deal was back up in the air. He went on GMA, got a lot of buzz going for his book, and did a couple talks at local Universities and colleges. Then Hollywood started knocking, and suddenly his publisher couldn't give a shit how many talk shows he canceled. A movie was going to be made on his life, they were almost as good as promised. His lawyer renegotiated his contract, and Jon's future looked considerably brighter.

Then the book dropped, and his future was damn near blinding. He made it onto every bestseller list there was, and even topped a couple. He was asked to do documentaries about amnesia. His doctors asked if they could write about him in peer journals, if he'd let their medical students ask him questions. He said yes to everything, so long as he didn't have to leave New York.

As long as he didn't have to leave Delaney.

It was funny, but after they got back together, *she* was the nervous one. She acted like she was dealing with a wild animal. Scared he was going to bolt some day. Just disappear. He still didn't have most of his memories back—when her birthday came and went without a word from him, there had been an ugly confrontation with a lot of crying.

It would take a long time to gain her trust back. She kept insisting she *did* trust him, but he was talking about a different kind of trust. Not in her brain—her brain trusted him just fine. This kind of trust was in her heart and in her bones, and it just wasn't there for him. Not yet. But it would be. He would earn it back through hard work and proof and love.

It was winter when the movie deal was offered, and he'd decided enough was enough. He needed to make an honest woman of her. Besides, having sex at Sloany's house creeped him out, and Delaney's bed was way too small for him and his lanky limbs. So he spent a few days with a realtor showing him around Midtown and Harlem and the Flower District, but nothing interested him.

Then one day he walked out the door and got on a train and somehow wound up in Brooklyn. He knew where they'd lived before, because she'd told him, but he didn't want to go back there. He wasn't Jayson Fairbanks anymore, he could never go back.

So he took another train to somewhere else, anywhere, and wound up in a neighborhood he was pretty sure he'd never been in before. After a couple hours of walking around, he saw a realty sign with the words "For Rent" on it—he called the number, did a walk through, then went home and met Delaney for dinner.

"*By the way, I got us a place in Brooklyn Heights,*" he'd said casually over appetizers. She'd beamed at him and only had one simple question.

"*Can we move in this weekend?*"

So in the chaos that is winter in New York, amidst an early December snowfall, they hauled all their belongings back to Brooklyn. Back to the beginning.

"Ooohhh, look, you look great in this one," she sighed, holding the developed photo out in front of them. He took it from her and peered at it. His grin looked crazy, and his green eyes were opened super wide. His hair was bushy and wild on top, yet still neat and trim on the sides. Mostly Jon Doherty, but with just a hint of Jayson Fairbanks.

"You don't look too shabby yourself," he called out to her as she got to her feet and skipped across the wooden floors. He kept looking at her image in the picture.

Her hair was in a messy bun on the top of her head, smooshed against the side of his face. Her big blue eyes were crossed, and she was making fish lips. She looked young and ridiculous, and so beautiful it hurt his heart.

He sat up and stared at her on the other side of the room. She was wearing a cropped sweater and black boy short underwear. It was freezing in the apartment, he was beginning to suspect their heat wasn't working properly, yet she still ran around half dressed. He smiled and stood up, slowly walking across the room to her.

Probably ninety percent of his memories were still missing. He didn't remember hardly any more about her now than he had when he'd missed his flight. Sometimes, it made him just a little nervous. Was she in love with someone who didn't exist anymore? Could he ever hope she loved him, Jon, as much as she'd loved Jayson?

Because it was no question for him—he loved her just as much as Jayson ever had, maybe even more. He'd loved her in two lives, and would keep loving her in however many more were to come. Nothing would ever change that, no accident, or drugs, or all the fog in the world.

"You have to get dressed," he breathed, wrapping his arms around her waist from behind. He was barely leaning over, so she was forced to stand on her toes.

"Why?" she asked, going through a pile of books.

"Dinner, remember?"

"*Uggg*," she groaned, dropping the books and leaning back against him. "How come you're the one with amnesia, yet I can't ever remember anything?"

"*Brat,*" he teased, pinching her side. "C'mon, we have a long train ride."

"Where are we going to dinner?"

"Harlem. I told you all this."

"Harlem? *Ug.* Fine."

She went to twist away from him, but he yanked her back and kissed her. Tasted some of his memories for a second, then let her go. She smiled up at him, brushed his hair off his forehead, then went into the only bedroom in the apartment and started rummaging through suitcases full of clothing.

Delaney was nervous whenever they used the subway. He'd teased her about it once and had gotten such an earful he'd never teased her about it again. He always stood well away from the edge of the platform while they were waiting, and hurried through the door-way when they were getting on, just to make her feel better.

But once on the train, she seemed to be fine. He stood and gripped onto a handhold, and she wrapped her arms around his waist, using him for balance. The car was packed, but he didn't care, and they spent the whole trip in their own little world, making plans for their apartment and their future. Once at the restaurant, they sat down and behaved themselves while they waited for their guests.

Sloany showed up first, rushing around the other tables to get to them.

"You look so good!" she squealed, holding out her arms. Jon stepped forward to hug her, but she ran right past him and practical-ly swallowed Delaney.

"Thank you!" Del laughed. "You, too! Your haircut is *amazing.*"

Sloany preened and patted her sleek new bob.

"Thank you, thank you. Seems like forever since I've seen you guys, sorry I've been so busy. I want to come to your new apartment soon. Immediately. Yesterday. I can't believe you're back in Brooklyn!" she exclaimed, finally letting Delaney go. Jon frowned.

"Hello! Your client? Guy with amnesia? Slept in your house? Nothing?" he asked, still holding his arms out. She rolled her eyes and shook one of his outstretched hands.

"Good to see you, Jon. Now, Delaney, I was wonder-"

Jon grabbed her and pulled her into a bear hug. She laughed, but hugged him back with a ferocity which took him by surprise.

"I always knew you'd do good, kiddo," she whispered.

"Thanks, *Mom*," he whispered back, and she didn't even get mad.

They all sat down and waited and talked. And waited. And then waited some more. Jon frowned again and looked at his watch.

"I hate it when she does this," he growled. Delaney laid her hand on his arm.

"Hey, cut her some slack," she suggested.

"I know, I know she's busy. But when we set a time, it shouldn't be so hard for her to make it on time. If she's *so busy*, she should just say she can't come," he replied. Del smirked at him.

"You're a hard man to resist."

He rolled his eyes, ready to give a smart ass comeback, but then the object of their conversation finally walked in the room.

Kitty Beaumont looked good, but then again, she always looked good. He knew for a fact she looked good first thing in the morning, and she looked just as good after a hard day of work. Yet he still continued frowning as she headed towards them.

"Who's that?" Del asked under her breath. Sloany shrugged.

"I have no idea."

But Jon knew. He'd been waiting for it to happen.

Kitty bustled up to them, towing a man behind her. She hugged everyone and gave them air kisses, then introduced her date. He seemed nice enough, but Jon forgot his name almost as soon as he learned it. After making room for another plate, they all took their seats.

"So where did you and Kitty meet?" Sloany asked in a polite, but all business, tone of voice.

"It was fate, I guess," the guy chuckled. "It's kinda embarrassing, though."

"No, no, it's okay," Kitty assured him, smoothing her hand down the front of his jacket. He took a deep breath.

"I got out of jail about a month ago. Boosting cars. I feel really bad about it, really. I got out on good behavior and was put into this halfway house, and they assign us jobs. I had to go clean these cat kennels at this vet's office, and Kitty was a vet tech there. It was like seeing an angel," he said.

Jon watched Kitty very carefully, noted the blush staining her cheeks and racing across the bridge of her nose. He couldn't be too upset for her, though. He could remember his first thoughts when he'd met Kitty. They'd been very similar. Jon Doherty may have been hard to resist, but in certain ways, Kitty Beaumont was much harder. He had no doubt she would build the car thief up. Clean him up and fix him up and then the guy would be ready for life.

And then Kitty would be all alone again.

This poor, poor girl.

He didn't let it bring him down, though. This rag tag group of people, who under normal circumstances would never have known each other, were his family. For better or for worse. He smiled as he watched Sloany laughing at something Mr. Car Thief said. Felt a warmth in his chest when he saw Delaney's dark head leaning close to Kitty's fair one as they shared some secret.

How could anyone ever forget this feeling?

As dinner wound down, they all made plans to meet for Christmas. Kitty would of course be spending the evening with her family. Jon and Delaney were going to Connecticut to spend the whole week with her parents. Sloany was going to Puerto Vallarta. But she would be back Christmas Day, so everyone agreed to go to her place.

After dinner was over, Del didn't say anything. Just put on her jacket and immediately walked over to Kitty's date. She started asking him everything about himself, just chattering away, leading him towards the door ahead of everyone else, and away from Kitty. Jon smiled after them.

She knows what I'm thinking before I do. She really is the other half of me.

"Kitty," he said, walking outside next to her while Mrs. Sloan took a phone call.

"Great dinner, Jon. It's always good seeing you guys. I'm sad we don't get to do this more often," she sighed, hooking her arm through his.

He could tell she meant it. Learning that Jon had never gone to L.A., and that he and Delaney were, in fact, going to be together had been rough on her. She'd taken the news well for her, with only a couple crying fits. Then she'd thrown herself into work and school, and almost a month went by before they spoke again.

It had upset him. They may have had a shitty ending, but Kitty was his friend. He wasn't going to force his friendship on her, though. He took a page out of Delaney's book and decided if he really loved Kitty in any kind of way, he would let her have her own space.

It worked. After that first month, Kitty had called and invited them both to lunch. Del had tried to get out it and Jon had to practically carry her to the restaurant. But it had been good. Being in school and having actual expectations put on herself had done wonders for Kitty. She'd seemed like a better, more confident version of her self. He'd had high hopes that maybe she could find her forever, too.

However, he doubted her forever would start with a car thief.

"So what's with the guy?" he asked point blank. Her blush came back, but she stared straight ahead.

"It's not what you think," she insisted. "I ignored him for the first two days, and I've barely helped him do anything. I'm *actually* attracted to him."

"Are you saying you were never attracted *to me?*" Jon feigned hurt, slapping his hand to his chest. Her blush got even worse and she smacked him on the stomach.

"I think we both know exactly how attracted to you I was," she said through clenched teeth. Then she glanced around and pulled him to a stop. "I think … I mean, *I know* I like him. Okay? I think about it a lot."

"Kitty," Jon sighed, turning to face her full on. "What are his plans for Christmas?"

Forget blush, her face was on fire.

"Why does that matter?" she asked in a snappish tone. He smiled sadly.

"I'm not trying to be a dick, but … do you always bring guys home for Christmas?"

There was a long pause.

"Oh my god," she breathed. "I never even realized I did that. I just … I mean, we have great holidays at home. I always thought who wouldn't want to be a part of them?"

"You're so sweet, Kitty. Too sweet. *Stop adopting people,*" he told her. She frowned at him.

"Hey, if I hadn't adopted you, you never would have met my friends, and they never would've taken you to Delaney's restaurant," she snapped. That gave Jon a moment of pause.

"Well, I mean … *I'm* a special case, duh," he finally said, and she burst out laughing. "I mean, jesus, Kitty, *I have amnesia.* I don't count."

"No, *you don't exist*, there's a difference," she replied, but she was teasing, so he allowed it.

They all huddled together as they waited for valet and rides. Sloany had a sleek new Acura, and after they brought it around, she got behind the wheel and gunned the engine, waving goodbye to them all through a sun roof. Kitty and her date dropped into a taxi, with Kitty and Delaney actually making a date to hang out together.

Del was going to do her makeup, spice her up a little.

Huh, maybe car thief bro **is** *good for her.*

Jon could've bought him and Del a car a long time ago, and then they could've just driven home. Even still, they could've taken a cab. But they held hands and made their way down to a subway stop. Tucked themselves into a corner of the train and traded grossly inappropriate kisses.

"I have a question," he breathed, pulling her face closer so the edges of his hood hid them both from view.

"What?" she panted, unzipping his hoodie and working her hands under the fabric.

"Did we ever have sex on a subway car before?"

She laughed. That beautiful song his soul remembered so well.

"Hmmm, I just can't seem to remember ..."

"You don't remember something like getting fucked on a train?"

"I think you need to earn the answer to that question," she teased. It was a game she played often, but she always lost. He *always* got the answer out of her, one way or another.

"We were dirty, dirty people," he sighed before nibbling at her bottom lip.

"Yes, we were, and it was *amazing.*"

"Now seems pretty good to me."

"Now is amazing, too."

They transferred to another train, then continued in much the same manner, making the two nuns sitting across from them very uncomfortable. Delaney winked at them, then straddled his lap.

It was a long trip from Harlem to Brooklyn, almost an hour in total. It would have been longer to get to Brooklyn Heights, but on a whim, Del decided to pull him off the train at Bedford Avenue. She suggested they walk the rest of the way to their apartment.

"Babe, it's over three miles, like another hour to walk it ... it'll be one in the morning by the time we get home," he pointed out, stumbling out of the car door after her.

"Who cares? It'll be fun, maybe we'll go on an adventure!" she laughed. "Night time in Brooklyn is magical. Maybe something crazy will happen, you never know."

"Last time I took a walk through Brooklyn at night, I wound up almost dying from tainted speed and a fractured skull."

"You're *such* a downer."

Delaney had told him all about their past together. The good, the bad, and the extremely ugly. She never sugarcoated anything, and answered every single question he had, no matter how awful or embarrassing. He had to admit, some of the stories made it sound like they'd had a lot of fun. But a lot of them also made him feel ashamed. Like he'd dragged her down into a seedy world, then kept her there. Locked them both in it, too high on drugs and too drunk in love to save each other.

I wasn't worthy of her then. But maybe I am now.

They made promises to each other to never go down that road again. Jon didn't mind having a drink on occasion, but only ever in moderation. Delaney wouldn't take anything, he had to beg her to take Tylenol when she'd broken a toe a couple months prior. She had such a strong sense of self, it was astounding. This tiny girl, built like steel. She could be pushed and bent and shoved, but she would never break. She held him and his entire world on her shoulders, and it didn't scare him at all. He knew she would never drop him.

When they finally got above ground, Jon had to admit, it was all pretty magical looking. Powdery white flakes were drifting down. Not in heavy, stormy sheets. More like delicate fairy crystals, turning the city into a winter wonderland. Making everything sparkly and clean and pretty.

"This won't be fun to walk in," Jon warned her.

He got a snowball to the face in response.

When he'd first gotten out of the hospital, he hadn't been able to remember whether or not he liked snow. He had a feeling he hadn't, and Delaney later told him she'd heard Jayson complain about it often, worrying about the impending winter when they'd been squatting.

But Jon loved it. Loved the crisp feeling in the air, making him feel alive. Loved the snowflakes when they got caught in Delaney's hair and long eyelashes. He laughed when she tilted her head back and stuck out her tongue, trying to catch flakes on it. Then he ran after he shook a tree branch and dumped about a ton of snow on her face. He almost slipped and broke his ass, barely catching himself when she tackled him from behind. They rolled around for a while, then stood up and shook off before continuing their walk, laughing all the time.

This is perfect. Walking with her. We did this before, I know it. I can feel it. Walked together. Walked everywhere. With barely anything to our names but each other, and it was enough. Just like this moment, right now.

He stopped walking and blinked in surprise. Sure, they had a lot to their names now. Their very nice apartment building was just down the street, he could see the Christmas lights on in their window. But right that moment, on that street corner, the only things he had were the clothes on his back, and Delaney's hand in his own.

*This **is** perfect. You will never be able to recreate a moment like this one.*

"Babe," he breathed. The word escaped on a puff of air, floating up into the night sky.

"Hmmm? What's up?" she asked, looking back at him. They were still holding hands, so he gently reeled her back in, making her slide to him in the frost. Everything around them glowed, the street lights bouncing off the fresh snow. It made everything soft and sort of hazy. Like a dream.

Like a memory.

"Can I ask you a question?"

It was a phrase he said a lot, and she never once got annoyed with it. She smiled at him.

"Of course."

"Scale of one to ten—how happy would you say you are with life right now?" he asked. She seemed surprised to hear it wasn't a question about his past, but she kept smiling.

"Eleven," she answered quickly, her smile growing into a grin. He didn't smile. She'd given an identical answer once before, when he'd asked the same question about their life prior to the accident.

"But what about ..." he took a deep breath. "Are you happier *now* than you were before?"

"That's an impossible question to answer," she shook her head. "They're two different kinds of happy. How about ... I'm *just* as happy as I was before."

"Really? I mean, *really?*" he checked.

"*You're* here," she stressed, pressing her hand to his chest. "You're with *me*. You plus me equals happy, okay? I don't care when or where or how, or even what name you have. You plus me."

Jon stared down at the hand on his chest. It was her left hand. She'd stopped wearing the mood ring a long time ago—not because she'd wanted to, but because the mood stone had gotten ripped off the band one day. They still had both pieces, and they kept insisting they'd get it fixed, but it just hadn't happened yet.

"I don't like this," he whispered, taking her hand off his chest and holding it in his own. His free hand dug around in his jacket pocket.

"What, my hand?" Delaney laughed, spreading her fingers out on his palm.

"No, *this*," he replied, stroking his thumb down her ring finger.

"We'll get it fixed," she promised in a soft voice. He shook his head as he pulled the object away from his coat.

"I don't want to get it fixed."

He'd bought it earlier in the week and had never taken it out of his pocket. Stupid, he knew. He could've gotten mugged or lost it or ... fallen on some train tracks.

But he hadn't. It was still there, still in the boring white box it had come in, waiting for this perfect moment.

"What are you doing?" Delaney demanded.

"I think … I mean, I can't really remember it all clearly, but I think … I told you once that I couldn't do any better than a mood ring, which I'd stolen. This isn't much better, but I didn't steal it, and it's real. It's for you, and only you."

It was a small ring for a small finger. A deep, deep blue sapphire was in the center, with two small diamonds on either side, all set into a white gold band. He slid it onto her finger, then watched her as she stared at it. Her eyes were huge, like saucers.

"Blue means love …" her voice trailed off. He smiled.

She always remembers.

"I wanted to do this at Coney Island, but figured I'd have to wait until the snow melted. I wanted to … I wanted to be him again, just for a moment. Just for you."

There was silence. She was still staring at the ring. Not moving, not speaking, not crying. *Not saying yes.* He took a deep breath and reminded himself that Jayson Fairbanks had been fearless, then kept speaking.

"But *this* moment … the snow, and you, and all this magic around us. It's perfect for *Jon*, and I can only hope it's good enough for you."

Still nothing. Jayson Fairbanks may have been fearless, but Jon Doherty was starting to feel scared shitless. Then she took a deep breath and lifted her eyes to his.

"You silly, silly boy," she breathed, stunning him for a moment.

"What? Why?" he asked.

"Why are you proposing right now?" she asked. He stammered, not sure how to respond, but she kept talking. "I already said yes, a long time ago."

"Seriously?" he asked, wrapping his arms around her. She nodded.

"What, just because I don't wear a ring, it means the engagements off? I'd never let you get off the hook so easily," she teased him, but her eyes were finally filling with tears.

"I should've known," he laughed back.

"You said forever," she whispered, coiling her arms around his neck. "Forever means forever, Jon. Jayson. Both of you. All of you. Forever and ever and ever and ever ..."

He closed his eyes and pressed his forehead to hers.

"I remember this," he sighed. "I remember this feeling."

"Do you remember this part?" she asked, then she pressed her lips to his.

"I could *never* forget that part," he replied, then he kissed her back.

They kissed all the way up the street to their apartment building. Kissed up the three flights of stairs. Kissed as they struggled to unlock their door, and kissed as they fell onto the futon mattress.

"I *hate* futons," Delaney groaned as she fought to take off her scarf. He knew all about the shitty futon from when they'd been squatting—she'd complained about it *a lot* when Sloany had given them the one they were now laying on.

"It's only temporary," he breathed, pushing her shirt up her body and kissing her stomach. "The bed is being delivered tomorrow."

"God, a bed. A *real* bed, like normal sized and everything."

"Fuck normal sized—I got us a king."

"I love you so fucking much," she whispered, pulling her sweater up and over her head.

They both laughed when she got trapped inside the material, the sleeves twisting together and getting wrapped around each other. While she begged for help, he went about taking off her shoes and pants, then stripping his own clothing off. She started twisting around in her struggle to free herself, rolling onto her stomach. He straddled her hips and then pulled the sweater free from her limbs. Then he stopped and stared down at her tattoo. Braced his hands on either side of it.

"I love this," he said, staring at it for a moment longer before unhooking her bra. She moaned when he massaged his hands down her back. "You don't have any others, though."

"You never said anything else worth getting permanently marked on my skin," she teased. He slapped her on the ass, then helped her roll over again.

"I say lots of good stuff," he informed her. She put her hands under her and started moving around, shifting further up the mattress. Only the Christmas lights were on, so everything was bathed in green and red and blue.

"You say the best stuff," she agreed, still moving backwards. "Maybe I'll reread your book and find something and—*ow!*"

Her exclamation stopped them both. She shifted around, then pulled something out from under her butt. It was the clunky big camera, the one she'd used earlier to take their picture. She got up on her knees and turned around, leaning into the light to see if she'd damaged it.

"You okay?" he asked, smoothing his hand over her butt while he looked over her shoulder.

"I'm fine. I think it's fine, too," she replied, wiping at the lens with her left hand. The lights caught the surface of the sapphire on her finger, making it shine and twinkle.

"Come here," he said, reaching around her for the camera at the same time he wrapped an arm around her waist. He pulled her back into him, then sat down so she was between his legs. She settled into his chest while he moved his arm from her waist to grab her left hand. He laced his fingers through hers, feeling the ring digging into the sides of his digits, then moved their arms together so they were covering her chest.

"What are we doing, Jon?" she whispered, then went stiff when he started lifting the camera. "No, no nude pictures."

"You used to take them all the time for me," he pointed out.

It was true. They still had a folder full of them on her laptop. He looked at them more often than was probably normal.

"That was a long time ago. Now it's different. You didn't even own your own computer back then. Now, you'll probably put this pic in your wallet and show it to people," she laughed.

"Oh no," he said, holding the camera up above them. "I would never let anyone see us like this, Delaney. This is *my* memory, and it's only for us."

He held down the shutter. The flash went off, then there was the whirring and the printing. He gently laid the camera on the floor, then wrapped himself around her while she held the tiny picture in her fingers. They waited while it developed.

"I thought of it," she suddenly whispered.

"Thought of what?" he asked, resting his chin on her shoulder. The white piece of film was darkening. Shapes and colors were starting to bleed through.

"My next tattoo. Your perfect words," she breathed. He took the picture from her and held it up closer to his face.

"And they are?" he asked, watching as they came into focus. It was actually a tasteful shot, from her chest up. They were both clearly topless, but her cleavage wasn't even visible. Their arms blocked it.

More than that, it was their faces that stole the show. Jon was looking down, a piece of hair curling over his forehead, and he was staring at their hands. At her ring. Delaney was looking up, her eyes locked on him. So big and blue and beautiful.

"*Muscle memory,*" she said. "You always said it's what brought you back to me. How you could feel me in your skin and your bones and your muscles. That they remembered me, even when your brain couldn't."

"It is perfect," he agreed, then he tossed the photo to the floor and bent his head down to kiss her cheek. "Now let's make some new memories with our muscles."

She laughed, then moaned when he gently rolled them around

so she was under him. His foot hit an outlet, knocking out a plug, and all the Christmas lights suddenly went out. She gave a throaty laugh and wrapped her arms around his neck.

"I know who you are, Jon Doherty. Even in the dark."

He took a deep breath.

"*You can call me Jay.*"

ACKNOWLEDGEMENTS

Okay.

I wrote a contemporary romance primarily from a male point of view.

That's a first for me!

I spend a lot of time in Oregon. My family is from there, my dad lives there, it's my second home. I just really enjoy it there. We were visiting there in the summer of 2017 and driving to the coast. I love to drive, and somewhere along the highway, I found myself thinking about the movie Cast Away and how—SPOILER ALERT—at the end, Helen Hunt has to choose between Tom Hanks, the man she thought was dead, and her husband, the man she married after Hanks went missing. And like, how hard would that choice be!? Like what would I do in that situation?

My brain, man.

Somehow, that got turned into me thinking about what if it happened to someone with amnesia. Like you bump your head, lose your memories, go off and have a life and get married and have kids, and then BAM, realize you've got a whole other life somewhere! How do you choose between the two? Which led me to wondering what DOES happen to amnesiacs? I guessed they were given new identities and whatnot.

Thanks to Google, I now know that's not what happens at all—it's assumed someone with amnesia obviously already has an identity, so of course they can't just be given a new one. This has literally happened to people before, I read about a man with amnesia who became homeless after being released from the hospital because he couldn't get a social security number.

Then I came home and played around with the Kanes for a while and refused to work on my actual WIP. The amnesia stuff came back to me, wondering what would happen if you had to choose, so I opened a new word document and started typing.

FOUR DAYS LATER I had written roughly 80,000 words. This is generally not possible. Nor is it smart, sane, or recommended. I didn't shower, barely ate, only left my bed to go sit on the couch and type.

Now, I don't know why my brain works this way. I wish it didn't. Some authors can plunk out 2,000 words a day solid—I would much prefer that way of working. Some authors only produce one or two books a year, and work on them for months and months. That would be nice, too. But this is the way my brain works, my creativity. And I have learned to trust it and go with it.

I don't know where this story came from, Jon was barely a thought in my brain when I opened the document, but he just spilled out of me. I've never written a book in a such a manic frenzy, not even Degradation. I am exceptionally proud of this story and its characters, and though I almost always prefer dark or strange books, this is one is easily among my favorites of mine.

LOTS of thanks! Everything around this book was a frenzy, including releasing it. Within an hour of emailing them a panicked "help I need to release this yesterday!" message, Give Me Books had a sign-up form drafted and sent out in their newsletter. How amazing is that? I know bloggers are busy and overwhelmed and worked hard, so it's really impressive and a true judge of their character that they would do that for me. Please follow them because they are true angels.

Najla from Najla Qamber Designs informed me this is our FOURTEENTH cover together! Count 'em—that's every single one of my covers (including one y'all haven't seen yet). I told her I'm excited for the next fourteen, and I can't imagine anyone else transforming my crazy ideas into works of art. She does it flawlessly and with a great attitude. Thanks for all the beauty!

Graphics by Erika for squeezing me in and doing emergency professional teasers for me, you saved me! And Liz Milner for making teasers just because that's what she does, and they're always beautiful.

Of course Champagne Book Designs, for dealing with my crazy date-changing-ass and squeezing me in and making the insides of my books as beautiful as the outside. I'm excited for their next adventure!

As always, Ratula Roy—the alpha and the omega reader. This bitch reads almost a book a day for her blog, and yet STILL fits in my junk, even when it's just basically drivel on paper. Encourages me and listens to me and laughs with me and talks shit with me and generally makes life a much better place.

Barbara Shane Hoover, for all the red marks and notes, and pointing out how I keep writing random things backwards. Why do I do that!?

ALL my beta readers, and there were a lot this time! I'm always adding new people, always wanting new and fresh opinions, and I thank each and every one for their help with this novel—Jennifer, Nanci, Paige, Teri, Deanna, Pam, Amy, Rebecca, Andrea, Lindsay, Reanell, Brittany, Jessica, Chandris, and Bex (say all that ten times fast!). I went through every single email, every single note you all sent. Thanks so much for helping make this story the best it could be.

Thank you to all the blogs that read and left reviews and shared for me. Thank you for promoting and taking time out of your busy reading schedules to fit me in and give this story a chance. Thank you for persevering in a community that doesn't seem to know which direction it's headed in from one day to the next.

Thank you to all my readers, especially the ones who've been with me since the beginning. What a crazy ride! Sometimes, I wish I could write in one genre. I wish I could control what I want to work on. I wish I could always give you something different and edgy and epic and mind blowing. But most of all, I wish I could always write what you want to read. I hope I continue doing that, and I hope you continue reading. We'll always have each other, and I'm so grateful for all of you.

Thanks to my friends. For putting up with my bad

communication skills and sometimes worse attitude. For my hermit ways and how much I resist doing anything ... pretty much ever. For laughing and being dorks and traveling long distances to see each other.

And of course, thank you Mr. F. For getting me special glasses so I could type for four days straight. For reminding me to eat, and for literally making me shower. For letting me stare dead eyed into a computer and ignore the whole word. And most of all, for understanding that it's just the way I am, and letting me be me.

Oh, and for helping me take that stupid boot on and off for a month straight.

And letting the dogs out because it hurt to walk downstairs.

You're the best.

degradation

Available Now

Tatum plucked at her shirt in a nervous manner. She had tucked it into a tight pencil skirt and even put on a pair of sling back stilettos. If someone had personally requested her, she wanted to make an effort to look nice. She had blown out her hair and put curls in the ends, and toned down her make up. Even she had to admit it, she looked presentable.

For once.

Men in expensive business suits began to file into the conference room and she stood still, giving a polite smile to everyone who entered. A team of lawyers was meeting with their client. Six chairs were lined up on one side of a long table, with just a single chair on the other side.

Tate had been positioned at the back of the room, next to a sideboard filled with goodies and coffee and water. She fussed about, straightening napkins and setting up the glasses. When all six chairs were filled on the one side, she stared at their backs, wondering who the big shot was that got to stare them all down. The person who would be facing her. A door at the back of the room swung open and her breath caught in her threat.

Holy. Shit.

Jameson Kane strode into the room, only offering a curt smile to his lawyers. His eyes flashed to her for just a second, then he looked back. His smile became genuine and he tipped his head towards her, almost like a bow.

She gaped back at him, positive that her mouth was hanging open. What was he doing there!? Had he known she would be there? Had he been the one to request her? Impossible, he didn't know what temp agency she worked for—but what would be the chances? She hadn't seen him in seven years, and now twice in two days.

Tate felt like swallowing her tongue.

"Gentlemen," Jameson began, seating himself across from the lawyers. "Thanks for meeting with me today. Would anyone care for any coffee? Water? The lovely Ms. O'Shea will be helping us today." He gestured towards Tate, but no one turned around. Several people asked for coffee. Jameson asked for water, his smile still in place. It was almost a smirk. Like he knew something she didn't.

She began to grind her teeth.

She delivered everyone's drinks, then carried around a tray of snacks. No one took anything. She moved to the back of the room, refilled the water pitcher. Tidied up. Felt Jameson staring at her.

This is ridiculous. You're Tatum O'Shea. You eat boys for breakfast.

But thinking that made her remember when he had said something very similar to her, and she felt a blush creep up her cheeks.

She was pretty much ignored the whole time. They all argued back and forth about what business decisions Jameson should, or shouldn't, make. He was very keen on dismantling struggling companies and selling them off. They tried to curb his desires. His tax lawyer explained how his tax shelter in Hong Kong was doing. Another lawyer gave him a run down on property law in Switzerland. Tate tried to hide her yawns.

They took a five minute break after an hour had passed. Tate had her back to the room, rearranging some muffins on a tray, when she felt the hair on the back of her neck start to stand up. She turned around in slow motion, taking in Jameson as he walked up to her.

"Surprised?" he asked, smiling down at her.

"Very. Did you ask for me?" she questioned. He nodded.

"Yes. You ran away so quickly the other night. I wanted to get reacquainted," he explained. She laughed.

"Maybe I didn't," she responded. He shrugged.

"That doesn't really matter to me. What are you doing tonight?" he asked. She was a little caught off guard.

"Are you asking me out, Kane?" she blurted out. He threw back his head and laughed.

"Oh god, still a little girl. *No.* I don't ask people out. I was asking what you were doing tonight," Jameson replied.

She willed away the blush she felt coming on. He still had the ability to make her feel so stupid. She had been through so much since him, come so far with her esteem and her life. It wasn't fair that he could still make her feel so small. She wanted to return the favor. She cleared her throat.

"I'm working."

"Where?"

"At a bar."

"What bar?"

"A bar you don't know."

"And tomorrow night?"

"Busy."

"And the night after that?"

"*Every* night after that," Tate informed him, crossing her arms. He narrowed his eyes, but continued smiling.

"Surely you can find some time to meet up with an old friend," he said. She shook her head.

"We were never friends, Kane," she pointed out. He laughed.

"Then what is it? Are you scared of me? Scared I'll eat you alive?" he asked. She stepped closer to him, refusing to be intimidated.

"I think *you're* the one who should be scared. You don't know me, Kane. You never did. *And you never will,*" she whispered. Jameson leaned down so his lips were almost against her ear.

"I know what you feel like from the inside. That's good enough for me," he whispered back. Tate stepped away. She felt like she couldn't breathe. He did something to her insides.

"You, and a lot of other people. You're not as big a deal as you think," she taunted. It was a complete lie, but she had to get the upper hand back. He smirked at her.

"That sounds like a challenge to me. I have to defend my honor," he warned her. She snorted.

"Whatever. Point to the challenger then, *me*. Defend away," she responded, rolling her eyes.

He didn't respond, just continued smirking down at her. The lawyers began filing back into the room and Jameson took his position on the other side of the table. She wasn't really sure what their little spar had been about, or what had come out of it. She was just going to try to get through the rest of the conference, and then she would scurry away before he could talk to her again. She didn't want anything to do with Jameson Kane, or his—,

"Ms. O'Shea," his sharp voice interrupted her thoughts. Tate lifted her head.

"Yes, sir?" she asked, making sure to keep her voice soft and polite.

"Could you bring me some water, and something to eat," he asked, not even bothering to look at her as he flipped through a contract.

She loaded up a tray with his requests and made her way around the table. No one even looked at her, they just threw legal jargon around at each other—a language she didn't know. She stood next to Jameson and leaned forward, setting his water down and then going about arranging cheese and crackers on a plate for him. She was about halfway done when she felt it.

Are those ... his fingers!?

Tate froze for a second. His touch was light as he ran his fingers up and down between her legs. She glanced down at her knees and then glanced over at him. He was still looking down, but she could see him smirking. She tried to ignore him, tried to go back to setting up his food, but his hand went higher. Daring to brush up past her knees, well underneath her skirt. He couldn't get any farther, not unless he pushed up her skirt, or sunk down in his chair. She dumped the rest of the cheese on his plate and started to scoot away. She had just gotten back to her station when she heard a thunking noise, followed by groans.

"No worries. Ms. O'Shea! So sorry, could you get this?" Jameson's voice was bored sounding.

She turned around and saw that he had knocked over his water glass. He was blotting at the liquid as it spread across the table. The lawyers were all holding their papers aloft, grumbling back and forth.

Tate groaned and grabbed a towel before striding back to the table. She glared at him the whole way, but he still refused to look at her. She started as far away from him as she could get, mopping everything up, but eventually she had to almost lean across him to reach the mess. She stood on her toes, stretching across the table top.

As she had assumed it would, his hand found its way back to her legs. Only this time he wasn't shy, and her position allowed for a lot of access. His hand shot straight up the back of her skirt, his fingertips brushing against the lace of her panties.

She swallowed a squeak and glanced around. If any of the other gentlemen lifted their heads, they would have been able to see their client with half of his arm up his assistant's skirt, plain as day. He managed to run his finger under the hem of her underwear, down the left side of her butt cheek, before she pulled away. She stomped back to the food station, throwing the towel down with such violence, she knocked over a stack of sugar cubes.

When she turned around, Jameson was finally looking at her. She plunked her fists on her hips, staring straight back. His smirk was in place—as she had expected it would be—and he held up a finger, pointing it straight up. *One.* Then he pointed at himself. One point. *Tied.* He thought they were playing a game. She hadn't wanted to play games with him, but she hated to lose at *anything*, and she never wanted to lose to a man like Jameson Kane.

An idea flitted across her mind. Tate wanted to make him as uncomfortable as he had just made her feel. She coolly raised an eyebrow and then took her time looking around the room. The lawyers all still had their backs to her—not one of them had turned around the entire time she'd been there. Blinds had been drawn over every window, no one could see in the office, but she knew the door wasn't locked. Anyone could walk into the room. She took a deep breath. It didn't matter anyway, what was the worst that could happen? She would get fired? It was a temp job, that Jameson had requested her for—he didn't even work there. Did she really care what happened?

She dragged her stare back to meet his and then ran her hands down the sides of her skirt. He raised an eyebrow as well, his eyes following her hands. When she got to the hem of the skirt, she pressed her palms flat and began to slowly, *achingly*, slide the material up her legs. Now both his eyebrows were raised. He flicked his gaze to her face, then went right back to her skirt. Higher, up past her knees. To the middle of her thighs. Higher still. If anyone turned around, they would be very surprised at what they saw. One more inch, and her skirt would be moot. Jameson's stare was practically burning holes through her.

Taking short, quick, breaths through her nose, Tate slid her hands around to her butt. She wiggled the material up higher back there, careful to keep the front low enough to hide her whole business, and was able to hook her fingers into her underwear. She didn't even think about what she was doing, couldn't take her eyes off of Jameson, as she slid her underwear over her butt and down her hips. As the lace slid to her ankles, she pushed her skirt back into place. Then she stepped out of the panties and bent over, picking them up. When she stood upright, she let the lace dangle from her hand while she held up one finger. Point.

Winning.

Jameson nodded his head at her, obviously conceding to her

victory, then returned his attention to the papers in front of him. Tate let out a breath that she hadn't even realized she was holding, and turned around, bracing her hands against the table. She leaned forward and took deep breaths. She had just started to gain some ground on slowing her heart rate, when a throat cleared.

"What is that, Ms. O'Shea?" Jameson called out from behind her. She spun around, balling up her underwear in her fist.

"Excuse me, sir?" she asked.

"That," he continued, gesturing with his pen at her. "In your hands. You have something for me. Bring it here."

Now everyone turned towards her. Tate held herself as still as possible, her hands clasped together in front of her legs, hiding the underwear between her fingers. All eyes were on her. Jameson smirked at her and leaned back in his chair. She took a shaky breath.

"I don't know what—,"

"Bring it here, Ms. O'Shea, *now*," he ordered, tapping the table top with his pen. She glared at him.

Fuck this.

She turned around and pulled one of the silver trays in front of her. She laid her panties out neatly on top, making sure the material was smooth and flat. She was very thankful that she had gone all out and worn her good, expensive, *"I'm-successful-and-career-oriented!"*, underwear. She balanced the tray on top of her fingertips and spun around, striding towards their table, a big smile on her face.

"For you, Mr. Kane," she said in a breathy voice, then dropped the tray in front of him. It clattered loudly and spun around a little before coming to a rest, the panties sliding off to one side.

As she walked away, she could hear some gasps. A couple laughs. A very familiar chuckle. When she got to the door, she pulled it open before turning back to the room. A couple of the lawyers were gawking at her, and the rest were laughing, gesturing to the display she had just put on; Jameson was looking straight at her, his smirk in place. She blew him a kiss and then stomped out the door.

THE BAD ONES

Excerpt

Available Now

"Constantine!?"

Dulcie groaned. *Frannie.* Since Con had come back, she hadn't seen the other woman. She'd begun to think maybe it was a sign, that her luck was changing. Con was her dark little rainbow, spreading peace over her world. But no. Apparently not.

"Hi, Frannie," he said politely, his politician's-smile making an appearance. No hint of the big bad wolf in that grin.

"It's been so long! How are you? *Move,* Dulcie, jesus, I'm trying to talk to my old friend," Frannie demanded, shoving her out of the way. The ice cream fell out of her hand and smacked into the floor.

"It's been a while," Con agreed, ignoring the incident between the girls. "How've you been? You look great."

Dulcie stared at their interaction, dumbfounded.

"Oh, stop. I don't. Do I? Well, not as good as *you.* You look *incredible,*" Frannie gushed. His smile got bigger and Dulcie watched as Frannie fell a little more in love with him.

"Thanks."

"Enough about me. What are you doing here? And god, is Dulcie bothering you? Townies, I swear. C'mon, there's a great coffee shop next door, it just opened. Let me get you a cup," Frannie offered, then linked her arm though his and began dragging him away.

"A coffee shop? Wow, Fuller's almost like a real town," he laughed, and she cackled right along with him as they walked out the door together. He didn't look back, not even once.

What. The fuck.

Dulcie stomped the whole way home. She bypassed her elevator and took the stairs, wanting to burn off some energy. When she got into her apartment, she slammed the door shut behind her and locked it. The knob and the bolt, even put on the chain. Something she rarely ever did; she pitied anyone who would be stupid enough to try and rob her. But that afternoon, she wasn't in the mood for anyone to come inside.

She felt like she was going to explode, she had to do something with all the tension that was threatening to blow her apart, so she tore around the apartment. The bed was a mess, blankets scattered everywhere—they'd stayed the night at her place, but hadn't slept much. So she changed the sheets and made the bed, then tidied up other parts of the room. There was a wash basin set up on a counter top, so she cleaned the meager amount of dishes she had and left them out to dry. She was rinsing off a chef's knife when she heard what she'd been waiting for—scratching, on the other side of her door.

"Fuck off, I'm not in the mood for you right now!" she yelled. Deep laughter rolled straight through the wood and brick, almost filling her apartment.

"That's a lie, and you know it."

She frowned and turned so her back was against the wall between the counter top and the door.

"I don't want you to come in."

"I wasn't asking. Open the door, or I'll open it myself."

She held the knife up, touching the tip of the blade with her index finger.

"*Go ahead.*"

The building was old, she didn't expect the door to put up much of a fight. She turned back to her wash station and went about drying the knife. There was silence for a solid minute after her dare, and she paused in her movements. Then the door almost exploded off its hinges as Con rammed through it, and she went back to drying.

"You can't honestly be mad at me," he said simply, brushing his shoulder off as he moved to stand next to her.

"You didn't think that was possible? I spent three years being mad at you. I'm really good at it," she informed him. He chuckled and put his hands flat on the counter top, leaning down so he was at her level.

"Dulcie, you couldn't be mad at me if you tried. *You're scared.* What are you so scared of, little girl?"

I'll show him scared.

She let out a yell as she stabbed the knife down in front of him. The blade lodged in the wood right between his index and middle fingers, and had gone so deep, it stood upright on its own. Con didn't even flinch.

"*Not her,*" Dulcie hissed. "You can do whatever you want, but don't *ever* play your little pretend act with her. *Got it!?*"

Almost stabbing him was fine, but telling him what do do? That was just going too far. His hand was around her jaw, his fingernails cutting into her skin, and he literally dragged her across the room. She cried out as he slammed her up against a window, the back of her head breaking out a pane of glass.

"If you're actually threatened by a girl like her, then I'm insulted. Then you're fucking stupid, and what's going on here between us isn't what I thought. Don't you ever fucking talk to me like that again," he snapped, baring his teeth against the side of her face. She held onto his wrist, trying to relieve some of the pressure he was putting on her jaw.

"While you were off playing pretend for those three years, I was stuck here listening to her voice. Dealing with her insults, her jabs, her digs. Watching as she sucked the life out of her husband. A guy whose only mistake in life was dating me, yet she won't stop punishing him for it. I've had to listen as she spread rumors about me, about you. Had to deal with not getting hired in places because she had her father forbid it. So you know what? *Fuck you,* Constantine. I'll talk to you any way I fucking want."

He was silent for a moment, his eyes wandering over her face. She knew he was attracted to her, obviously, but she often wondered if he found her half as beautiful as she found him to be. His blue eyes dipped lower, tracing over the outline of her lips, watching as she gasped for air.

"You are the most amazing thing I've ever seen," he said, reading her thoughts. She struggled to take in air and stumbled a little; his hand was still on her jaw, holding her up so she was forced onto her toes. His forearm was resting on her chest, making it hard to breathe. Yet she let go of his wrist. Let him push almost his full weight against her, and against the glass behind them.

"We're going to kill each other, aren't we?" she whispered.

"Baby ..." he sighed, his eyes fluttering shut as he moved to rest his forehead against her. "What a beautiful thing to say."

ABOUT THE AUTHOR

Crazy woman living in an undisclosed location in Alaska (where the need for a creative mind is a necessity!), I have been writing since …, forever? Yeah, that sounds about right. I have been told that I remind people of Lucille Ball - I also see shades of Jennifer Saunders, and Denis Leary. So basically, I laugh a lot, I'm clumsy a lot, and I say the F-word A LOT.

I like dogs more than I like most people, and I don't trust anyone who doesn't drink. No, I do not live in an igloo, and no, the sun does not set for six months out of the year, there's your Alaska lesson for the day. I have mermaid hair - both a curse and a blessing - and most of the time I talk so fast, even I can't understand me.

Yeah. I think that about sums me up.

19499576R00169

Printed in Poland
by Amazon Fulfillment
Poland Sp. z o.o., Wrocław